Parasites of the Universe

Hi Dodie,
Thank you for buying the book. I really hope you enjoy it.
Love,
Eve Moore

Parasites of the Universe

Evelyn Moores

Copyright © 2013 by Evelyn Moores.

Library of Congress Control Number:		2013900730
ISBN:	Hardcover	978-1-4797-7839-3
	Softcover	978-1-4797-7838-6
	Ebook	978-1-4797-7840-9

All rights reserved. No part of this book may be reproduced or transmitted in any form or by any means, electronic or mechanical, including photocopying, recording, or by any information storage and retrieval system, without permission in writing from the copyright owner.

This is a work of fiction. Names, characters, places and incidents either are the product of the author's imagination or are used fictitiously, and any resemblance to any actual persons, living or dead, events, or locales is entirely coincidental.

This book was printed in the United States of America.

To order additional copies of this book, contact:
Xlibris Corporation
1-888-795-4274
www.Xlibris.com
Orders@Xlibris.com
126174

1

From the stern, I could see the smoky folds of the mountains projecting from the western horizon. I stood staring in awe, gazing with the same look I had as a child, wondering in amazement. It was the same look that would bring those around me to say, "Why do you have that stunned look on your face?" when I stood daydreaming, immersed in my own pleasant thoughts.

I stared at the mountains with a stunned look on my face and could think of nothing but the word "majestic." I didn't really know why that word came to mind. It wasn't really a word in my vocabulary. Perhaps I had read it on a word paper that we had salvaged on one of our excavations. Majestic did seem to fit though. I had never seen them from that side, from such a distance into the Poison Sea.

At the foundation, there was light-tanned sand, barely visible from such a distance away, blending with the soupy green waters of the Poison Sea. With the sand and sea as their base, the stoic mass of the majestic mountains abruptly erupted, broken by clouds of mist midway up as they shot into a jagged peak. The dark coloured peaks appeared to pierce into the intense cerulean sky as if they had gained access to another world.

It made me feel other worldly. Or maybe the way I felt was more physiological than spiritual, and my imagination had once again burdened me unrealistically. For the next thing I knew my stomach convulsed, and I fell to the deck in a pool of vomit.

When I woke, the Moraines were dragging me back and forth across the vessel floor. It was far from comfortable, but they were strong and efficient at what they did. They were, of course, getting paid handsomely for it—three jugglets of mountain water for their personal consumption.

All they had to do was drag me around their sorry-looking vessel until one of three outcomes occurred: One, I was revived enough to tolerate the poisonous gases rising from the water, or, two, we reached Moraine Edge where I would be taken off their hands and placed in some primary treatment facility. There, the strongest treatment available was really rest and hope. And of course, three, they dragged me around until I died.

They appeared to have no preference to the outcome of my fate. At least, that was the judgment I made, impaired through my intensive toxic reaction. Reaction did not seem a strong enough description for my symptoms. I had been forewarned about the possibilities on this venture. And a reaction to the toxins in the water was one of them.

I had seen many people die a torturous death, and I had also had my share of pain. However, this was of no comfort or preparation for what I was going through now. In retrospect, previous affliction does not necessarily prepare you for future suffering. It may at best make you more tolerant.

On the other hand, what choice do you have but to tolerate the pain that you encounter? The options are limited. Besides, this "reaction" I was having was not a sickness or an assault by the ghouls. It was a direct strike on my life force. Unlike the bacteria and even the cancers, this poison had no benefit in keeping me alive.

Bacteria and cancers try to drain the life slowly and excruciatingly out of you. For the longer you live the longer they can exist. But my existence had no direct relation to the toxic unstable matter in the sea. It was simply reacting to me. I had disturbed its fragile stability by existing. With my termination, it would no longer have to react. It would return to its state of peace-fragile stability.

The assault had left me defenseless. I could not move, and yet I felt like my insides were about to explode. It was as though my organs were willing to abort as an entity in order to join with the toxins to achieve this stability. My body appeared willing to sacrifice my being in an attempt to achieve harmony in the universe. It would, of course, only be temporary peace. And my death would certainly not be enough to stabilize the universe.

Perhaps, I thought, my living might be of even more assistance to the universe. This was the argument my will was presenting to my body in attempt to convince it not to discharge at the command of the toxins. The Moraines also seemed to be doing their part to try and fight the toxins.

"Hold her higher. Her legs are dragging." commanded Daniel, the more robust of the two.

"So what? As long as we keep her moving," Pwanso responded.

"She'll lose circulation. We must keep the blood circulating to *all* parts of her body or the poison will accumulate."

Daniel had a point. Before I left on this journey, Denu, one of our leading healers, had stressed that the mountain dwellers who tried to cross the Poison Sea and never made it appeared to have high concentrations of toxins in particular parts of their bodies. The bodies brought back to the mountains after an unsuccessful journey had pronounced discoloration in specific areas, usually the arms or legs.

It wasn't a very comforting thought though. I had no control over the movement of my body at all. As consolation, the Moraines were doing their best to continue to keep my muscles moving. They dragged me to and from the bow, lifting my legs and massaging my feet and arms. I continued to drift from unconsciousness to a semi-comatose state burdened with excruciating agony.

The pain was intense. I recalled the travail my mother went through when she was dying of the cancers, and I wondered if I was experiencing anything similar. It ached so badly. I welcomed the unconscious with the terrifying visions of ghoulish creatures swarming around my decrepit body as death that inevitably takes us all ate away my flesh, leaving it raw for the demons to peel from my carcass and swallow. I stared motionlessly as I deliriously envisioned them amidst a feeding frenzy. The sheer terror of their demeanor made me forget the pain for a brief moment.

Pwanso and Daniel were certainly not ghouls. They were tending to me the best they could. Their large pale arms appeared increased in size, through the layers of salvage cloth that rested over their skin, as they contracted and strained their hefty muscles in order to keep my dead weight extended. But I sensed it was just a job to them, and they were somewhat hardened to the outcome of my fate. They did not know me personally, and they had seen several of my people lose this battle.

I then sunk deep into an abyss where I felt no pain or fear any longer. Was I dead?

2

Alexandra looked so beautiful when she was sleeping. Her hair glistened like the gold on the southwest side of the mountains that we had excavated on one of our salvaging expeditions. When her soft eyelids were lowered, they emitted tiny lines of blue and red, exposing her miniature veins and arteries through her translucent membrane.

With her eyes closed, her light skin seemed natural and tranquil. She reminded me of a delicate blossom on one of the fruit trees in the orchard: the soft pallid pedals that we paid homage to in hopes they would bring forth fruit for our consumption. Even in the dark, with limited exposure to the sun, the colour of Alexandra's hair illuminated our dwelling.

We were never able to marvel over Alexandra's beauty for long though. We knew that the rays shining on her, even when they were only a reflection from a wall, were lethal. They were more malignant to her than the rest of us. We would have to move her throughout the day when she slumbered, dodging the sun's rays which were in constant pursuit. Still, as she slept in the dark, she looked beautiful.

Suddenly her eyes opened and she cried, "Mommy!" It was completely dark around her except for her face, yet, through the pitch, I could see distinct figures scurrying about. There were noises uncomfortably audible. The sound was hard to describe, but it seemed similar to an amplified masticating, slurping, and chomping clamor that one might make chewing down a pine nut paste for medicine. The consumption sounds were echoing off a wall or two, and they were followed by gurgling and clicking noises that appeared to be some type of communication.

The sounds were coming from figures in the shadows. The occasional long spidery arm was raised to the limited light, just enough to show a figurine with a large head bent forward over the neck as though it had been mounted directly on the shoulders of the beasts. It was the ghouls! I had to protect Alexandra.

I reached for her but the distance between us had grown. Her presence slowly faded into the darkness. But her voice did not. Her cries for help grew louder, deafening, and haunting. I felt the pain of vulnerability deep within my spirit and I loathed myself for even considering my feelings when Alexandra was in such dire need.

"Mommy!" she cried. "Help me!"

I wanted to rip open my chest and expose the flesh that these creatures sought in an attempt to divert them from Alexandra to me. But I could not. I did not possess the power in this alternative world, the world that existed in the shadows of my darkest memories. In this world, all I could do was feel the pain of loss and no control.

Then I heard another quieter, more distinct voice saying, "She looks dead?"

I turned and looked toward the voice as I opened my eyes. I had made it to the landing. I was in a treatment facility at Moraine Edge, more dead than alive I gathered from the comments of the Moraines.

"You never know with those mountain people," another retorted in response to my apparent resurrection.

"How long have I been here?" I questioned in the groggiest of voices. I am sure I must have been slurring my words. Why that was of such concern to me as I lay immersed in my own diarrhea with fumes clearly noxious to the Moraines was certainly a mystery.

"A day," one responded. "We're going to try and get you to stand while we clean you."

They hoisted me up from the mattress, and slowly we made our way out of the compound to the creek that centred most of the dwellings of Moraine Edge. It was not the best conditions for observing a new village, a new region, or a new Peoples' habitat. Yet I was still able to study the Moraine territory.

Their huts appeared to be composed mainly of clay and they were situated on relatively flat terrain. In contrast, houses of the mountain people were constructed from trees and other foliage and were erected on ledges and small plateaus elevated in the regal crags of the mountains.

One other dissimilarity was the way the homes were located so closely to this small creek that meandered down towards the Poison Sea. Unlike the Moraines, the mountain people distanced themselves from the streams flowing from the mountain tops for this area was considered volatile with a less stable foundation for building homes. We only went close to the streams to retrieve the precious fluid that it contained. This Moraine creek was filthy in comparison to the purity of the mountain springs.

The Moraines doused me with the semi-clean liquid that was sometimes intolerable at best for drinking. Nothing was comparable to the mountain water of my people. The mountain water was the Moraines' lust. Why hadn't they attempted a hostile takeover of our land in order to gain unlimited access to the cleaner water? They were far more robust and known to be aggressive. They could easily overpower us.

Luckily, for the mountain people, these light-skinned inhabitants could not tolerate the sun's rays that permeated the mountains. Here in Moraine, the sun was far less intense, which became clear to me when I began to shiver uncontrollably in response to the shock of dirty cold water hitting my torso. That and the fact that I was still quite ill, malnourished, and dehydrated, from my venture across the Poison Sea encouraged the Moraines to escort me back to the complex.

Another mattress had been placed in my sleeping spot in the dwelling. Another salvaged piece of cloth was placed on dead vegetation. It was hard to assess how comfortable it was as I lay in my discomfort. I longed for my own mattress made of salvage cloth and sand. I longed for my home. I missed my children and grandchild dreadfully. I even missed their father. That, in itself, made it clear to me that I must be deathly ill. I drifted frightfully back into sleep and prayed not to witness another nightmare involving Alexandra.

3

I saw my first Moraine vessel when I was nine. We were generally forbidden to go anywhere near the shore of the Poison Sea, where the vessel docked, until long after we had bore children. But on that day, Stephin, Delta, Chris, and I, felt mischievously brave and had followed the adults to the meeting site. We stayed quite a distance behind, hiding in the wind-deformed conifers that grew sparsely along an invisible barrier that divided the tree line from the coastline. There, we witnessed our first look at a Moraine boat.

It was constructed of grey planks that appeared to be attached by bark-paste glue. It was approximately the length of three adults, and the hull was completely covered with flat timber. Toward the bow was a slightly raised cabin. Directly behind this was a small sail with a mast created from thick, sturdy-looking salvage cloth. Two sets of oars projected through the sides of the boat from within the hull, and one small rudder protruded from the stern. While the vessel was far from pretty, the technology was impressive to those of us who dwelt in the cliffs. Our only experience as seafarers was in our imagination.

"It doesn't look like much," Chris commented, as he peered from behind the bush to view the spectacle. He squinted his small dark brown eyes and then crouched back into his hiding spot.

"Be careful no one sees you Chris," cautioned Delta as she bowed her head forward. Her wire braids flopped over her shoulder, and her thin black eyebrows pushed down in a frowning motion. "Mom will kill us."

Delta wasn't kidding. Those two were beaten quite harshly sometimes. Once, their mother whipped them so badly, the council stepped in and took them away from her. It was in great violation to injure children among the mountain people. Even Violet, Chris, and Delta's mom, who was truly alone and, we later learned, dying of cancers of the brain, was not looked upon sympathetically by the council for her actions.

Violet was not permitted to even gaze upon her children until they were completely healed of all their physical wounds. Then she was only allowed to have brief visits with them under the close supervision of the elders and their adoptive parents.

By the time the twins had reached adolescence, however, it was somewhat of a peaceful outcome. Then their mother was clearly dying and in great need of their care. Then Delta and Chris could only recall a kinder, gentler Violet, who nursed them through infancy and early childhood, virtually independent of any assistance. Then, they only remembered a loving mom who washed them and hugged them and fed them.

Her fits of rage and erratic behaviour seemed a lost fable from an ancient people, as she lay in bed in intolerable pain with gray matter oozing out of her ears. She had no siblings, no husband, and no parents alive to help her. Poor Violet! Her pain in life and death was far greater than anything she had ever inflicted on the children.

Today, however, the twins were more fearless than either Stephin or me. They extended their heads above the branches and provided us with graphic coverage of the events.

"Ernest is leading a group of them on the boat," reported Delta from her perch in a small tree. Her little round bottom anchored her to a branch.

The three of us sat back and reflected on this. "I didn't think the really old people went on the vessel," pondered Stephin. His bronzed skin reflected the sunlight that beamed down through the openings in the brush where we were secluded. "I thought just people like Conan and Brad and people your parent's age went there."

"Must have to do some talking or something," I responded. "Donny says, usually, the old, old people only go on there when they have to talk. Our parents just go on to unload the salvages and the reactor metals."

"Wonder what they're talking about?" questioned Chris. "Do you think a Moraine might come live here?"

"Doubt it. More like one of our people will go there."

"Yea, sometimes they go there." Stephin reinforced my comment as he pushed the coils of his hair to the back of his head. "They check things out over there, don't they? I wish I could go there. I'd like to see Moraine's Edge. I'd like to sail on the Poison Sea. Jeeze, I'd like to see what a Moraine looks like. I heard they are really big and strong. And they have white bumpy skin like the sandbar over there. I'd like to have a Moraine for my bodyguard. If anyone bothered me, he'd kick their ass."

"They're coming off the ship," reported Delta as she squatted down further in her perch. She balanced delicately on the small branch in the dwarfed tree.

Ernest, Yucca, Louise, all elders, and Denu, a new member to council, walked briskly from the ship holding salvage cloth in front of their mouth as they did. The poisonous gases from the water were of greatest concern to the old and the young people of the mountain. The toxic effects of the invisible fumes that spewed from the water appeared most fatal to people in incline and decline.

"Who will we get to go?" Ernest bowed his head in a very concerned, solemn posture. The only portion of his body that was visible through the layers of salvage cloth was his black corneas emphasized through a grayish tint to the sclera. His weatherworn eyes conveyed a story of a long methodical life.

"Randil?" suggested Denu. Denu was smaller in stature and much younger than the others. She had become a member of the council at a relatively young age because of her skill as an herbalist. Randil, whom she spoke of, was a young adult male, one of a few mountain people at the time to have ventured to the land of the Moraines.

"No, Randil has gone before," Yucca interjected. Yucca's elderly body slouched forward at the base of her spine, as if her bulk was attempting to bow back toward the earth from where it came.

"But he was successful. He returned, didn't he?" Denu responded. Her small stature did not always communicate her feisty spirit. But her blunt words compensated.

"But at what cost?" questioned Louise. "We have no idea the extent to which the toxins have affected his longevity. We need him. He is a strong young man and has much to contribute to the people. He may be an elder someday. The people will benefit from his future guidance."

"Well, who then?" Denu returned.

"Nathan?"

"No. He is experiencing severe abdominal pains."

"How long has that been going on?" questioned Ernest.

"Four weeks."

Any ailment over three weeks was a very bad sign. It usually meant that cancers or strong bacteria would ordain its victim with an agonizing death. The sources for the cancer, the viruses, and the bacteria were numerous, and none of us were immune.

The elders continued to toss out a few names for the expedition. Apparently, the Stalites were withholding reactor metal because of an unresolved dispute with the Moraines. The Moraines hoped that a neutral party, namely a mountain person, might be able to assist at negotiating a resolve. The loss of trade between our peoples was not an immediate catastrophe, but we all believed that the goods we provided to one another were of great benefit, and many of us even ventured to suggest that it was the strongest component to our survival as a species.

"What about Anex," suggested Louise. Louise's tall, thin form towered above the others.

"A woman?" questioned Denu. There was a momentary pause as the suggestion was pondered. In the half-dozen trips that had been made across the Poison Sea, of which only four were successful, none were women. Women were assessed a very protective status when it came to dangerous activities, with the exception of childbirth of course.

"Hmm, she seems healthy. She has broad shoulders and upper body strength from carrying her anomalous son for so many years. She has displayed endurance on the salvage expeditions she attended. She is also quite learned and outspoken. She has made many contributions to our people," regarded Yucca.

"Yes, she is the one who developed the red citrus orchard through some innovative cultivation. It is a very productive plant around her dwelling. It provides food for many people and sun-dries well." The discussion revolving around Anex, who, at this point, had not or could not even express any interest in such a venture, continued for several moments. The mountain people found it uncomplicated to discuss the virtues of a person when they were not present. The contribution of the actual person who was the subject of the conversation was often considered a distraction.

"She has had four children. Two are successfully productive. I believe one may have already produced offspring."

"Yes, she has a young grandson."

Of course, none of this we could hear from the cliff behind the warped bushes, but our curiosity remained intense, not so much on what the elders were talking about because that always seemed to be blasé but on the thought that there were Moraines in the hull of that vessel, and we just might catch a glimpse of them if we waited long enough. Or, at least, we hoped we would. The challenge was that we had to remain rather still in our positions. This was a difficult task for any youngster. And we were restless by nature.

I was the first to be overwhelmed with boredom. I began to think there was no chance we were going to see a Moraine, and I felt we were wasting our precious playtime.

"This stinks. Let's go."

"Just wait, Letsi, jeeze you," retorted Stephin.

"Well, no one is coming out," I shot back.

"Maybe they will soon," Delta responded, almost pleading as she spoke.

"Yea, maybe one's dead, and they have to drag the corpse out on the deck. Yea! And the old ones aren't strong enough to lift a bug, let alone one of those giants." Chris added. His voice was very composed and focused on his thoughts.

"Why would they bring a dead Moraine here? Why wouldn't they just take him to his homeland?" I countered.

"I don't know. Maybe he's too heavy a load for the boat. Maybe it's a waste of precious cargo space. Maybe he stuck his head out too early and the sun parched him. Maybe he needs treatment or something. The first Moraine that died here was still alive when he was brought to shore you know.

That's what my mom said anyway. He was covered in cloth and kept in a hut on the beach. Mom said he had green and red sores all over and pus coming out of his face. It was like his face was cooked and his skin was peeling off. He looked worse than the old people dying. He groaned like some kinda monster animal being slaughtered, like one of those *dogs* they mention in the word papers in our lessons. His voice was really deep like a thunderstorm or something. It took him three days to die. He groaned and moaned for three days. No one was allowed in to see him except a couple of elders and old people. They brought him water and stuff, I guess."

We all knew this story quite well, but when Chris started talking, he had a smooth coherency to his stories. His small eyes lit up, and his thin-lipped smile looked sincere and confident. When he expressed himself this way, his self-esteem appeared to rise, and he did not speak with the timid tongue that usually presented itself whenever he answered questions posed by adults.

With adults around, he seemed to be on guard or in fear that he would get in trouble somehow or say the wrong thing. We all felt that way about the adults. It's just that Chris seemed in greater fear of them. With us, however, he was more confident. He often kept us captivated with his pattern of thought. Even when we didn't really agree with him, we found his stories very entertaining, and he often had us inside his head to the places and events he described.

It served him well to reduce tension in our minor childhood conflicts. And, sometimes, it was even enough to tame the raged beast that lived in the mind of his mother. When Chris began to tell a story, we would often lose track of the point we were trying to make in a discussion. And his story was so appealing that we usually did not mind.

But this time was different. For me, sitting and waiting was too much like work, and I wanted no more than I was forced to endure.

"No Moraine is gonna come out of that boat. This is a drag. I'm going back." I was so tired of just sitting there peering through the small scratchy trees that beat against my face as if commanded to do so by the wind. I was having no fun, and I knew I was in a place that would cause me trouble if I was caught.

"Letsi, can't you just wait a few more minutes? We never get to go here. Can't you at least wait till noon sun?" Stephin negotiated. He half-smiled displaying his dazzling white teeth. They stood in pleasant contrast to his smooth dark skin. To his friends, his look had an inviting social quality. To the adults, he was considered "cute." I answered by slumping down and pouting. I drew my long dangling legs beneath my salvage cloth and pulled them up to my chest.

Delta looked down from her perch in the contorted branch. "They're heading home." Quickly, she scurried down the tree, and we all left the shore area as swift as possible. Unfortunately, we discovered we were far less secretive than we had espoused. Everyone knew we had sneaked down to the shore cliffs. The twins were beaten, Stephin was put to work picking nuts in the orchards for extended hours, and I was given my usual humiliating and grueling lecture that left me feeling worthless.

Anex, on the other hand, became the first mountain woman to cross the Poison Sea to Moraine's Edge.

4

Daniel was careful to feed me only dried fruit and nuts as the Moraines nursed me back to health. He also gave me the most generous sips of mountain water. The others rationed me more skimpily. One microvessel would go to me and one to them. It was accepted that they would skim some for themselves. The taste was so alluring and clearly restoring to one's body. The Moraines were strong, but the mountain water certainly enhanced their endurance.

The Moraines had not offered any definitive study on the health of the people since the introduction of mountain water, nothing that compared to the proclamation of our reduced cancer rate and increased longevity since the introduction of reactor metal. But the anecdotal reports were convincing. The Moraines had stated that they had less death from disease among their young and old since they began to drink Mountain water. They had also stated to some of our council that the water made them stronger, although they did not elaborate.

Strength was never a great concern for the Moraines, at least not from the point of view of a mountain person or a Stalite. They were bigger and renowned for carrying enormous pack loads. For instance, to build the vessels that they traveled the Poison Sea in, they were required to retrieve wood from salvage sites on the other side of the Stalite Hills.

This area was dry and barren with a foul putrid smell in the air. A mountain person would most likely succumb to the pollutants on the trek to these barrens. Yet, the Moraines not only made such a journey, they hauled back heavy loads of lumber twice their weight. The barrens were known to contain many functional items.

The quality and quantity of retrieved material on Moraine salvage expeditions far exceeded that of the mountain people who excavated to the north of the range. The materials Moraines were able to retrieve had likely contributed to their ability to build a sea worthy vessel and entice us with items of trade.

Unfortunately for the Moraines, however, their sensitivity to skin cancer was taxing on their immune system. Furthermore, while they were more tolerant to parasitic diseases, their bodies were under far more distress because of the dirty water they consumed. So, while they possessed great strength and ability to endure attacks from toxins and parasites, their bodies did invest extensive energy in battling these plagues. Thus, there was little defense left to combat the ravaging effects of sun exposure. Their bodies appeared to have nothing left to recharge after such an attack.

The mountain water served to give their immune system a break. And they cherished it for this reason. Hence, it was understood that for every sip of mountain water I got, a Moraine was taking a little off the top.

Most of the Moraines gave me the impression that they were indifferent to my fate. They seemed disinterested in getting to know me, and I was puzzled by their lack of curiosity. They tended to me dutifully but made no effort to talk to me or spend any time with me as I gained my strength back. Daniel was the exception. He appeared to be generous and concerned beyond duty. I would hear him saying, "Don't try to feed her grassbake products. Mountain people aren't used to that. It could cause a reaction."

That was true. Mountain people rarely ate grassbake products, only when we were allotted some small portion from a supply brought over in a trade exchange between us and the Moraines. The two times I had consumed grassbake, I found it had a delightful texture. It certainly lacked the sweetness of all of our dried fruits or the density of our dried meats, but it was definitely more palatable that the sparse seed and bitter nuts we chewed on. Grassbake had the texture of a light bark or heavy reed. But, unlike bark, it completely dissolved when you chewed it. As I was still on the mend, I had yet to discover the variety of grassbake available in the Moraine region. Daniel appeared to be concerned with limiting any shock to my system.

I had not been sick often, nor had I ever been coddled or pampered. I was efficiently nurtured by my mother and even somewhat by my father in the early years of my life. But I had never really been sick, at least not this close to death. I had tended to my mother and Alexandra, but no one had ever really tended to me. Even post childbirth, I was generally left to fend on my own.

I was truly appreciative of the care I was getting in this foreign place, in spite of my pain and discomfort. I didn't even feel guilty about the attention. In fact, as I regained my health, I was really starting to appreciate the Moraines. They had been more than caretakers. They had been humane. Daniel had been particularly kind. I found myself starting to fancy him.

Daniel didn't smile or talk much, but a warmth exuded him. He was strong and solid but gentle when he lifted me from my mattress to walk out of the compound to wash. Our conversations were strictly about my health, but there was a kindness in his voice that transcended duty.

"Your balance seems much improved. There is no discolouration in your skin. Your appetite has increased."

I knew I was starting to have romantic inclinations for Daniel, and it was distorting my perception. Romantic love is truly the one sure falsehood of existence. I certainly knew nothing of Daniel, really. Yet, I longed for his visitations. Even though they were strictly service oriented. I started fixating on his mannerisms. The way he put his brow down over his green eyes when he was preparing my food and adjusting my salvage cloth blanket, it had seized my attention.

I caught glimpses of his physique beneath his cloth. His shoulders were broad, and his upper arms appeared larger in diameter than the thigh of any Mountain person. His neck was long yet thick, not slender like those of my people. His hair looked soft in comparison to my coarse locks. It was somewhat yellowish in colour, and he kept it bound up in a top knot. I longed to unfasten it and marvel at the length and softness of his tresses.

It was pathetic really. I knew where these feelings lead to, heightened desire with no earthly foundation. I just hoped I could continue to tell myself that and keep grounded. I was getting better, and I had tasks to complete. I hadn't traveled the Poison Sea and nearly died just to find a male companion. Perhaps, when I was healthier, the desires might turn to lust—a far more manageable emotion for a woman.

5

Among my friends, Chris was first to bring up the horrors of the adult world that we were about to be thrust into. He and Delta had been introduced to the topic through a dramatic confrontation with their mother. Usually, the twins never talked about their mother's rages. But since they had moved in with Lardes and Jamba, they seemed to be more open to discussing it.

"Once, when Delta went outside without any salvage cloth on her head, my mom lost it. She started ripping into Delta and I, calling us names and stuff. She said we need to cover ourselves from the sun and blah, blah, blah. It was kind of scary."

"Yea, but she didn't hit you. You got away. I ended up with a stick in my leg. It was bleeding and everything. Mom used up all the salvage cloth stopping the blood." This was a first. Delta generally left most of the talking to Chris, especially anything that might involve the personal commitment of talking about her own victimization.

She was very matter-of-fact about it, a little vague perhaps but strictly proficient in her execution of the events. The general village gossip version of the events was that Violet had dragged Delta in their dwelling by the hair, slapping her and kicking her as they went.

Delta was not a small girl. Her thighs and buttocks looked disproportionately large for the size of her upper body. Of course, when she developed an ample bosom postpuberty, it leveled out her morphology. Her lower body did possess power though. When we would play wrestle I always lost. I could never knock her off her feet, nor could Stephin or Chris. Her lower body seemed securely anchored. Yet none of this strength was present when she was being beaten by her mother. It was as if Violet's rage could neutralize Delta's strength and render her defenseless.

Violet's episodes of rage had conditioned the twins to feel helpless, and this incident was no exception. Chris, who was by no means petite either, huddled behind some citrus bushes in a catatonic state through the entire ordeal. However, most of the people around the twins' home were clearly conscious witnesses of the event.

Violet hurled vicious insults toward that young girl. The words were so austere and sharp in their meaning that they would surely pierce a young soul and take years or a lifetime to mend. It was name calling that no one should ever be burdened with. It made my complaints about my dad and mom's insults seem mundane in comparison.

Violet dragged little Delta into their dwelling with screams of fury from Violet, followed by cries of fear from Delta heard throughout the village, into the citrus fields, and far beyond the mountains. There was one final loud, clear, memorable outcry from Violet stating, "Don't you realize this is considered sluttish by our godforsaken people, and this will only bring unwanted suitors to our dwelling, you stupid girl?" Violet then grabbed a spear leaning on the inside of their hut and hurled it towards Delta. It pierced deep into the skin of her leg and penetrated well into the muscle. This was followed by an unforgettable shriek from Delta.

It must have broken the spell of the demon that possessed Violet because the next cries uttered from the twins' dwelling, as people ran from all directions to either intervene or observe, were, "Oh my God! What have I done to my baby!"

It took six months for her leg to heal, but Delta walked with a limp from then on. It was an injection of guilt to all that gazed upon her, from her mother to those of us who felt that if we would have just done more, sooner, this could have been prevented.

In spite of the dramatic occurrence, versus Delta and Chris's description of the events, Stephin and I welcomed the conversation. We were told not to ask them about their mother, ever. We were told only to listen if they chose to share with us. We were under fairly strict regulations about it from our parents who had it handed down by the elders and leaders.

While her account was far from vivid, it was clear from the expression on her downward-hung face that the memory was indeed still very painful. In an attempt to dress the wounds of the past for both his twin and himself, Chris added, "She did say sorry though, eh Delta? I mean she was crying and everything and telling us all about what's gonna happen in a year or so."

"What do you mean in a year or so?" Stephin's interest was heightened and mine was extracted from the images of how Delta met her misfortune.

"You don't know? Really?" said Chris with heightened pitch in his voice. When his audience had limited knowledge of a subject, this was generally a blessing to Chris. It gave him a freer rein in his explanations.

"I've heard a bit about it," I piped in. Generally, I left detailed explanations and credit entirely to Chris as he did seem to have a particular talent in this area. But for some reason, I wished to vocalize my knowledge of puberty.

My mother had told me that, soon, I would start bleeding between my legs; and, as soon as this happened, I was to tell her and not another soul. The whole prospect seemed dreadfully frightening. But I yearned to know more.

I knew it had something to do with childbirth as I had witnessed blood-drenched salvage cloth at many dwellings where a baby had been born. We would often hide in the shrubs around the dwelling of woman known to be bearing a child until a midwife such as Anex or Denu came out with blood and cloth. They generally caught us at this point and shooed us away to suffer the wrath of consequences for disobedience at a later point in the day.

However, not before we were subjected to the moans of pain from the woman. My mind desperately wanted to make the connection between the blood and the moaning and the baby. I dared not approach it with my mother as I would surely be subjected to some sort of punishment for my inquisitiveness. However, if Chris had some information that could provide me with a fragment of enlightenment to these mysteries, I wanted to draw out as much detail as he could possibly offer.

"I know that Delta and I will soon start bleeding, and then we will have babies. We aren't supposed to tell anyone."

Chris looked surprised and made an unusual hesitation before proceeding. "Well you're supposed to stay indoors too and cover up even more than we do now. That's what mom told us." Again Chris hesitated in his speech as his mind seemed to wander back to the first meeting between him, Delta, and his mother after Delta's injury.

"I'm sorry babies. Please forgive me," plead a frazzled-looking Violet. "I do love you so much. I don't know why I act like I do. I truly am glad you were taken from me. I'm not deserving of you. I am proud that you are living with such good parents."

Violet looked old for her age. Large folds of skin sagged below her eyes. The wrinkles in her forehead looked like permanent grooves carved into her skin from a constant frown of pain and confusion. Her black eyes seemed grey and lifeless.

When her children were taken from her, she began to venture about the community lost and confused most of the time. She had some good days, but most were bad. She was noticeably thin at this time, and it was suspected that she was forgetting to eat. She had become dependent on the charity of neighbours to call her in and give her a few morsels. She was becoming more and more incoherent and seemingly lost. She had no close relative living except an aunt who was not well and busy with her own children.

Delta and Chris's dad had died when they were toddlers. He had been lost on one of the salvage expeditions. He hadn't been of much help to Violet previous to that as he had been preoccupied suiting with other young girls. Violet was alone and lost.

While she spoke to her children, a rare spark seemed to emit from her face, and for a brief moment, she looked intent and focused. "Do not feel guilty. You deserve the attention you are getting. I love you both so much. I hope someday you know that." That speech, of course, went on until the children felt renewed but dreadfully uncomfortable. All this was simply the image in Chris's head. The story he gave was of a visit much later, after their reconciliation.

"Mom came by one day with some fresh fruit and nuts and salvage cloth for us. We really miss that about Mom. She sure has a nice orchard round her house. When we lived with her, she used to let us pick our own citrus every day. We could eat a whole one, fresh, as long as we saved the seeds. Lardes and Jamba make us work like slaves before they feed us.

Anyway, we sat to eat in the dwelling, and Lardes and Jamba left us for the first time since we moved into their house. Mom was talking quite a bit, and then she started asking weird questions about whether Delta had started to turn into a woman. She asked several questions, and Delta never answered. She just sat real quiet."

"So did you Chris," Delta piped in.

"Yea we both did," Chris quickly conciliated. "So mom just looked at us and started to try and explain what was gonna happen when we turned into adults. She said, soon, Delta would start to grow breasts. Then she would start to bleed. Then men would come and bring gifts to Lardes and Jamba so they could have sex with Delta."

"Sex?" questioned Stephin. I felt a hot piercing stria variegate through my body. It was always scary when someone mentioned sex, and I really didn't know why.

"Yes, you know when old guys get to have sex with all the young girls when they start to bleed. Mom says the girls don't really like it, and they try to get out of it. Mom didn't want Delta to have to do it if she didn't want to. She just wanted Delta to cover up as much as possible and not to tell Jamba when she started bleeding. She said, the longer you can put off having the men come and visit you, the better."

"When do we get to have sex?" asked Stephin. The gleam in his eye and the slightly furrowed brow indicated Stephin's playful inquisitiveness. We knew he was half joking, half serious.

"Whenever we want I guess," answered Chris. "Why, are you planning on getting your own place and becoming a suitor?"

"No," hesitated Stephin. He bowed his head forward and smirked. "But I am thinking about having sex."

We all responded with laughter and directed our discussion to the race we were about to have. We had challenged each other to reach the summit of a small cliff on the east side of the dwellings. It was a fairly straight facing with a few cracks and ledges to hang on to. We had inspected the site prior to the race, looking for a path way to the top.

We mentally planned the execution of this event. We stepped back to a lower ridge for our starting point.

Delta, who could not participate because of her leg, raised her hand and called, "Ready, go." The three of us ran for the cliff. Stephin reached the facing first and secured a hold on the ledge that I had eyed up previously. Chris and I reached the bottom at approximately the same time.

We each dug into a crack. Stephin was now a body length ahead of both of us. I scurried up to within an arms-length of Stephin's lead but could not find a ledge or crevices on which to advance. I sited a small slit close to the top and reached for it.

Stephin tried to secure a foothold in the same groove and stepped on top of my hand. I pushed his heel away, which caused him to momentarily lose his footing. He dangled by one arm swinging into the air and looked down at Delta, whom from this distance looked the size of a small bird. His recovery seemed effortless as he swung back and re-secured a foothold in the crevice I had now advanced from.

I do not recall ever hearing of a mountain person falling from these cliffs. I was now only slightly behind and below Stephin and, with one extended reach my arm, touched the base of the summit pathway. I swung my body upward and rolled onto the trail. I looked up to see both Chris and Stephin in similar positions.

We lay there briefly, catching our breath. None of us claimed victory over the feat. The fun was in its execution. There were many such events in our playtime. As I lay on that pathway panting, I looked to the sky and wondered how much of this I would have to give up when I was deemed an adult.

My parents had not been as explicit about the future as Violet was, but they had left an imprint upon me in regards to my role as a woman. It was clear that I was due for many unpleasantries involving sex.

"Letsi?" my mother questioned. "Come and sit here beside me." I moved to her side in the dwelling and reached for her arm thinking she needed some assistance standing. She had been having some trouble with dizziness and fatigue. Instead, she put her arm around me and began to straighten my hair with her fingers.

"Tell me what you know about being a woman."

"It is a lot of work," I retorted, hoping the conversation would not last long.

"Yes it is." She smiled. Her tone then became more serious. "But becoming a woman is even more enduring than just work."

She paused before continuing. Then explained several milestones associated with puberty and asked if I had noticed any of these. Of course, I had, and I'm sure she had also. You would have to be blind not to know I had gone through some developmental changes. I was still quite skinny, but I had sprouted up in height to where I was towering over many in the village. And there were two little bumps protruding from my chest despite the thickness of my salvage cloth. However, I answered innocently as I thought this would make the conversation shorter and less uncomfortable.

"I haven't really noticed anything, Mom."

Again she smiled and looked somewhat awkward. I wasn't sure if it was the fatigue of her illness or the weariness of the discussion that caused her to terminate it and allow me an exit.

"Letsi, please come to me as soon as it happens."

Our conversation was abruptly ended when my father entered the dwelling demanding I refrain from my sloth-like ways and prepare a meal for him and my brother Donny.

About six months later, as I was relieving myself in the bushes, I noticed a small dribble of blood trickling down my leg. I didn't tell my mother though. I just spent long hours alone in the tree line and stayed close to the streams, bathing in the cool waters, fully clothed. It seemed the most effective divergent; but, unfortunately, it only drew more attention towards me, not only from my parents, but also from the elders and leaders as well.

"Letsi, has it started?" My mother looked up from her mattress in the dwelling with tired kindly eyes. It was the first time I remembered seeing anything but pain or anger in her face since I was a tiny girl. Even my Dad seemed different, uneasy perhaps.

"What?" I said, fully aware of what they meant and scared to death.

"You know what," my Dad jumped in. "Don't give your mother a hard time." He raised his hand to my face as if to strike. He hesitated, and my mother continued to talk.

"You need to tell us. We're the only ones that can help you with this. We will protect you as much as possible, but you need to tell us. It is your family that really cares about you." Tears were flowing down my mother's cheeks, and she buried her head in her hands. I had never seen her cry. She had always seemed too fatigued to have any excessive emotion. But, now, she was actually sobbing so much that she couldn't continue to speak. My fear changed to sympathy.

Poor Mom, she fed us and clothed us when she could, and I guess she really did care about us. I felt a strange sense of guilt and wondered what I had done wrong. I wished I could be good so that everyone would be happy.

As my mom lay weeping quietly, my dad began to talk. I was expecting the usual lecture marbled with degradation, but, instead, he seemed almost sensitive. "Letsi, do you know that soon you will have to let men touch you in ways you may find uncomfortable? At first, the stage of womanhood that you are about to enter will be quite awkward and put you ill at ease. You will become accustomed to your new life eventually.

But it does take time. As you get older and more mature, you will become secure in this new life. But, now, it is indeed discomfited."

I looked at my father as he spoke. His long thin face housed a slight mass of short curled whiskers that he often shaved off with a quartz scraper. His hair was a tight mass of plaits braided tautly. I was told that when his hair was unleashed from its braids, it sprung up similar to sage brush and launched from his head in every direction, just like mine. I was often told I inherited his hair, his height, and his stubbornness. He was a lofty figure that commanded and demanded authority. I looked at my father and dutifully absorbed his directive as if it was all there was to believe. I had been well trained to do so.

"We want to delay this event for as long as possible, but, because of the way you've been acting this past week, the leaders are quite suspicious about you. They believe you have begun bleeding, and that is why you've been hiding. They have given us three quarter moons to begin your visits or to prove that you are not bleeding."

I really did not want to talk about this. I was erupting with feelings of fear and anger mixed with curiosity. "I don't want any men touching me," I blurted out. "They're old and mean. Leave me alone."

My father blocked the doorway to the dwelling and prevented me from exiting amidst my rant. "Letsi, you really have no choice. The leaders insist upon it. Our people could not survive without it. You must bear children, and, to do so, you may have to indulge in this behaviour. Submission is a respected quality."

In the middle of this conflict, I noted my father's particularly eloquent language. Generally, it was so offensive. He would usually say things like do as you're told and prove you are not worthless for once. But, now, he appeared to be using more than his brute size and dictatorial practices to convince me of my course. He seemed to be actually trying to reason with me.

"If you do not, we will be banished."

"What is banished?" I murmured through a brine of tears.

"It is the consequence for not following certain rules." He paused for a moment as he searched for an analogy. "When Violet mistreated the twins, the leaders stepped in and took them away from her. If you do not submit to the suitors, the leaders will step in and force us to live on the side of the tree line by the Poison Sea. We will not be considered mountain people."

"How can we not be what we are?" I questioned.

"In our laws, the rules state that we must make every effort to procreate. It is necessary for the survival of the people." My dad truly sounded like someone else now. Never had I heard him talk with such efficiency. He usually seemed so judgmental, opinionated, and fanatical. Now, he sounded neutral, reflective, and effective. He sounded like a leader or an elder. He sounded like a person, not a dad. He sounded like he could care less about me. "If all girls do not have children, we will not survive as a people. There are so few of us. We need to have more children. The best chance for us to have more children is for the girls to have suitors as soon as they are fertile. It is deemed necessary."

At this point my mother dragged her body up to a semi-prone position, leaning on both arms for support. "Letsi, we will do everything we can to make it as easy as possible for you. But you must trust us. We really do care."

Whether I believed anything they said at this point was irrelevant. What was my alternative?

The next two quarter moons were filled with fun. I was allowed to play for longer periods than usual with the twins and Stephin. I did not have to do much citrus or nut picking, and I hardly ever had to go and get water.

My friends would inquire about my situation. Stephin seemed the most inquisitive, Delta seemed to be listening the closest, and Chris appeared to want to talk about anything else.

"What kind of things will you do?" posed Stephin. "I mean, how will they start? Has anyone told you?" He looked at Chris and Delta. "What about you two? What do you know of it?"

"Jamba mentioned once that the men show the girls what to do when they get them," offered Chris hoping it was enough to quiet Stephin.

"Nobody tells me anything." Stephin pouted. He lived with Ella, one of his sisters. Both of his parents had died by the time he was about six years. His sister had a young toddler that kept her busy. She lived with Brad, a man at least twice Ella's young age. He provided well for them, but Stephin was required to work hard for his keep. He laboured arduously in the orchards and went on many hunting and trapping excursions with his stepfather.

However, neither Brad nor his sister saw it as their duty to discuss adulthood with him. Whenever Brad had intentions of intimacy with Ella, he banned Stephin from their small dwelling. Stephin spent many nights sleeping in the storage hut. Stephin was enthusiastically inquisitive about the future prospect of male adulthood, but he dared not approach Brad about the subject. Brad was never cruel to Stephin. But he was never open and inviting to him either. There were clear unchallenged boundaries in their relationship, and Stephin felt inclined not to push them. Instead, Stephin tended to vent his intrusive nature around his friends.

Fear had stolen my sense of curiosity. I feared my new role, and I feared I could not live up to the expectations thrust upon me. I felt guilty because I wanted no part of this new life that was supposed to be considered an honour and rite of passage. I wanted to forget about it and immerse myself in the games that gave me joy and obliterated my worries.

"How do the men learn what they are supposed to do?" questioned Stephin. "Who teaches them? They must have to practice to learn." Stephin leaned on my shoulder and rolled his eyes upwards at me. He batted his thick lined eyelashes and suggested he practice with me. I responded by jumping up and heading for the north facing of the incline we were playing on and proposed that he practice trying to race me up one of these cliffs.

We climbed up a gentle slope that we had not explored before. There we came across an unusual gouge out of the rock. It had vertical column-like grooves beginning at the bottom of the rock section projecting well above our heads. The projections were approximately a finger's length in diameter. The columns stopped at what appeared to be the entrance to a cave or tunnel. Peering down the dark passage made our hearts race.

We knew we had stumbled on a forbidden area. We knew that this area was one of the sites created by the ancient people. The ancient people were sites to be avoided. While adults ventured much further into unstable territory to excavate some of the technologies that the ancients had left behind, children were not permitted to explore such sites. They were considered both dangerous and evil.

We peered in the tunnel as our hearts raced. Terror prevented us from continuing. Fear of both our parent's wrath and the wrath of malevolence that might be inflicted upon us by these wicked primeval ancients encouraged us to turn and head back in the direction of our dwellings.

On our way, I spotted a small concave hollow in a rock. I sat myself down in it and proclaimed that I was a queen and this was my throne. My friends laughed recalling a word paper during our schooling hours that spoke of a queen that ruled the land from her throne. The lesson was presented as a sample of the wrong way to live. In this particular lesson, the village elder, Yucca, was trying to demonstrate the shortcomings of the ancient peoples.

"Children, look at this picture." Yucca held up a drawing of a woman whose hair was adorned in beads and shiny rocks. The mountain people all wore some jewels but nothing as excessive as this lady had on. Her clothing was trimmed and superbly fitted to her body unlike the salvage rags that we draped over ours. Soft metals and shiny beads encircled her neck and brightened up her pale skin. Her eyes were small, her lips, thin, and her expression, lifeless. She was raising her hand. The caption below this picture read, "Queen of the Land."

"This is the idol ways of the ancient peoples," began Yucca. "They sat on thrones and worshipped each other. They did not work for their sustenance. They paid homage to those with such light skin that the sun burned them up. They suffered a deserving wrath for their idol ways. That is why it is important that you children work and not waste your time. Help your parents with the chores. Gather fruit and nuts in the orchards. And be thankful for these wise ways that the mountain people have been blessed with."

As I sat on my rock carved throne, Stephin grabbed a stick and touched my shoulder with it. "I crown you Queen of the Mountain People." He proclaimed as he knelt before me in a mocking behaviour. We all laughed heartily and ran to our homes in hopes that we were not late or in trouble for not adhering to some rule we didn't understand.

I loved the extra free time. Once, when the twins and Stephin were not available and when I was too bored to amuse myself with the younger children, I set off on a trek to a mountain peak. We were discouraged from such ventures as they were considered dangerous alone.

However, by myself, there were no voices discouraging me from my venture. And I was still young enough that any conservative voices in my head were well overpowered by a thirst for adventure and discovery. When I reached the top, I was astounded with the view. At the peak, I could see a mountain range that extended in three of the four directions.

On the west side was a deep desert-like canyon separating our region from a distant range. The steep cliffs of the landforms on this side were considered impenetrable. It was said that those who tried to venture in this direction perished either from dehydration or exhaustion. To the north and south of me was a long range of similar mountains extending as far as I could see. The site was inspiring and tugged at my spiritual centre.

I wept as I perused the arrangement of rugged slopes, arising abruptly from the land below. There were petite incisions throughout the range carved by small streams. The mass was decorated with sparse green vegetation and grooved and sculpted with plateaus, mesa, and cones. I saw two ravens in the distance. They looked like specks as they encircled one of the far off intrusive features.

How I wished at that moment I could have been one of those birds and viewed the spectacle from their eyes. To view the world from that distance above the earth would be all-knowing. I sat down and closed my eyes and tried to envision what they saw. I prayed that I might keep this moment to carry me through the more difficult times I was about to endure.

On a day soon after this venture, I returned from the orchards to find my parents sitting in the centre of the dwelling. My mother was actually upright. She had generally been bedridden for most days that year.

She sat leaning against a wall covered in salvage cloth. Her thin face still seemed attractive despite her lack of colour and her drooping eyelids. She still maintained well-etched cheekbones and full lips. It gave her a dignified quality. My father was to her left. On the other side of him was Rondo.

Rondo was at least ten years my senior. I went into a state of numbness immediately. My father began to explain that Rondo was going to be my first suitor. He went on to describe all the food Rondo had brought us and then to explain what was to occur. Waves of heat rippled through my frame.

I knew Rondo as a man who always kept his hair short and seemed to spend a lot of time working out in the orchards. My friends and I often saw him when we were playing by the stream. He would be loading jugglets. We always commented on how full he made them, yet he spilled very little. Occasionally, as we peered at him through the trees, I would catch him staring back at me. I always responded by slinking into the trees and bowing my head as if I had done something wrong.

Rondo seemed quiet. He generally just looked at us. His skin was relatively light, almost olive in colour. His shoulders were broad, but he was not very tall, perhaps a bit shorter than me. He had been living with Stephin's older sister, but she had died in childbirth.

After an explanation, I barely heard I was instructed to go with Rondo to his dwelling. I submitted without dispute as I was resigned to my fate. It took a millennium to walk the few paces to Rondo's quarters, and it seemed as if production in the village had stopped so that all could stare at me. I perceived everyone glaring as though I was guilty of an unspeakable deed. I walked next to Rondo never lifting my head. I followed the direction using his feet as a guide. When we reached his dwelling, I was thankful despite the fear of the events that were abutting.

In the dwelling, Rondo offered me some water and fruit. I had very little appetite, but I indulged myself part in effort to show respect for Rondo and part because I knew that my body craved nourishment. I looked at the floor as I nibbled my fruit, and I sensed Rondo's glances. I continued to ruminate the small portion wishing it would last forever.

Rondo began to speak. "I don't wish to rush you. I will be as kind and gentle as possible. I do not wish to hurt you or anger your father. I would just like to hold you and kiss you for a moment. Please don't be frightened."

He took my lack of response to mean I was prepared. He sat next to me and put his arm around me. His arm felt similar to what I had experienced with friends and relatives, but his kiss was more forceful. His grasp was strong, and I sensed he had to fight his preferences. He did indeed leave it at that though, much to my relief. He directed me to a mattress on the other side of the dwelling. Somehow, the anxiety of the night served to help me sleep.

I slept adequately stirring only two or three times when Rondo arose to leave the dwelling. I saw my mother standing over me after I had spilled some citrus and it bruised. And then I thought I envisioned her scowling at me when I had piled the sun-drying fruit too high and it rotted? My impropriety was unclear, but the response was typical. My mother grimaced in a look of total disgust directed at me, and my father's voice was heard in the background suggesting what a little asshole I was turning into. I awoke from my dreaming discomfort to Rondo noisily repairing a small hole in the thatch of the dwelling.

I sat up and rubbed my eyes to which Rondo immediately responded by offering me water and pine nuts. I went to relieve and refresh myself and returned to eat. Rondo remained in the dwelling the entire time. Upon my completion, he came and sat beside me and, once again, kissed me and held me promenading his efficacy. He held me, and, this time, he moved his hands about touching me. He pulled his torso from me as his arms seemed affixed to my body. Somehow he was able to loosen them and then looked at me. My averted eyes and timid appearance signaled him to let go.

The next day, Rondo went about doing simple tasks such as carrying water and dried citrus into the dwelling, inadvertently kissing and fondling me increasingly throughout the day. I remained in the dwelling mending salvage cloth, an assignment offered to me by Rondo. I had no desire to surface from the abode to the examinations of the surrounding village members. By that nightfall, Rondo had entered me.

6

Rondo's desire did not lessen postacquisition. In fact, it increased. The first night, Rondo lay with me all night and entered me twice more. The next morning, I arose early to relieve and refresh myself in hopes of not being detected by the other villagers. As I sat on a rock close to the dwelling and scooped water from a small bark container to splash on my face, I reflected on the loss of my virginity, trying to discern wisdom from the very little my mother and father had forewarned me about. It had been less discomfort than I anticipated, but it had not been arousing either. Perhaps it had been my perpetual state of numbness that prevented me from feeling anything, good or bad.

I remained numb for the next ten days, but Rondo's desire only increased. He held me possessively. He began to pull the salvage cloth from my entire body and explore me with his mouth. For the most part, I remained detached from my situation, as if I was some type of observer of the events that were occurring. I felt comforted in this state.

I remembered hearing one of the elders telling us during a lesson that "you could discern much from observing." And so I told myself I was learning as I endured my fate in a dazed dilemma. However, occasionally,

I would be brought into the physical reality, and then I would react. I felt overwhelmed and confused. I found myself crying uncontrollably in one afternoon without being able to give a verbal reason for my state.

Rondo walked in on me. He came and sat beside me and put his arm around me. I buried myself in his chest searching for comfort. It was the first time I had done anything other than put my arms around his neck out of fear during intercourse.

"You're so enchanting. I feel like you have put a spell on me." He lifted my chin to direct our eyes to meet. He was a sincere-looking man with light brown eyes. I focused on them as he gazed at me. There was no sparkle to his eyes, but, occasionally, a reflection from the sun or water seemed to lighten them to a different shade. They had a pronounced slant that extended out into a line at the lateral edge. He smiled slightly expounding the fullness of his lips. "I do not want to hurt you."

I replied with nothing. I did not know what to say. I didn't know how to feel. I missed my friends and family. Rondo seemed to be aware of this though, as it had likely all been discussed previous to arrangements made with my parents.

"Would you like to go home for a couple of days?" Rondo asked.

"Yes." I wept.

My mother was actually walking around. Her pace was slow and methodical, and she hunched over a bit, but she appeared to have gained some physical strength. She had even been out tending to the citrus orchard. We sat to eat some dried raven meat that my father had captured and prepared. Fortunately, Dad had given us some privacy. I concluded that it was probably at my mother's request.

"It is a good sign that Rondo permitted you to come home for a while. It shows he does have some sensitivity. It is rare in a man you know.

He could have kept you for the entire ninety days with no retreats." My mother projected a weak smile with downcast eyes.

She looked up at me and motioned me to come and sit close to her. I moved beside her and she touched my head, sliding her fingers through the tightly bound fastens in my hair. She skillfully loosened them and began to braid my hair. "You know, if you have conceived, you do not even have to return, but that would be hard to tell at this point. Let me check anyway." She put her hand on my breasts and then my stomach to check for swelling. "Hmm. Maybe." She smiled. "I'll have someone else come in tomorrow. If you'd like, Letsi, you could go visit your friends. I'm sure they've missed you."

During my absence, the twins and Stephin had been working fairly hard picking pine nuts in the southern valley. Young teens were considered the most suitable for such a task as we were strong enough to climb great heights yet limber and agile enough to burrow through the tightly clustered branches.

We would scurry to the top of the conifers and pull the cones from the branches. We dropped the seeds down to the youngsters and the adults that were below us on the ground. They collected them in sacks and brought them back to the village to be pried open and dried. We worked our way down the tree. Sometimes, we would step out too far on a limb or reach too close to the edge of a small branch, and the stately firs would respond by snapping one of their arms and we would tumble from our perch. Generally, we would not fall very far before grabbing hold of something secure within the concentrated branches.

When I arrived at the site, they were all taking a short break sitting in the damp soil at the bottom of the incline. Their dark skin was a mesh of red and white striations from the cuts and scratches they endured with the battle against the mighty conifers.

"Hey, Letsi!" exclaimed Chris. "Come and join us. We're taking a break while Donny and Randil carry back the baskets."

"You want some nuts?" Delta directed me to some warm pine nuts that had been baked by the noon-hour sun. I grabbed a handful and sat with them under a fir tree. The nuts were bitter from the limited sun exposure. It was preferable to dry them for several days, but they were palatable after opening the cones and pulling the bark like meat out. The more they dried, the less they were bitter. However, the dryer they were, the tougher they were to chew. So it was a choice between taste and texture.

Stephin smiled and nodded a greeting when I sat down, and then Chris filled me in with all the details of their past week and a half, which really amounted to them working fairly diligently on the harvest. No one mentioned my situation, probably because of strict instructions from the adults. We had so little time to visit, and we were all exhausted: they, from their regimented labourious schedule, and me, from my physical and emotional turmoil. Our chat remained superficial, centering on a description of the cones.

"It is hard to believe that one of these little cones can give birth to so many gigantic trees." commented Stephin. "I wonder how it grows into the shape it makes." He lifted the cone to his eye. "It certainly doesn't look like a tree now," he paused for a moment and then looked up with a gleam in his eye. "And it certainly won't look like a tree when it passes through my bowels."

We all responded with an eye-closing, silent chuckle and assumed to eat the tartly morsels. Several similar lines of thought were expressed in our brief meeting amidst the firs, but none sparked into a swirl of youthful dialogue. There was a suppressive guard about us. Perhaps it was brought on by the change that was being thrust upon us. We were metamorphosing into a mode that we did not know how to share. At least, that is how I felt. Perhaps it was the vibe I was projecting to them that dampened the sparks. We did appreciate seeing one another though. I'm sure of it.

I left when the men returned.

I didn't wake up until the sun was well into its climb upward the next day. My dreams had been warm throughout the night. My mother was laughing and swinging me around. My dad and my brother Donny took turns carrying me on their shoulders.

"Letsi," Mom whispered softly. "Louise and Anex have come to examine you."

Quickly, I exited to relieve and refresh myself. When I returned, the women were quick to usher me to the mattress. The procedure was discomforting but no more so than what I had already been through. Anex looked empathetically toward me. Then she turned her attention to the women. No one said a thing, which answered the question. The next day, I returned to Rondo. He was sensitive for a man, I guess. He fed me and limited my workload to sewing and sparse food gathering. He had never actually hurt me, but I was dreadfully uncomfortable and lonely. I began to dread nightfall.

A month later, I exhibited clear signs of pregnancy.

7

It had gotten to the point of being pathetic. I was planning a dwelling for Daniel and me. In my fantasy, I had us living together. I was preparing meals for him and mending his salvage cloth. I knew that men rarely fantasized in such a domestic manner. I knew their thoughts generally centred around sex. I wondered if Daniel was fantasizing about me right now.

On a realistic note, I was given the badge of full recovery in the Moraine Treatment Facility. I had only lost two days of travel time. I felt fairly healthy, and I was looking forward to my journey. I would be meeting with the Stalites to discuss the death of one of their people. Though I hardly felt qualified to act as an intervener, apparently, I possessed qualities that would make me suitable for this position. At least that is the status that had been awarded me by the mountain elders.

"First," stated Randil, "you have had three children, two of which have reached adulthood, one of which has bore offspring. Second, you appear to have insight and innovation when it comes to finding use for salvage equipment."

By this, he was referring to the uses I found for the metal I had salvaged on my excavation ventures. First, I had begun to use thin threadlike bendable wire to prop up plants in the orchard. It had provided increased strength to weak-stemmed plants, which assisted them to stand tall. This, in turn, allowed them to maintain more branches filled with fruit. Prior to this, weak-stemmed plants were generally pulled from the ground before they even had the opportunity of developing. Their future was predicted by those who tended to the orchard. However, with my procedure, more small saplings and tree grafts were starting to have a chance to flourish. This was noted by our people.

However, the most significant invention for which my community acknowledged me was my discovery of a bendable metal paper. This paper allowed us to radically speed up procedures for sun drying and extracting medicinal oils. Quick sun drying was a sought after technique, particularly with meats. Insects often laid eggs in our food products only to be discovered when a person grew deathly ill from consuming them. Quick sun drying practices limited opportunity for maggots and parasites to invade our measly morsels. Also and perhaps even more important, this paper allowed for an increase in medicine. I had been fortunate to have been the one that found it. Or at least that is how it was described by the elders.

What I considered my most noteworthy talent, however, was my ability to decipher the written codes in the word papers found on the excavations. The word papers used such eloquent language. Words never used by our people. I wondered if our people had ever engaged in such language. In the past few years, young mountain children had begun to approach me with word papers in hopes that I might explain their meaning.

"Letsi, we found these papers up on the south face. Do you know what they are?" questioned Ethan, a friend of Mika, my second son.

I perused the specimen presented to me:

The fear of the Lord prolongeth days:
but the years of the wicked shall be shortened.

"It says that if you are good, your days seem long. But if you are bad, your life will be shorter."

"Why would you want to be good if you were gonna live longer with the days dragging on and on? Why not live wicked and not be so bored? We're all gonna die anyway," retorted Mika as he scowled down his mouth. "Those people that wrote this stuff seem very foolish."

As a youngster, Mika came out with many of these profound melancholy thoughts. I rarely could do anything but smile as I usually had to tend to chores or Douglas if Rhondo was out hunting. His doldrums never seemed anything serious though. It did not prevent him from playing with his friends and, in later years, chasing girls. Perhaps his dark humour blended with his carefree attitude had some connection to the fact that he was the youngest male known to have fathered a child.

I did enjoy the opportunity of finding out the meaning of the word passages, however. It seemed as though I was solving an enlightening puzzle like a little chunk of divinity.

Alas, while the ability to decipher word sequences had increased my own self-identity and given me recognition among the people for *being smart*, it had not increased my social status. It was my retrieval of bendable metal sheets from the salvage areas, which had given me elder recognition for something other than childbirth. Although it could be debated as to what gain in status one was getting by being chosen for a trip across the Poison Sea given the highly unlikely survival probability.

"You also appear in good health," added Yucca. She coughed and sputtered as she spoke. She paused to spit and wipe thick, coloured saliva from her mouth with her boney hands. She looked frail and ready to pass, but she, as did we, took comfort in her long full life. It was a positive sign for our people.

"As you know, the Stalites have ceased to trade with the Moraines again," began my father, who had just recently become an elder. The grey in his hair gave him a stately and wise presentation. "The Moraines suggest that it is because of unresolved issues involving the death of a young pregnant Stalite girl. According to Aquill, captain of the vessel docked here last full moon, the Stalites insist that the Moraines have not made just amends for her death. While the Moraines, on the other hand, insist it was an accident. They are deadlocked over the issue, and it has halted trade between our nations. This has caused great inconvenience to our people."

It truly had. The Moraines had much to offer us in diet supplement by way of grassbake, herbs, and tubers. Even more significant though, with halted trade, we no longer had access to the Stalites' reactor metal. The reactor metal had induced us into becoming involved with the conflict between the Moraines and the Stalites. This metal had properties beyond our comprehension. The children referred to it as "the magic rock." The composition of the metal was such that when rubbed moderately, it produced enough energy to serve as both a light and heat source.

Other than the sun, this was the only alternative for heat. Although we knew of fire and knew how to create it, fire was strictly forbidden for the mountain people. It was considered a competitor for our breathing air.

Following a storm, if lightning struck and caused a fire, we would spend several days gasping for air, even if we put it out immediately. A lightning fire was attributed to the death of two small children and an elder in our community and contributed to the illness of numerous others. There did not seem to be enough air for both fire and people to breathe. The reactor metal did not appear to be in competition for our air, and, thus, we welcomed the opportunity to use it.

The metals had proved to act as a positive catalyst for many of our life ways. They did not seem to deprive us of breathing air, but, because they allowed us an extra supply of heat and light, many of our life funds had increased also. Our food supply was greater because we could use this metal to cook some of the fruits and nuts that did not dry well yet were toxic when eaten fresh. We could also use the metals for lighting to extend our harvesting hours into the night to retrieve more fruits and nuts that, otherwise, might spoil.

Furthermore, the heat and energy emitted from the reactor metals allowed for more efficient extraction of medicines from various plant sources. Death was often less painful, and an occasional illness was being cured, particularly in young children. This was attributed to better medicines. And the reactor metal was certainly a factor in producing them.

Our only access to this metal was through the merchants of the sea, the Moraines. The Moraines were no longer bringing over reactor metal because the Stalites were no longer trading with them. It was imperative that a settlement was achieved so that all might benefit. The remuneration to continued trade far outweighed the risk of my death in crossing the Poison Sea. Well, perhaps not for me personally but definitely for the continued existence of the mountain people.

Daniel's light skin looked pale and somewhat sickly alongside my dark skin as we packed supplies for our journey to the Stalite Hills. Yet his muscular robust form, which protruded through layers of salvage cloth, truly made him look more virile than me.

Daniel and two other Moraines, Jaffy and Suz, were assisting me on the journey. Jaffy was a guide who traveled the Stalite route on many trade missions. Suz was a respected and effective negotiator. Her role was similar to mine among her people. Daniel was on the mission because of his medical experience and most likely because it was probably clear to the Moraines that I did fancy him.

The Moraines did not express emotion to the extent that mountain people did. Hence, I had probably already given away several readable gestures and signals of my infatuation. It was so embarrassing.

We set out on the journey the next day. The trail was lenient, relative to the trek across the Poison Sea. The entire terrain was so level in comparison to my homeland. We would cross the Moraine, take a small vessel across a water-filled gorge. By nightfall, we would be at the base of the weatherworn hills that hosted the caves of the Stalites. And, there, we would camp until morning. When the sun rises, we would meet with the Stalites in a common area at the edge of their habitat.

The Moraines had no central village, and we passed patches of dwellings all along the route. Houses varied from the clay huts at the treatment facility to plank hovels created from wood similar to that of the hull of their boats. Small orchards, consisting of a tree or two, were situated at each home. As well, there were small gardens close to the huts with a variety of bushes sprouting up. These bushes were of great interest to me.

Many of these plants contained edible products on not only their fruit, but on their leaves and roots as well. The mountain people had great interest in trying to grow these products in their own habitat but, to date, had been unsuccessful.

Periodically, between dwellings and along the shoreline of their dirty creek, large areas displayed sections of tall reeds and grasses.

"Are these the plants that produce your grassbake products?" I questioned Daniel as I trudged along beside him.

"Yes. But they require our help." Daniel hesitated in his explanation as if frustrated with what he had said. I expected him to continue offering further explanation, but, instead, his face began to turn a reddish tint, and he clenched his fists. His chest heaved, and he let the air out of his lungs with a huffing sound. He then simply rushed ahead of me passing Suz on the trail, bumping into her shoulder knocking her off her stride. He made no offer of apology to her but rather kept up his hurried pace. My perplexed look persuaded Suz to wait for me and walk by my side.

"We, the Moraines, sometimes have trouble expressing things in words. It is particularly frustrating for our men," Suz explained. I nodded trying not to show the level of upset I felt from my exchange with Daniel. Suz continued to speak. I imagine it was an attempt to minimize any friction on this journey.

"The grass is not simply cut and cooked to make grassbake. It must be reaped, dried, and shook. Then only what is left after shaking is pounded. Water is added to the pounded seeds to make a paste. The paste is then cooked with reactor metal. It involves much work and time."

The process seemed fascinating and so foreign to our food gathering practices. I had so many questions about it. I wondered when it was picked. How long was it dried? How was the paste made? I wished I could stay and witness the whole procedure to satisfy my private inquisition. As curious as I felt, I dared not ask too many questions in fear of offending anyone.

Daniel's response to my questions about the grassbake procedure had been very bizarre and somewhat frightening. I had no intention of probing these people to the point of insult. However, I continued to contemplate my query in an introverted manner. I believe it left an expression of incredulity on my face. From this, Suz concluded that I had been put at ease with her brief explanation about both the grassbake and the mannerism of her people.

We continued at a hurried pace along the course. I found the walk easy to adapt to but not typical for me. In the mountains, our pace would slow on the inclines and speed up on the declines. Here in the flats, the rate was quite steady. I was having a tendency to slow down without the mountains to guide me. My traveling companions, however, were used to the flats and ensured that I kept pace with them.

In the night, we camped at the edge of a gorge. The terrain had become desert-like. At the campsite, there were mainly sand hills, sparse bushes, and clumps of grass varying in colour from pale green to brown. Most of the limited flora looked dry and brittle. Yet the Moraines paid close attention to this vegetation as though the scarcity of it had deemed it sacred. I was instructed to walk carefully in this area and not step on any of the vegetation, even the small blades of grass that encircled the site where we were to make our camp were to be avoided.

"These plants struggle for their existence in this harsh land. Their success holds the prospect to our future success," offered Jaffy as an explanation for the strict rules involving where my feet walked. I was by no means sure what he meant, but I certainly wasn't about to ask him to expound his statement since Suz explained the difficulty with communication that I may encounter. I certainly did not want to insult my hosts. But I was so intrigued with their customs; I yearned to understand more.

We put our sacks down in a location that the Moraines had proclaimed was acceptable for our night rest. Daniel brushed the light-coloured sand in one spot and motioned me to sit there. The other two headed towards an unusual-looking plant with a single stalk and a thick green trunk about the size of my leg. They knelt before the large stem and started to chant in a soft melodic voice. Jaffy raised his voice slightly and recited a short incantation:

> *Flourishing growth attached to our home, the earth.*
> *Share with us that wisdom you maintain,*
> *That, which allows you to thrive in such a seemingly inhospitable land.*
> *Nourish us with the blood of the earth that you possess.*

Suz and Jaffy then stood while Daniel continued to kneel. Jaffy took out a small stone scraper and cut four small pieces out of the top of the plant. He passed one to Suz who bowed her head in a motion of thanks. He proceeded to Daniel and then to me. I watched the others intensely as I wondered what I was to do with this offering. Slowly, they put the plant to their mouth and sucked the juice from its shoot. I mimicked their actions. The juice had virtually no taste. It was bland like warm water. However, the taste elicited a sense of thirst in my body, and I was awakened to the fact that we had traveled a great distance without consuming any water. And, hence, I realized water must be a rare and sacred commodity in this region. Constructively, this plant had developed a mechanism to store a large supply. I began to suck the morsel rapaciously. I tried to bite into the plant to squeeze the remaining juice from its pores, but I felt a sharp puncture in my lip.

"Be careful of the thorns," cautioned Daniel. "You must be patient and gentle with this plant, or it will strike out against you. This plant offers you a great gift but demands that you accept it with humility." I thoughtfully absorbed there surprisingly eloquent words and then continue to gently suckle the remaining juice from their sacred offering. I watched and followed as the Moraines took their finished morsels and tenderly buried them in the sand.

We had a small supply of mountain water with us, but, for now, we could postpone using our rations. The plant seemed to have quenched our immediate thirst and stifled our basic needs.

We took our extra cloth from the sacks we were carrying and spread them on the ground in the area that had been staked out as the campsite. Suz sat on hers and I on mine. The men spread out their cloth and left the circumference and headed toward the approaching horizon. I leaned back on my cloth and welcomed the rest.

Suz began to give me more details about the incident involving the Stalites.

"There was a cave-in at one of the Stalite chambers. The Stalite girl was in it, and she was crushed by the rocks. It is not clear how the cave-in was caused. The Stalites accuse that some Moraines were in the area pounding."

"Pounding?" I questioned.

Suz bowed her head and paused for a long time. I did not think she was going to answer my question. I wondered if she had taken offense. I found the Moraines behaviour quite confusing. However, after a noted long time, she did continue.

It is said that some of our people have been crushing rock on the south facing of the Stalite Hills in hopes of discovering reactor metal. The Stalites believe that the quarrying, or the "desecration of their sacred stone" as they describe it, caused the death of one of their children and future offspring."

Suz was a relatively thin Moraine but not nearly as slender as a mountain person. She carried a heavy a load on the trip, comparable to the much larger and younger men. Yet she never seemed to falter. Her emotional state appeared just as stoic, or else she was emotionally removed enough from the situation she was describing, to have a sense of detachment about the loss of a young fruitful Stalite woman.

I wondered about the Stalites' position on having the hills quarried. I had numerous thoughts and questions, but I asked none out of concern that I might insult Suz. Often in reflection, I had resented my mother and father's training on "concern for the feelings of others at the expense of my own." It had frequently made me a self-loathing pushover in my own description. But in this case, I was quite appreciative of the character flaw. I did not know enough about the dynamics of these people to be too aggressive in my questioning. Furthermore, I had clearly been warned that they did have difficulty with expression that could manifest into anger. I chose to listen.

As the sun fell, Suz pulled the salvage cloth back from her eyes. Her ashen face was more weatherworn for her age than mine. The limited sunlight accentuated the wrinkles and grooves on her cheeks that radiated from her mouth. She looked strong though. As she arranged a small mattress in the corner of the camping circle, I went to relieve myself and prepare for bed. I took a small capsule of mountain water with me. In the short time I had been in the Moraines, I had grown tolerant of the restrictions on water use, but I had a mounting desire to purify myself by bathing in mountain water. Of course, I could not sit in a pool along a mountain stream and pour water over my naked body or immerse my bulk into the cool, clear water flowing from the peaks of my homeland. Here, someone would end up with shivers, fever, and death within a couple of days if they immersed themselves in the tainted waters of the Moraine creeks. But I could fantasize. I envisioned myself home, bathing in the spring close to Rondo's old dwelling. I dipped my finger in the tiny capsule and outlined my lips and traced over my eyes and then my entire face. The liquid sparkled like gems against the dark silhouette of my features. It was peaceful, but it made me dreadfully homesick.

I was startled from my visions of the homeland by some unfamiliar noises. It was a grunt or a moan followed by mewling. The noise resembled that of marm, a small rodent that lived in the mountains. A marm had a very deep voice, which was a masquerade for their small size. The intent of the marms was to frighten off predators by their hoarse wails. They were good for eating though and easy to catch if you found their location. This, of course, was not always easy as their calls bounced and echoed off various rock faces in the mountains. Here, however, there was much less echo. I surmised I could probably locate the rodent if I tried hard enough.

I should have gone directly back to the campsite but felt that if I could hunt down this animal, it would raise my status among my traveling companions. It would win me their favour and perhaps motivate them to share their knowledge with me despite our difficulty conversing. I had hunted on occasion in the mountains, mostly when I was younger, before being inducted into the role of bearing children. I had hit a raccoon with a sling before and clubbed down a rat that Stephin and I had cornered. Once, I had almost hit a raven with a rock, but they were so crafty and intimidating. Anytime I had ever been successful at hunting meat, it had always elevated my status, briefly.

I followed the noises, which at this point had quieted down. I was frightened, but the adrenaline kept me going, and the notoriety from securing meat from a small mammal was of greater and more positive a consequence. Besides, most mammals were small and had limited defense against people. I had little to worry about except that I must tread very lightly so as not to disturb the sacred grass. There was still a sliver of sun left. It was enough for me to distinguish movement in the brush ahead. I crept forward steadily, and I slowly pulled back the branches and poised my spear stick.

I almost crumpled from what I saw. My knees were weak. I shifted from leg to leg to keep my balance. It was Daniel and Jaffy, together, in the bushes. I ran back to the dwelling and curled up on the small mattress I had made, wishing I had not seen what I had seen.

8

I knew that those of a similar gender engaged in sexual acts together among the Moraines. Anex had described this and many other dissimilarities among our peoples.

"Well, how do they have children then?" I questioned Anex as I switched Douglas from one breast to nurse on the other. Douglas quickly took hold of the new source of sustenance. He had no trouble feeding. This was a good sign.

"The Moraines do not have strict rules governing procreation. They do not focus on having children from what we know of them. They say they have a high birth rate. They are more concerned with their mortality rate. Their rules and laws seem to centre more on prolonging life rather than giving it."

"Do they suffer from cancers the way our people do?"

"Well, yes," replied Anex. "Cancers of the skin seem to be particularly prominent. But other sicknesses seem to kill them as well. On my venture across the Poison Sea to the Moraine Edge, there was a young Moraine man in my traveling party who complained of a sore stomach. Within two days, he was dead."

"Isn't that how Coral died?" I questioned. Coral was the second of our people to cross the Poison Sea. He was the first to die.

"I believe so," Anex replied. "He recovered from the trip across the sea but then developed a fever on his way to the gorge. The Moraines said he never recuperated completely. The Moraines never go into great detail in their explanations, but it seems they believe that some bugs can inhabit our bodies for years without causing us much discomfort. And then they may suddenly cause a rapid death. This is usually the person we look at with retrospect saying, "Well, he did pass a lot of gas. Or he seemed to have a very active bowel." Anex paused to reflect for a moment as she often did. Anex was about my mother's age, yet she looked much younger. I wouldn't say she was as pretty as Mom, but her healthy complexion gave her an attractive quality. She wore her hair up, bound together in a weave of thin salvage cloth. It was hard to distinguish her hair from the cloth. She pulled it back tightly which elongated her round face and kept her eyebrows in an expression of enthusiasm. She was adventurous and had tales of journeys to support her nature. She continued to speak.

"None of us really know when we are going to die. I guess it helps to rationalize the death by reflecting back on the person's life. And it could very well be that life-threatening insects live inside us." Anex stopped again as she seemed to realize she had strayed from my initial question without giving it ample explanation. "Yes. The Moraines have significant health problems from what I understand, but bearing healthy children is not among them."

Anex took the baby from my arms. "He seems healthy, eating well, getting fat." She paused. "His eyes seem distant though. I wonder what he is thinking about." She looked at me solemnly. "We won't know for a couple of years yet."

The conversation ended as my father entered the dwelling and handed me a sling to carry the baby in. It was made of animal hide, but it was soft to the touch. "Rondo sent this for the baby. It's been cured to relax it. He would like to see the baby again. He should be entitled to that. He could help you over there you know. Here, you are a burden. Your mother is sick, and she cannot help you."

I replied with nothing. It's most likely he would not have slapped me in the mouth for any retort I made, like he had so many times before. Surely, a woman or a girl holding a baby was off limits and had enough status to respond to his remarks. I wished to say, "I want to stay with my Mom to keep her company. I don't want to go to live with Rondo." But instead, I put my head down and said nothing.

My Mom began to stir on the other side of the dwelling. She now spent most of her time sleeping with the aid of the medicines and herbs. It seemed to be a good thing as she did not appear to be in too much discomfort or pain. My father rushed to her side and grabbed her hand.

"She needs water." he commanded. I reached for a small wooden flask and passed it to him. Anex took Douglas out of the dwelling. I reached down and kissed my mother's forehead as my father put the flask to her lips. I followed Anex out of the hut.

She passed the baby back to me and continued to talk as I walked her toward her dwelling.

"Your father is like many men. He thinks he is responsible for everyone's wellbeing. When you are here, he does not see you as a contributor. He sees you as his responsibility. Men do not often recognize that women are industrious. Right now, he wants to focus on caring for your mother. When you are here, it disrupts his focus."

"But I could help him with mother," I countered.

"Not really," replied Anex. "You could help your mother, but you could not help him. With you there, your mother does not receive the full extent of his devotion. He feels he must devote some time to you as well, not only that, but when he cares for her, it not only helps her, but it also helps him cope with his grief." Again she made a characteristic pause. "He is right that Rondo could use your help."

It is not that I didn't value Rondo. In fact, I had grown very appreciative of his generosity. I ate well the time I spent with him. And I lived in a comfortable dwelling. He was a good provider. I was especially grateful when I learned of the hardship Delta had been put through with her first suitor.

Lardes and Jamba had paired her with Salyut, a man at least fifteen years her senior. After the second night with him, Delta had fled from his dwelling. She had been beaten and brutally raped. Although Lardes and Jamba lived fairly close to Salyut's home, Delta ran to the other side of the village to her mother's empty dwelling. Though Violet had passed over a year earlier, the hut was still relatively stable. And, apparently, the spirit of Violet still lingered there and offered a safer haven than with those of the living. The general gossip forum concluded that it was probably a combination of Delta's troubled upbringing, Lardes and Jamba's limited negotiation and instruction for both Salyut and Delta, and, the strongest factor, Salyut had lustful and uncontrolled desires that caused the incident.

In comparison, Rondo had been kind.

As for me, I just longed to be with my mother. I knew she was dying, and I just wanted to stay with her. I didn't think of the baby as a burden to her. He only cried to be fed. I thought she appreciated me by her side, despite her delirium and discomfort. However, she didn't actually say that she wanted me there. She probably didn't actually. At least, she never ever said she wanted me.

On the many occasions, when my father made it clear that I was just a nuisance, she never contradicted his remarks. In fact she supported him. "Why do you have to act so stubborn? Don't you appreciate all your father has done? He cares for you and Donny when I'm ill. He has given you extra privileges among the people. I hate to think about the way you're turning out."

I realized then, I would be going back to Rondo.

I continued to walk with Anex, but I did so with my head shamefully down, pondering my future relocation. I felt so alone and unloved. My soul was grieving also. Anex's wise words had not given my young ears and heart solace.

Anex spoke softly, "Love your baby the way you long to be loved. It will be the greatest gift you can give yourself." She kindly embraced both Douglas and me then parted with these final remarks, "You will be the best mother you can be for this baby. We all are." The acclaim the words offered me at this time was as meaningless as their content.

Two days later, I moved to Rondo's dwelling. My mother died within the month. My father refused assistance preparing her body. He wrapped her in his finest salvage cloth with sage brush and soft needled conifer. He bound her body in swaddling strips of roots and bark. He sewed her favourite shells and beads to the cloth. Her body was carried by my father's peers to our ceremonial mesa on the north side of the dwellings.

The mountain people gathered at the mesa and formed a small circle around my mother's body.

Yucca began the homily: "Joan was a woman of high quality. She bore two healthy productive children. She respected the ways of the mountain people and shall be rewarded in the afterlife."

The speech was so generic. It offered no personal reflection on her life. I was grateful it had been brief. Neither my father nor I appeared to have the competence to deliver a worthy eulogy. My father was uncharacteristically speechless in the midst of his grief. He stood with my Auntie Dana who tried to offer him some consoling. But as she held tight to his arm it likely served to comfort her for the loss of her sister rather than help my father. She stepped forward to make a testimony.

"Joan suffered for many years. She did not complain about her illness. She tried desperately to avoid drawing attention to it. She will not have to avoid it any longer. The suffering is over Joan." Dana swallowed a large lump in her throat, and then her face began to crumble as she wept. Dana could not continue. I began to weep. Rondo took Douglas from my arms and stood by my side in an awkward attempt to comfort me.

Others stepped forward to pay tribute to my mother. Most were tales of her youth, before her sickness. I could not recall a time when her illness wasn't a factor. So the tales were of no value to my grief, at least, not at the moment. I now wondered how much of her pain affected how she raised us. Was her apparent indifference to our struggles as children a lack of love on her part? Or was it the most her weakened body would allow her to express?

It was a sad procedure.

The sorrow found an outlet in my Brother Donny's short accolade. He and the other young men of the village had gathered around her remains as they prepared to take her to the top of the mountain peak. There, her body would stay until the ravens and the beetles dissected her, permitting her soul to enter the Oneness. But before they lifted her with their strong young arms, Donny motioned them to wait. He raised his head to the sky and began to speak as if in a trance:

> *Mother, whose soft hands cleansed my face and braided my hair,*
> *Mother, whose smile warmed my heart and soothed my wounds,*
> *Mother, whose arms gave me comfort from my fears,*

Mother, whose heart gave me strength when I was despaired,
Mother, I will miss these things about you and more.
I feel your presence in my spirit.
May the love that you shared with me guide me on my journey.
And may your love steer you on your journey to the Oneness.

Donny then motioned for his peers to gather up her body and carry it to the resting place. The rest of us stood and wept. Some women brought capsules of water and offered them to my father. My father left the mesa when he saw the young men declining from the peak. I don't think he was aware of anyone around him. He certainly never made a motion to comfort or to seek comfort in me as he scaled down the rocky ledges. Auntie Dana came to embrace me and then followed him down the mountain. I walked home slowly. Rondo reduced his pace to accompany me.

I never returned to the dwelling where I was born.

9

I huddled in my salvage cloth, curled up in a ball, lying on the desert sand of the poorly vegetated gorge. Had I really seen what I had seen? I felt so uneasy. I was embarrassed and not looking forward to my encounter with Daniel and Jaffy in the morning. I had to laugh at myself about the romance I had fantasized about. It seemed unlikely that Daniel could reciprocate any feelings I might have expressed towards him. I had no idea how they would act when they reentered the campsite. Mountain people tended to leave problems or conflicts at night to rest and then review them in the morning in hopes that the sun would burn away the evil and help illuminate the facts. So I was unprepared for the way Daniel marched into the campsite and picked me up and carried me out into a distance clearing. The swiftness to which he transported me and the tightness of his restraining hold highlighted the strength that his large physique suggested. And the prospect of my possible fate, should he chose to exercise his physical power, left me terrified. I was very frightened but I remained in a petrified state of calmness.

"Why were you watching us?"

Amidst my fear, I tried to explain the situation. To my astonishment he just held me and listened. His chest heaved and he looked bellicose, but he made no harmful maneuver toward me. His eyes were piercing and intent. And his face seemed to swell as I stared at him through the light of the stars. He was not a person I would want to have to lie to at this moment. As I spilled out the story, innocent as it was, Daniel's face and grip relaxed while my emotional state intensified. When he finally let me go completely, I ran to the edge of the gorge and sat behind a small bush, desperately hoping no one would find me, at least until I had stopped crying. I'm not sure what was ailing me most, the shock of seeing two men in an intimate position, the fear of Daniel's size and anger, or the fact I had been so off with my fantasy about Daniel. It had certainly elevated my homesickness if nothing else.

I buried my face into my salvage cloth and wept profusely. Every sad thought I could recall throughout my life served to fuel the anguish. I wondered why I had agreed to come here. Why had I risked my life to venture to this unfamiliar place when I had people at home that yearned for my love and care? Why was I not home helping my son, Mika, with his new responsibility of fatherhood? Why was I not home caring for Douglas? Why was I not home trying to get to know Rondo? The sadness of my thoughts mixed with the physical exertion of the day served to sedate me as if a large hand had reached down from the sky and scooped me into its arms. I felt a gentle rocking motion as I curled up in my cloth and lay my head on the side of the gorge.

I'm not sure if they couldn't find me or didn't look, but I remained at the side of the gorge all night. I dozed off at the foot of one of the few sacred bushes. It was a terrible sleep. I awoke several times to brush off the masses of cockroaches and flies that attacked me chronically.

I drifted off to sleep, and Alexandra appeared about a cluster of fog and haze. She looked so radiant with her shiny blond hair and sparkly blue eyes. I moved toward her to give her a hug, but something held me back. It was the ghouls, their long scaly arms pulling at me and mauling my flesh. They were making unusual ticking sounds in the mix of their usual gurgling. It startled me awake.

I realized that the ticking was tiny creatures burrowing into my flesh. I brushed them off frantically and ran around rubbing myself with dirt. It stung as they clenched their incisors into my skin. I took off my salvage cloth and applied the dust directly to my flesh. I shook my cloth and beat the ground in the direction from where the insects were advancing. Quickly, I rolled further down the gorge and wrapped my salvage cloth around my body. I huddled into a crouched up orb and prayed for sunlight.

I dozed off again but it was a guarded sleep. Soon, I awoke to find Suz, Daniel, and Jaffy standing at the top of the gorge. Daniel descended to my location and assisted me up the steep incline. I was weak from lack of sleep and bug bites. The three of them worked under Daniel's instruction to clean me up using some of the dirty Moraine water. They made no mention of the incident the night before, but they were overly attentive to the trauma I considered fairly minor. Perhaps they were genuinely concerned about my state. Many of their people died as the result of an infection inflicted by an insect. Or maybe it was their way of dealing with the discord that occurred that previous evening. I surmised it was both.

I was weak though, and the day's journey was grueling. Had it not been for my years of running and climbing in the altitudes of my homeland, I would not have been able to complete the challenge of reaching the foot of the Stalite Hills. There was little rest that day, but neither was there any attempt to discuss the incident from the night before. It was as if incidents from the past had not occurred. It seemed as if there was only the present to deal with. Indeed, we did need to focus our energy on the journey. And it was becoming clear to me that Moraines expended a lot of energy attempting to communicate verbally.

I had always attributed Rondo's lack of verbalization to lack of interest on his part. I felt I was only there to serve his lust. That was my duty. He seemed to have no interest in me otherwise. He worked hard and provided well. He expressed an interest in his children by taking them with him and explaining many of the tasks he indulged in. He would even take time to try and show Douglas how to plant seeds and carry water. With me, however, he said or did very little beyond attempting procreation. When I would sometimes disclose to him some of the activities I engaged in while he was gone or talk about the people I had spoke to that day, he rarely responded. He would usually just change the subject and request the whereabouts of some object in the dwelling. I began to resent my submission to him. I had once feared it, but, now, I begrudged it. Because there was so little verbal feedback from Rondo, I never attempted to engage in much conversation with him. At times, I allowed my needs for verbal communication to be expressed with Delta or Donny or even Anex. But generally, I just tried to achieve a state of homeostatic harmony through withdrawal.

As I continued on the level pathway, I reflected on my mindset. Maybe I should look at other ways people try to communicate with one another besides words.

I decided to look for signs of reconciliation in the actions of the Moraines. Certainly, they made every attempt to ease my journey. They offered me generous food portions, asked about my insect wounds, checked my skin for a rise in temperature, and even offered, at times, to carry my pack sack.

Perhaps they were making amends in their own way. Or perhaps they were reacting to the fact that I did not look well. By the time we reached the Stalite Hills, it was close to midafternoon. Suz indicated that we would have a brief rest, a small meal, and then we would head to the meeting place.

I was too exhausted to even prepare my mattress. Daniel generously assisted me in my struggle. I felt so lonely at this time that I was practically unaware of the help I was receiving or the help I required. Loneliness is a derivative of alone, and, at this time, I saw no distinction between the two. It wasn't simply a case of pouting or feeling sorry for myself because of my satiation of unusual customs or my revelations of the value of my family; it was beyond this. I genuinely felt profoundly disconnected from my environment. I feared I was slipping back into an all-consuming depression.

Suz peered deep into my eyes. I returned a glance staring at the small speck of red and brown pigment that stained the sclera of her eyeballs. She turned to her companions and spoke.

"It appears to be the venom. We will need to prepare a treatment." Suz gently pushed me to the ground on top of a thick piece of cloth she had pulled from her satchel.

I fell asleep within moments. I slept soundly and remembered nothing. When I woke a short time later, it was still light but close to dusk. The Moraines had prepared grassbake with dried fruit and a small portion of dried meat. Jaffy offered it to me on a piece of dead bark with a full flask of mountain water. I consumed the offering rapidly. Daniel appeared with a small caplet of water and a small piece of very clean-looking salvage cloth. I hadn't noticed, as the journey had been so tasking over the past day and I had been so hungry, but several of the insect bites I had endured the night before had started to fester. My extremities were sporadically adorned with pus filled boils.

Daniel proceeded to clean my wounds frugally but with very expeditious use of the clean water. "They lay their eggs in you. The rachnals do. The maggots can make you very ill if they hatch. This might hurt a bit."

It hurt plenty. He had taken a thin piece of obsidian and commenced to scrape every abscess on my body. He then cleaned my wounds again and told me to rest. He took out a small blanket made of the smoothest salvage cloth I had ever seen. It slid over his skin in a frictionless motion. It was a light shade of blue that shone like the reflection of the sky in glistening water.

"This cloth is very soft to the flesh. It will make your rest much more comfortable." He placed the cloth on the top of a mound of sand and directed me to lie down on it. He placed a smaller sheet on top of me and looked me in the eye. This time it exuded softness and compassion. The raged fury of the previous night was no longer a demon in his spirit. It was this kindness and tenderness in his personality that had charmed me in the first place. I now embraced it as friendship, a quality far more enduring than romantic love.

I rested briefly on the smooth cloth while Suz and Jaffy prepared a small snack of water and nuts. I felt better rested and in much less pain owing to their skillful treatment. Daniel entered the campsite as well, holding a small handful of maroon berries and spoke to Suz, "There was a small patch along the rock face." He proceeded to grind the berries on a rock and mix them with dirt. He dabbed the pasty mixture on all my sores. "This should reduce the pain and the risk of infection. You should be able to travel now."

The paste mixture was cool to the skin and clearly reduced sensation in my extremities in the areas it was placed. I wrapped the smooth cloth around my naked body and added a layer of salvage cloth on the outside. Our journey continued. We began to climb the Stalite Hills in a quest for a small cave that would be our meeting place.

10

For a period after the birth of my second son, I had begun to grow fond of or, at least, comfortable with Rhondo. He continued to be hard working and committed to the children. He was generally unspoken though. His conversation was generally limited to discussing foraging duties, water requests, and questions about Douglas and Mika. "I'm going to the wetlands to get some moss to repair the roof thatch. He's starting to walk now, eh?" He would comment, referring to Douglas toddling around the dwelling.

He often took the children in arm and coddled them. I even saw him kiss Mika once. Overall, he remained quiet and unexpressive though. I rarely saw him smile. Occasionally, when Douglas would copy his actions, such as pressing his palms to the sky in a mimic of his dad's stretches or taking a stick and rubbing it with a flat stone in response to observing Rondo shaving the bark from a frame pole, then I would catch him looking with a warm glow toward his son.

I had started to look forward to his touch. I had begun to initiate conversation with him as an expression of appreciation for his devotion. It pained me when he did not reciprocate the conversation.

I watched Rondo repair the roof as I tended to the children. "You're doing a good job." I remarked. He just looked at me perplexed as if to say, "Who are you to judge my work? You, who does so little." At least, those are the words I ascribed to his silence. I wondered why he was so mean. Was I that valueless?

My self-depreciation was interrupted by Anex, who came to look at the children. I had the privilege of her visiting several times over the past couple of years. I was particularly impressed learning about the excavation journeys she had made.

"I believe Louise was the first woman to attend an excavation," she once explained. "I was the second. It is a fairly grueling expedition but not as severe as the Poison Sea. I would go again if need be, but there seems to be several young men that are more efficient at the task right now."

"Were there not several men that could have gone in your place back when you took on the exercise?" I pondered out loud.

"Maybe," she replied. "Well, I guess there were now that I think about it. Perhaps it had more to do with my insistence. I was quite forceful about my desire to go. I had worked very hard to raise my children, two of which grew up to be healthy enough to bear their own offspring. I was one of the first women to be able to make a claim of productivity to that extent.

My daughter, Winnette, had two children and my son, Barren, had four with three different women. Although my son, Scout, did not bear children, I would say he too was fairly productive. Even though he was branded as anomalous, unworthy, and not encouraged to breed, he was hardworking and smart.

He certainly assisted me at sorting the citrus fruits. He is the one that identified the small ridge on the most productive seeds. I was simply sorting them by shape and colour, but it was my son who had them divided by ridge and nonridge. Because he didn't speak, it was assumed by those observing us that he was obstructing my work.

They left us be though, mainly because they didn't want to deal with my hostility, I guess. Anomalous children are so shunned among our people, especially those considered feeble and unable to support themselves or contribute to the group. It was worse back when Scout was alive. The population was even less stable. The people more or less blamed him and all the anomalous children for our problems."

"But why?" I found myself interrupting to say.

"Because they could, I suppose. It was clear, I guess, from our conception as a people, when we migrated from wherever it was we came from, that, in order for us to survive, God had insisted that we have many children; they needed to be dark skinned, and they could have no defects that would prevent them from being productive to the group or from having future offspring."

I noted her indifference about the subject of our ultimate purpose. Whenever my father spoke of it, he stressed the seriousness of it. When we were children, it was emphasized to the point of putting a deathly fear into us. In childhood, we were terrified of not adhering closely to this instruction. There was elevated anxiety among us when it came to these principles. I could recite the entire doctrine of these principles practically by heart. I had grown up accepting that the mountain people were here for a divine intention. And, thus, many of the principles in the doctrine, I took for granted as truths.

> *In mythical times, the land was covered with a blanket of inferior people. They had some skills and an abundance of tools and textiles but very little wisdom and absolutely no spiritual direction. Their frivolity, of course, had led to their demise. The land and water became poisoned, and these people became sick or were burned up by the sun. Only a few chosen ones remained and it was their preordination to preserve distinctive characteristics among the race. It would clearly not be an*

easy task though, as the demon spawn could still exist among us. And it would be our duty to follow the strictest of regulations to ensure that this evil does not pervade and cause our downfall. These laws include that every effort be made to have all fertile females give birth to as many fledglings as possible. Through abundance, we will be able to search out the desired seed.

As a child, I often feared that at some point I might be centred out as an impure seed. It horrified me to think what fate I might meet if I did not meet this standard.

Because of the belief in these principles, many precepts were set in place, many of which I had already been subjected to through the arrangements between my family and Rondo four years ago. The premise to this arrangement seemed fairly straight forward to me now after having endured the initial trauma of intercourse and childbirth. I was expected to bear as many children as possible. However, now, as I tended to my tiny children despite the arduous demands, I reflected on the marvel and wonderment of the gift of bearing offspring.

The area of doctrine that Anex spoke of, however, seemed much less clear to me, even though I knew that it was one of her main motives for visiting me. It was the designation of "anomalous" among our people that officially brought her to my home. Children who exhibited any signs of "abnormalities" were closely monitored as there was concern that they would be defective.

As Anex had told it to me, when our people first came here, children with obvious impediments, such as those born with profound restrictions on their muscle coordination, were put to death. A few mutant children had been eliminated in the beginning, but, by the third or fourth generation, the law had been adjusted. Now, a child deemed anomalous was simply not permitted to procreate.

Anex had mentioned that she thought the shift in procedure was due to a tragedy of protest. She believed that few women had accepted the infanticide of their children in our early times, regardless of the dogma. Because most women were exhausted after childbirth, they were resigned to the fate of having their child taken from them and disposed of as something beyond their control. They did not do so compliantly though. There was a famous cliché metaphor among our people that had surely stemmed from the practice of infanticide.

"You scream like a woman having her baby taken away" was used to describe someone in terrible agony from a painful accident such as a gash wound or broken bone being reset. Or it was also used to make fun of someone who appeared to be overdramatizing their pain. It was believed that the phrase came from the early people who had to endure the screams and wails of those misfortunate women who had their babies stole from them as they lay helpless post delivery.

Nevertheless, when the women became stronger, some reached elder status. These women opposed the fate that had beset their own babies and damned the law that had allowed them to be taken. They expressed this by vocally protesting the judgment and the doctrine.

In fact, Anex had been told this by her mother who stated that it was her great-great-grandmother, Serene, who was in the forefront of amending this law. She lobbied hard for change when she became an elder. The council responsible for this act had taken one of her babies, and it had left her devastated. Serene's niece was not so strong, or perhaps she was stronger as it was her actions that put a final demise to the infanticide practice. Anex told the story adeptly.

"While the midwives cleaned up the newborn, Greta, Serene's niece, mustered up all her strength to oversee what they were doing with the infant she had just bore. The women looked at one another, and Greta knew something was alarming.

She took the baby from them and cradled her in her arms. She looked upon her beautiful daughter, so tiny and frail. Her skin was light and had not had time to darken up. That tiny baby had delightful facial features and eyes that sparkled and fixated on things as if they could focus like a baby that had matured and been out of the womb for a time.

Greta took that baby to her breast and would not part. As the baby suckled, Greta outlined her face with her finger and moved her hand down the baby's extremities. Where there should have been legs, there were two little stumps on that child. Fate had forgotten to put legs on that beautiful baby.

No one dared to take that child from her breast. But a meeting was called to discuss the situation. Greta held that baby in her arms all night, knowing she would have to fight to keep her. While she lay sleeping, the child was pried from her grasp by a nameless man. She woke but was unable to struggle free from the restraining hold of another man. The screams were haunting and resonating throughout the dwellings of all mountain people.

"My baby! Bring me my baby!" The man continued to hold her as his strength was greater than a woman in this state; she could not loosen his grip. Eventually, she quieted and the man left the hut. Greta complied by lying still; but a solemn, determined, almost catatonic look was on her face.

In the morning, Greta was gone. She had slipped out of the dwelling and past the village compound without anyone hearing her. It seemed next to impossible that a woman in this condition could walk past the midwife sleeping in her hut and creep by so many dwellings after just having had a baby. Yet no one was stirred. Some have described this as the time the mountain people were put under a sleeping spell, unable to wake in time to right the wrongs done to a young woman.

The only clue to Greta's whereabouts was a spotted trail of blood from her hut to the east cliffs. She was still hemorrhaging, and the people feared she would lose too much blood to recover. Alas, she would not recover, but it wasn't from blood loss. When they reached the cliffs, they saw Greta's mangled body at the bottom of the jagged rocks close to the passage toward the Poison Sea. The loss was so devastating. The people went about their business for months, jolted by the atrocity. Greta's death was never mentioned in any public forum, but never again were mutant babies murdered."

Anex looked up, pondering the power of the tale she had just revealed. Her eyes were clearly saddened and distant. "That is not to say they are treated well now. Scout was always looked down upon. Other mothers told their children not to play with him. Scouts own siblings often had to choose between staying with Scout and leaving him behind to join their peers. The older they got, the more the peers won the decision. I felt like no one else except me and my kids ever really gave Scout a chance.

I felt like he was perceived as the cause of the woes among the mountain people. In fact, when he drowned, although people were cordial to me, I'm sure, amongst themselves, they thought our race, me included, were better off without him." Anex looked at me with her imperturbable features showing a slight hint of emotional pain. I was so often honoured that she would share her stories with me. I knew she did not with everyone.

"The irony is," she continued, "Scout was far closer to purity and wisdom and Oneness, than most of the People. We are just too pathetic to realize it." Her eyes turned from pain to empathy. "If it turns out that Douglas or even Mika is deemed anomalous, it may be very difficult in the beginning, but I think you are strong enough to deal with it. And I think you are sensitive and insightful enough to realize that this world loves all children."

I loved to talk to Anex. She always seemed so warm and down to earth. As I began to have more trouble with Douglas, I wondered in retrospect whether her talks were just spontaneous conversation that she trusted me with or lectures geared specifically to prepare me for the woes I may encounter as my son got older but did not grow up.

Douglas still wasn't talking and his legs did appear to be a little too wobbly for a toddler. Anex had made mention of it and did watch him very closely. But that was her official reason for visiting. The elders had assigned her to visitations with me precisely because Douglas appeared to be experiencing difficulty with his milestones.

After she left, Rondo reentered the dwelling. "Do you think Douglas will be okay?" I questioned him.

He gave me a warm but pensive look. "He's perfect. I am a fortunate man."

And I, in that brief moment, felt like a fortunate woman.

11

By Douglas's fifth year, it seemed clear that my first born was not achieving the milestones well enough to suit the regulations of the mountain people. He barely walked and still babbled like a baby. He understood little instruction, and Rondo and I had to watch him closely around the cliffs, the streams, and the poison fruit. Mika, our second son, was only two, yet he seemed more mature than Douglas.

Anex's visits had switched from observer to counselor. Although I made no note of any real distinction, I was aware of the protocol from years of my father's instruction.

"When a woman has a child, an elder woman is assigned to look over the baby. If she makes no immediate note of any mutations, she will return on a moonly basis to assess the progress of the child. When she is completely satisfied that the child is not anomalous, she will cease in her visits. If she finds clear signs of mutation, she shall counsel the woman in the purpose of our people. There is always the fear that a young woman will refuse to bear more children once it is exposed that she carries spoiled seed. The role of the elder is to convey to the young woman that she must continue to bear children.

Purity is not a gift that all are blessed with. Yet, within even the most tainted individual, there are some remnants of the image of the Oneness. With proper nurturance, guidance, prayer, and hope, even these people can produce regular children. Thus, even for those with spoiled seed, it is imperative that women continue to procreate and attempt to produce acceptable children in order to ensure the preservation of the mountain people."

All of this was transmitted by my father in one of his many lectures. He was not just our father but one of the instructors in the ways of the people. He was responsible for this instruction to many of us when we were children. It was always very difficult to sit and listen to his lectures. They did not have the same inspiration for me as the letter and number lessons that my Aunt Dana, and Berma, Stephin's aunt taught us. Yet we dared not show any signs of ennui, regardless of how banal we found his lectures.

If we so much as drifted into daydreams, let alone acts of disruption, his wrath was swift. Many times, we had been hit with a switch for putting our head down or kicking at the sand as he spoke. Occasionally, some of the boys received a thrashing for attempting to talk during his addresses. Had I understood how closely those lectures would be a testament of my own life, perhaps I might have been more of a keen listener.

In contrast, the women who taught us had more hands-on learning. We were able to work with the numbers and manipulate them. It always seemed like magic to me how two and three could be transformed into five.

My greatest fascination, however, seemed to be with the word books that they salvaged from the excavations. We learned how to read through them and developed an insight into the people of the past. To me, these ancients often seemed so similar to us, not wicked as it was supposed. The stories we salvaged contained many common emotions and feelings.

While there did appear to be many tragedies in these word papers, there was also love, sensitivity, and joy. Of course, there was no doubt that many examples of profane work among these papers would support the belief in their great wickedness. We would be exposed to long descriptions of gruesome murders with details that appeared glamourized as though the storyteller took pleasure in the description. There were also passages that appeared to deface the sanctity of the act of procreation. These and many other passages were generally used to support the concept that the ancient people lived a contemptuous lifestyle.

On occasion, however, there was a whole book that hadn't been deciphered. And I would have the opportunity to use my own ingenuity and creativity to try and decode its mysteries. Our time in the learning circles was limited as it interfered with work schedules, but the brief periods were certainly appreciated by me.

And while I detested my father's learning circles, I had discerned enough from his lectures to know what Anex's intent was with her visits. As a result, I began to resent her intrusion on my life. But I said nothing. There was nothing I could do anyway. To show any resistance to her would simply draw more attention to me and likely more visitors, intent on enlightening me and showing me the true path.

My interpretation of their "enlightenment" meant breaking my spirit and resigning me to defeat. Since I did not have an option, I tried to make the best of it. This is the time I learned about cynicism and searched for the uselessness in everything.

During this time, I also learned that I was a vocational listener. I could sit for an extended period of time and reveal little about myself while giving others the impression we were having a conversation. I had also learned a skill of manipulating dialogue. I found that people who generally talked a lot could be steered from the original goal of their talk because they often didn't take appropriate time to think about what they were saying. I noted that Donny did this quite often with my father. And, now, it appeared to me that I might also have the ability.

While I had not originally thought of Anex as a long-winded person but rather a skillful storyteller, I now found our conversations very hard to endure, especially whenever I detected that she was subtly trying to give me advice. Despite how much I liked and respected her, I viscously resented her assumption that she knew how I felt.

I found that intolerable in most people. I felt that in order to know someone, you had to listen to them, absorb, and discern. In contrast, I found most people did not do this, and Anex was no exception. At least that is how it appeared to me. I felt so invalidated as if no one understood me.

It was the misinterpretation that was most frustrating. It was as if people, Anex among them, thought they knew how I felt, what I was going through, and what was best for me. There was ignorance about such an assumption that disturbed me deeply.

Anex was likely out of her comfort area when she gave these talks because she knew first hand that I would have to go through the experience myself for no one else possessed the ability to go through my life for me. She also knew, however, that her duty was to try and shed some fragments of experienced wisdom on my situation that I might hear now, discern later, and apply someday. So, as awkward as the meetings had become, Anex felt obligated to try and fill the void of my silence and throw out lifelines in the form of possible scenarios for my future.

I, on the other hand, began to focus on the parts of the conversation that suited me. Ultimately, I guess that is all any of us really do, attempt to discern wisdom from the information we are presented with. The motive of the speaker seldom factors in to our listening. We may dispute some of the facts and disregard others, but the goal of language appears to be a search for meaning hidden like a riddle amongst the mundane.

Anex spoke, "When Scout was little, I didn't believe anything was wrong with him. And I had a hard time accepting that he was not really wanted by anyone but me. I wondered; what was the point of having children if the people didn't include you or accept you?

Sometimes, people just don't realize that a mother's children often feel like an extension of herself. We are not only physically of the same body but, somehow, connected closely in soul. Children are connected to us with some kind of a spiritual umbilical cord. Through bearing children, something is not taken away, but, rather, you are extended.

New children you might bare are also connected in the same manner as your children deemed an anomaly. In fact, they will be of more support to you. You will gain status for having them and, thus, gain status for your mutant children as well. There was certainly no misfortune for me in having Scout; nor was there any setback for me in having two more children that were more accepted by the people."

I wondered what elevated status really meant. We had a child that depleted most of our energy simply by tending to him and preventing him from offending others and injuring himself. That was compounded by the emotional strain of coping with rejection and feelings of unworthiness, which accompanied having an outcast son. How could tending to another child somehow relieve our exhaustion?

Mika was a beautiful addition to our family, but he had not lightened the burden of our plight. In fact, he not only became another mouth to feed and body to care for, but also attending to Mika began to tax my emotion as well for I felt guilty that I could not take time to give Mika the attention he deserved and the attention I would like to give him. I felt remorse over the fact that I did not have the energy to care for him the way I would like.

Thus, I was not only physically strained and in grief, but I was also emotionally guilt-ridden and overwhelmed. I mused over this self-pitying trend of thought and let Anex's continued word leave my notice. Occasionally, the odd word or phrase would drift into my consciousness.

"It is truly an endowment to bear children. We are truly bequest with that." I thought of the gift as more an encumbrance. Anex continued as I preoccupied my own thought that varied from planning my harvest activities for the next day to the futile existence that we all seemed to succumb to.

"It is my greatest accomplishment. I know it probably seems pomposity to you at this point. It certainly did to me at your age. But now, in reflection, I realize it was a consummation not measurable. To beget children is verily a spiritual fulfillment."

Here, I recognized the opportunity to maneuver the dialogue. "What did you think about at my age? What did you do? What kept you happy?"

"I kept very busy, preoccupied I guess," Anex replied. Her response was always forthright.

"How? I mean, what type of activity did you engage in? What kind of adventures and goals did you pursue?" I queried, hoping she would focus on the excavations. I yearned for knowledge about these expeditions and romanticized about them as wondrous adventures. As she described them to my well-suppressed elation, I began to realize the travail that such an enterprise encompassed.

"It is a truculent journey. You have to bypass the mountains, to the dry delta. It is very unstable ground, and people have been lost to mudslides and washouts. The terrain changes so abruptly. There is no warning. On my second trek, we were walking along a ledge below the tree line on the east side of the mountains. It was the silence, the stillness that I recall, then a gust of such great magnitude I could never have imagined." There was a pause as Anex recomposed. It was characteristic of her whenever she wished to speak of something that bestowed her with discomfort or pain.

"It was the rocks and boulders, which I remember, striking us with such great force. And we couldn't breathe as we were swept away in this light brown soup of sand, mud, and boulders. That was my last conscious memory until I awoke on a resurrected sand spit.

It was evidently the next morning or some subsequent morning. It was hard for me to discern how long I had lain there or how long I remained drifting in and out of sleep, but when I tried to walk, I noticed that my ankle was virtually severed, hanging only by skin and perhaps some muscle and tendon. I tore some of my salvage cloth and braced my leg with a couple of sticks that lay amongst the debris from the landslide. Then I hobbled forward with the aid of a small log. I oriented myself with the sun setting and headed out on a northern trek for home.

I noticed my hands were dreadfully bruised and cut as I raised them to my face to feel the swells around my eyes, cheeks, and mouth. I was in major trauma. I kept trudging along though and managed to reach what appeared to be a newly formed summit as result of the washout. The geography was much kinder on my jaunt home, but the journey was far more grueling. I hobbled over rock ledges and crawled on all fours whenever I was required to descend or ascend a mountain strike.

There were plenty of unfamiliar springs sprouting from the mountains in the form of miniature waterfalls. I'm sure they were connected in some way to the great tributary that caused this washout. I have often wondered where the source of our clean water begins. Many people have tried to trace it but have given up the search because of rough terrain. In some places, the streams just seem to disappear inside the mountains. Some of us wonder if some mountains are just a hard exterior encircling a pool of precious liquid inside. We wonder if it is possible that some mountains are merely vessels for our precious commodity. I guess this is why we hold the mountains in such great honour.

The springs along route allowed me to cleanse my wounds and keep myself hydrated. I am sure that is why I did not suffer any major infection or, worse, lose my leg.

When I reached the orchids, I found out Faren had made it back, but Ori had not. Ori never returned. He was devoured by the mountain gods I suppose. I never really grieved for Ori, at least not properly. I was just too busy recovering from my wounds I guess. But while I lay healing, I did have plenty of time to ponder over why I had chose to endeavour on such a difficult journey.

The journey had been a great risk on my part. I believe it was because I was trying to escape the reality of caring for my children. The constant barrage of judgment because of my son Scout had taken its toll on me.

You see, I truly believed and still do that I possessed the truth when it comes to Scout and that he *was* a mountain person, just as worthy as any. Because of this, I had thought that I was invincible to the constant intolerance. Intolerance, such as the comments behind my back, would infuriate me. It was particularly hard because they would not say things to my face, so I had no means of challenging them or defending Scout. However, what they did say in front of me was far worse, even though it was not their intent. People would approach me on occasion with remarks disguised as sincere condolences. "I am so glad I do not have to endure what you endure. You must be a special person to endure such a hardship." There remarks sounded so patronizing. It disgusted and angered me. It was especially maddening to think that these people thought they were saying something in any way "helpful." I tried to convince myself that these things didn't bother me by rationalizing them. "The people that say these things are assholes. They are ignorant and they are wrong. So I will not allow their thinking to sabotage my happiness." But the comments did bother me. They left me feeling sad and lonely.

However, it also made me crave to escape the situation. The excavations seemed just the divergence with enough duty to preoccupy myself. But, of course, we cannot escape ourselves."

I thought to myself, "Yes. That is what I crave also, a divergence." As I pondered these thoughts, my attention drifted from Anex's words, but I did register one of her final thoughts.

"As I lay healing after the washout tragedy on my second excavation, I realized that these trips only served to reaffirm me, how important my function was to devote love and nurturance to my children. I think my survival was a testimony to that."

Although I registered these final thoughts, the words of apparent wisdom met my ears with indifference. It was the adventure that enthused me.

12

The tree line of the Stalite caves was not adorned with the wind-deformed foliage that graced the footpath of our stately peaks. The hills of the Stalites look so obscure in comparison to the topography of my homeland. Of course, I did have a bias for the mountains, especially since I was chronically homesick. Nevertheless, the pastel shades of the Stalite swells, traced by the contrasting hues of green shrubbery, had an alluring soft calm about them.

The night sky was approaching and the sunset presented an array of red and violet shades spread across the horizon. There were occasional breaks in the colour arrangement by tints of yellow, orange, and shadows of sparse clouds. The painted sky appeared to extend into infinity. In the mountains, we were never exposed to this much uninterrupted sky. The atmosphere was always broken at some point by one of our stately peaks, even when we ventured to view the world from the top of a summit.

The Moraines and I began to venture up and through the incline caves, cliffs, and tunnels in pursuit of the Stalite home. The undertaking became more difficult as we hazarded further into their domain. As we ventured forth, the tunnels became longer and narrower. The caves darkened. Paths were littered with cracks and crevices that presented the threat of a bottomless drop to any unsuspecting intruder. It was a challenging trek, but Suz and Jaffy were quite familiar with the trail and able to guide us safely along.

Finally, however, after several gruesome maneuvers, our journey came to a halt. We had reached an impenetrable end pass that was virtually absent of light. We crawled into a small fissure which served as the opening to a small dark cave. Both Suz and Jaffy forewarned that there were several gaps in the floor of the tunnel and that we should remain seated on the ridge close to the entrance. Apparently, many Moraine travelers had been swallowed and devoured by these unassuming crevices in the ground.

We waited quietly in the darkness of the cave. It was frightening. It reminded me of my dreams except that there were no voices calling in the distance. There did appear to be tiny lights flickering in the void, however, that were starting to catch my attention as my eyes craved stimulation. As I began to focus on them, I realized they were growing. They were moving closer. I looked to the Moraines to see if they were aware of the image I saw developing. They seemed to know, but were not alarmed. I continued to stare at the increase in illumination.

The lights pulsated, escalating in size and drawing nearer to us. As the lights grew near, shadows began to appear. The shadows commenced to take form, and it seemed they were shapes similar to ours but darker in the blackness. Then what appeared to be an arm slowly threaded its way through some small crack in the wall of the cave, counter to where we sat. Then another arm slithered through another crack and then another.

Slowly, tiny bodies began to immerge through the slivers in the wall as though they had osmosed through solid rock. Next, the images were in their fullness, one followed by the next. The green lights appeared fastened to their hands. They shone them toward me and then pulled them back toward themselves. The vision was startling. I saw them amidst the shadow and light. It was the ghouls. My body went weak and I collapsed to the ground.

13

I had not had thorough preparation for the appearance of the Stalites. Only a handful of mountain people had ever seen them. Anex was one of them, but we had never really discussed their facade in great detail. She said that they were small thin people. She also mentioned that she wasn't sure of their skin colour and did not give me much detail about their features.

She alleged that it was difficult to describe them because she only saw them briefly, likely in the dark cave in which I now found myself. The conflict she was involved in was solved very quickly, and she returned home having accumulated very little observational data about the Stalites.

Anex's assignment had not involved a murder. It had only involved trade issues with all parties looking for more goods. Anex's main task in crossing the sea was to introduce mountain medicines to the Moraines. They negotiated a settlement through a brief meeting. Thus, she had spent little time observing the people. Most of her assignment was spent talking to the Moraines, explaining how to use certain herbs and oils. Furthermore, Anex had been quite ill for the entire trip. It is likely she barely made it home. Thus, her description of the Stalites was next to none.

Through a glazed-over eye and up-close, face-to-face observations, the Stalites really didn't look like ghouls at all. Their skin glistened with a cool, light green tinge by the illumination of their beacons. Around their faces was a soft glowing aura. They looked peaceful and warm. Daniel, in contrast, looked hard and brawny but with a rustic charm as he felt my forehead. As I saw the faces of both people above me, looking down and discussing my situation, I surmised that they had come to the conclusion that the insect assault had been the cause of my collapse. Despite the fact that my sores were healing nicely, they had grave concerns about my health. I wondered if perhaps it was simply the prominence of my scars that had them aghast. The light skin of the Moraines did not seem to pronounce their scar tissue with the same distinction as my darker hue. I was sure this was some of the cause for alarm. It was simply one of the very few disadvantages of my relatively dark skin. We could not hide our scars.

While the others were concerned with my insect wounds, I attributed my weakness to being an emotional ambush that overtook me when I thought my most ghastly visions and dreams were confronting me in a new form of reality. I did not share this story with my hosts though; but I held it deep in my heart. I thought that perhaps the death of Alexandra was finding a new way to haunt me. Besides, I did not want to think of any alternatives such as insects invading my body. It seemed much less desirable at the moment.

I sat up indicating I was all right. Immediately, I sensed a clear animosity in the small enclosure between these two peoples. I was aware there were more conflicts between the Moraines and Stalites than between us and either people. The reasons were fairly obvious. We simply lived further away and had little contact with the Moraines and virtually none with the

Stalites. It was generally accepted that the territorial borders between the Stalites and Moraines made the two more antagonistic toward each other. However, when confronted with the state of affairs directly, it certainly made things uneasy. In fact, I concluded that my weak spell had served the purpose of alleviating the tension a bit by drawing the focus away from their conflict and toward my condition.

It lasted only briefly though. Once I sat up, a small circle of people was guardedly constructed on the cavity-ridden floor. The green glowing lights were placed in the centre of the ring. Suz began the discussion by suggesting we all introduce ourselves. The Stalites appeared compliant but not overly enthused.

"I am Neil," began the first Stalite. His hair appeared soft and fine. In fact, all the Stalites in the cave appeared to have similar hair texture to that of their giant neighbours. And it seemed to be fairly light in colour, although this was difficult to make conclusions about beneath the emerald glow. Neil's eyes were a warm but piercing hazel, and his skin was clearly fairer than both mine and the Moraines. "I examined Lauren following the trauma that took her life."

Vanel, announced herself as an observer, and Alan and Tonaldo proclaimed themselves as council members. Because of their apparent senior years to Vanel and Neil, I concluded that their status was analogous with our elders. My inquisitiveness appeared to be overpowering my self-control as I found myself staring at these "exotic people," as I termed them.

In the glistening light, it appeared that their skin was covered in a mix of oil, and earth and a faint pattern could be observed through the shadows. The painted skin appeared to be a substitute for clothing. Their stature was clearly petite. They were tiny in comparison to me and minuet alongside of the Moraines. They seemed fragile.

I noticed myself staring and hoped I hadn't been observed doing so to the point of being offensive. Occasionally, I would meet glances with a Stalite. It made me think that perhaps the Stalites too were checking me out with the same inquisitiveness.

"We would like to talk to the mountain person alone," Tonaldo spoke in a soft but assertive voice.

"If that is what you wish," responded Suz somewhat abruptly, as if she half-expected it. Daniel and Jaffy looked somewhat alarmed, but Suz seemed confident in her reply. Since she was the one most familiar with interacting with the Stalites, the Moraine men nodded their head in compliance. I, for the most part, appeared so baffled and foreign during the brief discussion that any alarm I exhibited was not at issue here. Suz turned to me and stated, "We will return for you in a day and a half. We have other things to tend to on this journey. We will continue beyond the hills and meet with the Moraines that live on the east side. We will secure supplies for the trek home. In two mornings, we will be here in the meeting place waiting for you."

She noticed the apprehension emerging on my face and felt compelled to say more.

"Do not be distressed. They have no issues with the mountain people."

Issues? I pondered to myself. The point was supposed to be reassuring, but it left me perplexed and apprehensive. While, indeed, I was hesitant, conflictingly, however, it also aroused a sense of curiosity inside of me. How did the Stalites and Moraines usually deal with issues? Nothing more was said on the matter. The Moraines rose to leave. Daniel looked gently at me as he left my supplies and gave directions on applying the paste to my insect wounds. He gently lifted my arms.

"I think they will heal," he said with what appeared to be a smile on his face. And then he exited the cave.

I sat alone with the Stalites glowing at the green embers, which began to have a trancelike effect on me. It was quiet and calm. The lights seemed to generate a soothing force. Still, I felt somewhat uneasy. I continued to sit silently and focus on the rays of the light. The discomfort in the situation began to fade as my eyes fixated on the brilliance in the centre of the cave. From the centre, both the Stalites and I radiated like rays of the sun that break from behind a cloud. I was surprised at the calmness that was overtaking me. It was like I was thinking of nothing and reveling in the splendor of nothingness. I felt quelled. It was in this omnipresent calm that the Stalites began to converse with me.

"The loss of Lauren was a great tragedy for our people," began Alan. Alan had an oval-shaped head. He bound the front sections of his hair posterior to his ears, leaving the back sections flowing behind his shoulders. "She was young. And she may have been with child. The Moraines must take responsibility for their culpability."

Several questions entered my mind at this point. Two main ones being how, exactly, were they responsible, and how should they take responsibility. The Moraines had mentioned that she was killed when a cave collapsed and that the Moraines may have caused the collapse because of the mining assignments they were undertaking as an attempt to retrieve some reactor metal on their own. From what Suz had said, the "pounding" as she referred to was in no way related to the cave-in. And the Moraines had been sympathetic to their loss and bestowed many foods and medicines upon the Stalites as an offering of peace and goodwill.

I was quick to correct myself, however, as that was the Moraine's version of events, not necessarily the facts. Now, I was about to be immersed in the Stalites' account. I was thankful for my listening skills. And the experience with the Moraines had reinforced my inclination to keep quiet in order to understand. In spite of this, I sensed that the

Stalites were waiting for me to respond with some statement indicating I acknowledged their position.

"To lose a young woman with child is a devastating loss among our people as well." I spoke out. As I did, I realized it was the first they heard my voice other than the slight sigh following my fainting spell. I picked up on their intrigue in hearing me although it was ever so subtle. It was only a slight quick shift in the eyes toward my direction. These emerald eyes had only maintained a strong relationship with the centre light up to that point. It was a warm and inviting look of interest though.

They appeared to want to maximize our encounter. They seemed to be interested in me or curious at least. I had not picked up on any curiosity from the Moraines. I'm not sure if it was misinterpretation, or they general had no intrusive inclinations about Mountain People, or me in particular.

Alan looked with an ardent and stoic blend. His straight grey hair was long and thin. It fell like string from the sides of his head. There was a small goatee protruding from his chin. His well-traced eyes were small and sunken in. Wrinkles encircled them and the lines around his mouth resembled ripples extending from a pebble when it is dropped in the water. "Among your people, was anyone murdered?"

My first thought was of Greta. Although she took her own life, the dogma of our people had really been responsible for her death. And laws were changed as a consequence of the loss of this young woman. As quietly introspective as I generally was, I found myself relaying the story of Greta to the Stalites and my interpretation of the events as well.

The Stalites listened so intently and respectfully that I found myself opening up and sharing my knowledge and thoughts even more. It was rare for me to trust anyone enough to do anything like this. Occasionally, I had shared with Stephin and even Rondo, some of my personal feelings, but I generally found that they, as well as others, used knowledge of one another as a weapon, if they listened at all.

The only people I truly shared with were Alexandra, Douglas, and Mika, but they of course were children. The connection I shared with them, as sacred as it was, was far different from sharing with an adult. Children are deep spiritual beings. Sharing with them is like sharing with the Oneness. It is easier and unconditional.

Sharing with adults is a much more difficult challenge. Adults can relate to many of my situations more because they are struggling through the same stage of life. But as adults, we often see ourselves as competitors. And, thus, we compare when someone shares a story. We feel threatened when others are successful and vain when some speak of travail. There is little solace in our sharing, so we tend to build up barriers.

With the Stalites, I was not divulging the most intimate details about myself, but I was committing to a story that would convey some of my values and beliefs. I felt free to do so partly because of their attentive mannerism and also because there was a very limited relationship between me and these people. And, thus, I did not have to invest very much personal emotion. At the same time, I could let my guard down a little. Even if they were judging me, their standards were alien.

I relayed how I thought our laws, while there to protect, preserve, and enhance our people, were often not flexible enough to deal with the reality of our random world. Or, at least, we were not superior-enough beings to have a reliable blueprint that could be utilized to all interactions within our society. I realized I was getting off on a tangent, but their gaze was affixed to me as I spoke, and I felt very comfortable sharing what I believed with them. Neil in particular was actually staring. He did not even avert his eyes when I looked back.

I then began to recall the only murder I was aware of among the mountain people. It involved Lardes's brother, Thomas. Occasionally, I could recall running into Thomas on the mountains where Delta, Chris, Stephin, and I would play when we were nine or ten.

We all had been warned several times to stay away from Thomas. We were also told to return to the dwelling area if we saw him while up in the mountains. Generally, the handful of times we had seen him, he was at a distance and we ran down the mountain quickly excited and enthused over our adventure.

"That was close," expounded Delta. "He could have reached us up there, you know?"

"What do you think he would do to us if he did?" questioned Stephin.

"Most likely eat us," replied Chris. We all responded with laughter. But Chris did not recant. Instead, he expanded on his theory. "Well, why else would our parents and the elders be so concerned about us around him? It makes sense doesn't it? Think about all the stories we have been told involving witches, ogres, and ghouls. All those evil creatures ate children didn't they? Thomas is off by himself. His clothes are ragged. He is short with long spindling arms."

"His arms aren't spindling," responded Stephin, grabbing my arm. "This is a spindling arm." He perused me intently. "You're not a ghoul are you?" I responded by kicking him as hard as I could. I aimed for his crotch but missed and got the inside of his thigh. "Iee-yow! Watch the jewels."

"Actually he isn't that tall, but his arms are quite thin," corrected Delta, attempting to focus the topic. "He looks very strong though. I'm sure afraid of him."

"Strong and evil, just like a ghoul. Why else would we have been told to stay away from him? And what does he eat really? He is never gathering with the people." Chris did have a fairly convincing argument as usual. Nevertheless, we did try to challenge it.

"He could hunt. He certainly spends enough time in the mountains," I suggested.

"Well, I heard he beats and rapes people. That's why he's so dangerous," included Stephin. Sometimes Stephin startled us, both with his bluntness and his knowledge. At this young age, I really knew nothing about the concept of rape or even a beating for that matter. And even Chris and Delta had only relatively minimal experience with beatings in comparison to what we later found out that Thomas was guilty of committing. It was described to me, by Anex, years later.

"Why was the murder of Thomas sanctioned by our people?" I questioned Anex on one of her visits to check the progress of Douglas who was now six, barely walking and still not speaking intelligibly.

"It was not considered murder. It was considered justice. Of all the children that have been murdered among our people under the guise of protecting the species, no one to date was more deviant and worthy of such a proclamation than Thomas. At least no one deserved to die more." Anex always spoke with a mix of sensitivity, analysis, boldness, and authority. Her stories left room for reflection and thought, as well as personal reaction. "I guess it was about his time of puberty that I and the community at large were first made aware of Thomas's serious aberrant behaviour, although I'm sure his parents recognized things much earlier.

It was my daughter, Winnette, who brought him to my attention. He was about her age, a little younger perhaps. One day, my little Winnie came running down the mountain frightened to death. She was crying. Her skin was all pasty and her eyes were puffy. She was panting and sweating from sprinting so quickly down the hill. She began to babble fairly incoherently mentioning Thomas and Dana, but it was very hard to follow.

I grabbed her hands in an attempt to calm her, and when I turned to her palms, I saw blood on them. Eventually, she eased in her state enough to explain the events that led to her circumstances.

Apparently, Winnette, Thomas, Lardes, and Dana, your auntie, were all playing in the mountains one day. The girls were having a game of hide and seek, and Thomas came to join in. Dana and Winnette welcomed the extra player, but Lardes, Thomas's sister, said she was tired and not feeling well, so she left, down the mountain. In retrospect, I wonder if Lardes was trying to avoid her brother because she had lived with his deviance first hand.

Dana, Winnette, and Thomas had played several turns of their game and were immersed as children often get. On one turn, Dana was "it." She had found Winnette fairly easy as she was always very determined and competitive in her pursuit. Winnette sat by the home log while Dana went in search of Thomas. She was off quite a while, evidently, then returned and went to search in another direction.

Winnette said she waited quite a lengthy period and then decided to go and search herself. She wandered in the direction that Dana had gone and began to hear noises. As she got closer, she realized they were screams and bellows. She followed them to a shrub-covered crevice where she found the horror of Thomas on top of Dana. Their bodies contained limited salvage cloth, and their skin was exposed to the sun.

According to Winnette, he was punching her very hard in the face. Dana being a strong girl, like you Letsi, was fighting Thomas very aggressively in her defense. She was kicking him and mustering all her power to try and push him off. But Thomas was much stronger and was forcing himself upon her. Luckily, Winnette quickly recovered from the shock of what she was witnessing. She grabbed a large rock and bashed Thomas in the head as hard as she could.

It appeared to be enough to knock him off Dana. Dana rose quickly in a rage as Thomas grappled to gain his senses. She kicked him in the face with as much force as she could. Then she grasped a large stick and began to beat him. Winnette grabbed Dana by the arm and tried to pull her down the hill, away from Thomas. She felt their best move was to run to the protection of the adults.

They moved swiftly down the incline and entered your grandmother's dwelling. Your grandmother tended to Dana as her half-naked body appeared red and swollen in many places.

She sent your mother out with your Uncle Harol to escort Winnette toward my house and retrieve water to tend to Dana's wounds. That is when I received Winnette crying at the door.

Thomas's reprimand was mild on that occasion, in hindsight. He had not achieved intercourse with Dana, although it was accepted that was his intent. While the assault had been severe, it had not interfered with her child-bearing capabilities; thus, his crime, according to the elders, was regarded as assault. He was required to engage in services to your family, mainly hunting and gathering food. He did become an avid hunter after the incident and began to spend days then weeks in the mountains alone."

Anex picked up little Douglas. "How can a beautiful boy like you be given less rights and status among our people than a beast like Thomas?"

Several incidents regarding Thomas occurred in the next few years, all similar to Dana's ordeal. Each time, his punishment and banishment increased. By the time I was old enough to run around in the mountains with my friends, Thomas was more of an evil entity than a person. When he was spotted up in the high hills, he resembled more monster than man.

His hair was outgrown like a tattered clump filled with knots, tatters, dirt, sticks, and pieces of bark. It seemed he had lost any sense of grooming. Hair grew on his face in scruffs. Dark circles formed under his eyes, likely from poor diet. His ragged clothing was even more hideous. The site of him was so repulsive that it supported the need to keep away from him.

Many felt that it was just a matter of time before Thomas seriously hurt someone; but no one knew what to do, more than what was already sanctioned. Many hoped that he would meet his own demise with an accident in the woods before he inflicted any more tragedy upon the mountain people. Alas, that was not how it ended.

Ingrid, a girl, of six or seven, had been out foraging for herbs in the mountains with her mother. She was still in the reminiscent age of childhood, the time before a girl began to bleed and was instructed to bear children. It was a time when a girl would love to wander in the mountains looking for the biggest toadstool she could find or look for shiny rocks among the layers of gravel. At this age, everything in the forest seemed so new and fascinating that one thirsted for the knowledge it possessed.

Ingrid had left her mother's side to do just that, explore the splendor and wonder of the mountain. She walked carelessly along the path, occasionally tripping on her salvage cloth that drooped down to her ankles. Her hair was neatly tied back in dreads, and her eyes sparkled underneath her thick lashes. She had wandered quite a distance from her mother, unfortunately, following a small quartz vein embedded in the mass of metamorphic conglomerate.

In places along the stream of rock, the quartz was so lucid; it glistened like a large droplet of mountain water. Ingrid bent down to brush away a light powdery layer from the surface of a gem-like portion of the vein.

From behind, Thomas pounced on her, bashed her in the head with a rock, and dragged her deep into the woods.

Her mother called for her, unconcerned at first. The calls increased in alarm as there was no response. She quickly yelled for help. The search was immediate and intense. Despite the swiftness of the search party, they were unable to find her in time. The years alone in the mountains had served to make Thomas a more seasoned criminal as his navigation skills had become superior to the rest of us.

Ingrid wasn't discovered until late that evening. Her defaced body covered in blood. Apparently her entire pelvic area was in shreds. An uncharacteristically thorough investigation of her body postpartum concluded that the hemorrhage from this ghastly occurrence was not the cause of death but rather a fatal blow that she received at the onset of her attack. It was the most accepted explanation—she was dead or close to it before the ravage attack was heightened. People were more than willing to accept this explanation as it served to project an image that minimized her suffering during the assault.

The horror of the incident left people in shock. Not so much though that they were not moved to respond. The elders had a meeting to discuss the situation, but before they made any recommendations, a group within the community had formed on their own to hunt down Thomas.

Thomas by then had become an accomplished mountaineer, probably more sophisticated than anyone on the mountain. He managed to elude the tracking of the people for several days. But the mountain people were too numerous, determined, and vengeful for him to divert forever, and he was captured heading toward the excavation lands.

When he was caught, he was tied by the arms so tightly that his arms were blue from lack of circulation. He was dragged, pulled, and pushed back to the village. He was even thrown down a section of a steep strike. By the time the posse was within two kilometres of the dwellings, with

Thomas in tow, the group had doubled in size, and they were moblike in their treatment of him.

It was Lardes, Thomas's sister, however, who pushed them over the top. When she caught sight of him bound and staggering under the uncharacteristic punishment that he had been inflicted with by the assailants, rather than offering him sympathy, she reached down and grabbed the largest rock among the gravel she could lift and struck a mighty blow to his head. It clouted him just above his left eye, and blood squirted out as though she had severed an artery.

It sparked a frenzy among the people where more followed suit, picking up stones, smashing them on him, hurling them at him, and pelting him with rocks and sticks of every kind. With every blow, Thomas plummeted until, finally, his body descended to the dirt that he was."

Amazingly, I found myself revealing this story to the Stalites. They listened intently.

There was a brief pause and then Vanel spoke up: "It is rare for us also to seek vengeance. But we feel the circumstances here warrant such a response. The Moraines wish to gain direct access to the reactor metals. This would be acceptable if they had been provided this access by the Creator of Life; but they have not.

They choose to try and take what is not theirs to take. They choose to try and steal the gifts of others. The Moraines were raping the hills with their attempts to steal the reactor metal by "pounding."

And they treated our people with dishonour and disrespect. Their actions have resulted in the death of one of the children. It altered our future in the most negative of ways. We must honour the death of this child. We must heal the wound that pierced the heart of our people. We must address the wrongs that the Moraines have done and are committing."

Her message was sincere, heartfelt. I felt myself swayed toward her position. She was a handsome young woman. Her hair was long, brown, and shiny. It reminded me of the soft salvage cloth that the Moraines had bestowed upon me. My cloth clearly seemed out of place in a location where people wore no garments. I stopped to think about the message Vanel was trying to convey.

I knew I was not in command of enough of the facts to make a judgment in favour of the Stalites. Furthermore, I knew it was not my vocation to make a judgment. I was just supposed to help resolve the situation, not take sides.

As I continued to contemplate the state, I was surprised how similar my rationale had become to the way my father spoke. I seemed to be able to distance myself from the conflict. I was not overtly affected by hearing about the death of this young woman. I did not appear to be reacting emotionally to the situation. This type of detached observation was characteristic of my father.

I was often amazed and sometimes hurt, by the fact that my father seemed to make rational judgments without becoming sensitively involved. As he was now an elder, he often sat in judgment of many people. In particular, it was his ruling that forced a young woman named Katrinka to leave the man she proclaimed to love to form union with another older man.

The logic behind the ruling that my father yielded was that Katrinka had failed to conceive after six months with her lover. Therefore, she must perform with other suitors. The sad part was that the man she loved was my childhood friend, Chris. And he and Katrinka were apparently very happy together despite the fact that they had not yet borne children.

I would not have been able to approve of such a decision. I was sure that the happiness of the people was also a blessing from the Oneness. Besides, Chris was a close friend of his daughter. This should count for something. But, apparently, it did not. He was also responsible for approving the union of many young girls with older men.

As I grew in age, the girls seemed younger, childlike. I wondered how my father could detach himself from their plight. I wondered how he detached his self from mine. Did he really believe that this was the ultimate purpose? Did he think it was all that simple?

The Stalites' loss was great. And yet I seemed to be functioning very logically about the circumstances. I did, however, recognize the seriousness of the situation.

"What would the Stalites consider an acceptable consequence for the results of this incident?" I questioned, attempting to put it as sensitively as possible.

Alan looked at me fastidiously. His body drooped in the front, and his spine rounded in the back. It looked as though his body ached. His lower lip sagged, exposing his sparse grey teeth arrayed on his lower jaw. "Perhaps the death of one Moraine or perhaps the life of a new Stalite."

Again, I found myself considering a judgment. The first part of their request gave the impression of revenge for the sake of revenge. There seemed nothing to be gained. Another death would only contribute to this toll. The second part of the request made little sense to me, but it did seem relatively constructive.

I pondered their thoughts, but I said nothing.

14

Now it was clear that Douglas was an anomaly. And our people had ordained him as such. It was his tenth year. The superficiality of such a label would have been comical had it not been so cruel. The purpose of categorizing anomalous children was to prevent them from procreating.

Douglas did not even know how to relieve himself on his own. It was not likely that he was of the capacity to share his seed. He walked funny. He talked very little, except basic commands. He had unusual facial features as though some of the muscles under his skin were either missing or inoperative.

He was handsome though. At least, I thought so. Rhondo appeared to think so too. I guess I was truly blessed to have someone who stood by and supported his children. Rondo would not confront anyone who challenged Douglas's status as a mountain person, but he never balked on his devotion to his first born.

Rondo often was accounted for down by the mountain streams washing feces from Douglas salvage cloth after a day out scavenging with him. Occasionally, they would be taunted by children hiding in the bush. Douglas would be running back and forth in the stream, babbling, naked from the waist down.

"Ooo! Get that shitty ass misshapen kid out our drinking water." This was followed by laughs and children running away through the woods.

Rondo said nothing. He would bring Douglas home after tending to him and tell me what happened. He was cold and expressionless when he mentioned it though. He was always distant with me with the exception of union. He rarely expressed his thoughts or desires, more so, even than I. We were both very withdrawn.

I wondered if he would have preferred to catch those kids and give them a thrashing for their insolence. He might have been able to get away with it. Or would he prefer to just walk away from the cruelty and leave his son and problems behind? I wondered what my dream was to do. Would I walk away from my reality if I could?

Now, however, Rondo seemed particularly cold. He seemed bitter. The bitterness seemed directed toward me at times. That is how I interpreted it. He was efficiently attentive, dutiful, and dedicated but clearly distant.

"Do you think it was something he ate?" I questioned Rondo one time when he returned with Douglas, half his salvage cloth in hand and the rest sparingly placed around Douglas's skinny body. "He seems to be sensitive to certain foods. Perhaps he can't digest it properly."

Rondo said nothing. He just averted is thin eyes and furrowed his slender brow. Next, he walked across the room and grabbed some more salvage cloth.

Because of the difficulty Douglas experienced, I found myself in excess need of cloth. It was taxing to barter for. I had begun to fancy extracting some salvage cloth myself. And this in turn drew me further into my dreams of attending a salvage expedition.

15

I felt completely disconnected from Rondo. He offered me no sentiment, and I reciprocated. We were not disobeying any creed by our resolve. We were not required to support each other in a spiritual sense. Our only duty to one another that the mountain people recognized was our obligation to try and procreate. This we had done. If it suited us, we were free to part ways and seek out new unions.

However, there seemed to be a tie that bound us together. We never discussed it, but it was clear that we both felt we must put the needs of the children first. We both knew it was best for their livelihood if they had two people tending to them rather than one. We did not see it as a sacrifice of our happiness. At least, I did not.

My only joy appeared to be sporadic moments when the children would do something that sent a surge of love through my soul. It might be attempting to help with a chore such as trying to carry a bag of pine nuts that weighed almost as much as them or simply the elicitation of the cute response that would force me to feel delight, despite myself, when I gazed upon their soft smooth delicate faces. These tiny trickster youngsters insisted upon it. I was sure that Rondo's presence had little bearing on my misery or elation.

Other than the brief moments emitting from the children, there seemed very little to be happy for though. Everything appeared meaningless. What was the point of becoming an adult, having children, and preserving the culture? Was it so that more could suffer in this cycle of struggle?

While the thought did seem depressing, for me, it instigated a challenge.

> *To prove that life is meaningless,*
> *Go out and seek happiness.*
> *See if it exists.*
> *If it does not, then you have confirmed your darkness.*
> *If it does exist, however, then you are happy.*

Since I found little happiness at home with Rondo, I had once again began to focus on extended family and friendships. Anex was no longer visiting regularly. Her counseling duties were not required according to the elders; although our visits had clearly become more than counseling, Anex had other duties and less time to spend with me. She also appeared to be somewhat failing in health.

It was different from most of the mountain people. She didn't seem to be in the same level of agony that inflicted the others, certainly not like my mother. Anex just seemed tired and in need of more rest. She often became short of breath and was unusually hungry and thirsty at times. I envisioned Anex dying in her sleep one day.

I still went to visit her sometimes, mainly because I saw her as a valuable resource for knowledge of the salvaging that I yearned to know more about. There was so much more I wanted to know about the excavations. Often, I would enter her dwelling and find her motionless. I would gape at the salvage cloth on her chest to see if it rose for it often appeared that she was no longer breathing as she lay there. Then, suddenly, she would give a great heave with her chest, cough, sputter, and turn.

I would not wake her when I saw her this way. I feared that one day her chest would not heave but rather sink forever. As gloomy as the notion was, it did seem the most desirable way to die—abruptly, in your sleep.

So, as my time with Anex was limited and my time with Rondo seemed limited in pleasantness, my gregariousness was directed toward Donny who had taken up with one of my closest childhood friends, Delta.

Delta had not had it easy, ever. And postpuberty was no exception. The first suitor she was presented to was Salyut. Salyut was a cousin of mine on my father's side. Salyut's father, my dad's brother, had died when Salyut was an infant.

Salyut, apparently, had a vicious temper that flared up on occasion. That in itself was not unusual for a man, but there was a heightened level of unpredictability surrounding Salyut's episodes. Donny was close in age to him yet never wanted to hang around with him. Donny barely talked about anything negatively, yet he did make a couple of uncharacteristic comments about Salyut.

Donny rarely showed signs of frustration. Even when my father was on one of his rants, Donny never seemed to react adversely. In fact, I can recall my father specifically belittling Donny and Donny still appearing unaffected.

"Working in the fields and hunting is certainly a necessary chore, but that, in its entirety, hardly constitutes a man. Even an anomaly can accomplish some of those mundane tasks. You won't amount to much if that is all you do for our people, labour about like a simpleton. We need leaders, thinkers, creators, and supporters, not more indifferent harvesters . . . Worthless!" My father would often express frustration with Donny's apparent lack of commitment to the people and their doctrine.

He could not force Donny to engage in these activities that he considered nobler.

Furthermore, my father likely felt as if Donny was a failure on his part. It is likely that my father saw Donny's indifference and lack of ambition as a reflection of himself. Donny had modeled little of Dad's apparent vocation. But my father could certainly vent his frustration by raging at his son.

As my father continued to yell, Donny began to walk away, out of the dwelling. My father saw this as the ultimate disrespect, and his anger escalated. He shoved Donny in the back of the head, and Donny slammed hard into one of the frame poles of the dwelling. Donny turned and looked at my father as he kept one hand to his forehead to minimize the flow of blood that was gushing from his wound, as head wounds always do.

Even then though, he did not appear to exhibit any signs of hatred or anger, unlike me when my father had committed similar assaults against my person. Donny just looked at my Dad and softly announced, "Perhaps you're right," and then left to tend to his lesion.

Donny's behaviour bewildered my father.

Donny was truly a peaceful person, at peace, with peace. His words were always warm. He was not obtusely optimistic but, nonetheless, positive and reflective. In fact, the time I had heard him speak unkindly of Salyut was one of the few times I had ever harkened a negative remark about anything from Donny.

My mother and I were sitting in the dwelling. I was just a youngster, still not old enough to venture into the village on my own. My mother was braiding my hair, and Donny walked in. I recall her questioning his arrival; "Hi honey! I'm surprised to see you here in the middle of the day when you don't have to be."

She finished my last plait and then turned her attention to Donny's hair as he sat kind of slumping on the dwelling floor. "What's the trouble?" she questioned in a soothing voice as she attempted to pull the wooden fork through his coils. Donny had thick curls that spiraled down his back. My mother let it flow free as the tresses remained tidy and in place. His hair was so unlike my mass of wire when it was unleashed.

"Salyut is an ass. He doesn't have the right to live," he blurted out with limited emotion. He just seemed to state it so matter-of-factly. My mom appeared taken by surprise. She did not respond in a surprised manner but gently pulled the comb through his hair and reached for a small jugglet of seed oil that she massaged into his scalp. She gave Donny a small hug and looked over at me and winked. Donny said nothing further, but, through the next few years, I picked up on more utterances about Salyut.

"His temper goes beyond the normal fights for teenage boys," commented my Auntie Dana one day when she came over to bring my mother some medicinal plants. "And he's always been like that as far as I can remember. He put Dijan's eye out when he was ten."

"That was an accident," my mother interjected.

"Accident? Not likely!" Dana responded. "He threw a spear right at him, just because he lost a running race. Besides, that was only one of many incidents. Don't forget the tooth he knocked out of Manuel's mouth or the time he smashed Ophelia with a log. And these are only some of the occurrences we are aware of. I can't imagine what is never mentioned by the kids."

Dana was always quite outspoken and down to earth. She differed immensely from my mother who always appeared to put a positive spin on any character assault presented by another individual. The irony is that my mother would often character assault whoever spoke to her making negative reference to others. I recall several times being chastised for any complaint against my father.

"He is so mean, Mommy! He says I'm worthless and useless and of no help to the people. And he hits me all the time!"

"He only tells you the truth Letsi. He does it for your own good. You should feel lucky that he cares so."

I guess you could say my mother offered isometry to those who chose to express a judgment. If you judge others harshly, I shall judge you harshly. There was no solace in that thought for me though. I craved validation for the pain I perceived that was inflicted on me by my parents. I sought empathy from my mother but, generally, received rejection.

Now, Dana, on the other hand, would present her case so strongly that my mother would generally concede to it. That really seems to be the general trend of all things though. Is it not? An idea or thought is generally validated not so much on its merit but rather on how well it is presented.

"He may be your nephew Joan, but that does not exonerate him of the evil he has inflicted on people at such an early stage of his life. He should receive a severe reprimand for his actions. If his mother will not correct him, then the council should step in." Dana's point would be supported with several more examples and little airtime for anyone else to speak. At the end of the presentation or perhaps simply when there was a pause, my mother clearly tired, conceded to Dana's position. Well, perhaps it is better to say she endured it.

"Well . . ." Mother started with clear fatigue in her voice. A ray of light pierced down on her face that accentuated her frowning wrinkled forehead. It cast a shadow below her eyes that made her face look skeletal like. "He has clearly made some bad choices."

"Joan." Dana changed the subject with a less assertive tone. "Have the herbs been helping? Has the pain remitted?"

"It hasn't made much difference," my mother responded wearily.

"Have you tried any crimson flower seeds?" posed Dana.

"A few, but they are so potent. I cannot think clearly with them"

"But they will help you sleep."

As I recalled these events, I wondered if perhaps my mother wasn't intentionally judgmental to minimize conflict. Rather, she was sharp in her rebuttals in the hopes that the energy expended on conflict would be curtailed. Perchance, she longed to focus her finite amount of energy on more productive activities such as maintaining her health. Perhaps all she wanted to do was rest.

Nevertheless, Salyut's reputation of violence was secured in my mind. I was saddened when I learned he would be Delta's first suitor. Salyut was striking looking and naturally athletic. His muscular structure was marked and well-defined. His facial features were distinct and handsome as though they were chiseled from a rock. It was a wonder why he was so developed physically given his poor work ethic.

Donny not only hated to play with Salyut in his youth, but he also loathed having to do chores with him. Salyut seemed to have trouble following the simplest of directions such as separating fruit from seeds. He often left the food source in a mess. And, despite his obvious agility, he would never pick all the fruit from a tree when he climbed it. Salyut would often scamper up the branches and spend most of his time dangling from limb to limb. And, by midafternoon, he would often claim fatigue and fall asleep on the ground in the shade, leaving Donny to finish the tasks.

Donny felt he spent more time picking up after Salyut than getting help from him. Moreover, Donny would sometimes get the blame for their lack of productivity when working together. Salyut never displayed any signs of aggression toward Donny. But that likely had more to do with Donny's passive nature than Salyut's ability to control his impulsive aggression.

The time when Delta was suited to Salyut was lost to me. I was restricted by my pregnancy and knew very little of her time with him. I knew of her leaving his dwelling, apparently beaten and raped; but, following the incident, more directions were given to both of them, and she was instructed to return. He did not appear to repeat such an episode with her again. Or another rumour was that she learned how to avoid his aggressive behaviour. Nonetheless, she left him for good as soon as the ninety days were up.

She talked very little of that time. She seemed content now that she had conceived with Donny. Delta liked to leave the past in the past and pray that it didn't manifest itself in the future in some demoralizing manner. Donny was her third suitor, and this was his first attempt.

Donny was very late to attempt procreation compared to his male peers. There was no enforcement of such action for men or boys mainly because they did not generally seem to need much encouragement. While it did seem of concern to the mountain people, especially my father, it was not an issue of priority. Occasionally, some males were slow to take on the role of suitor. Ultimately, there was limited means of enforcing a male to procreate whether he was able to or not.

With the issue of conception now at rest, Donny and Delta actually looked happy. They smiled at one another, and Delta even showed open signs of affection for him. She would wind the spirals of his hair around her fingers forming short lockets. She would lean on his shoulder when they sat together. And he would often reach for her hand. They would even walk to the orchards arm in arm on occasion.

For many, their mannerisms were perhaps annoying as other's happiness often tends to make us bitter with envy. However, for me, their company was a haven. It was contentment. It was hope for us all.

"Mika is such a sweetheart isn't he," remarked Delta one day while we were sorting citrus seeds. He had large dark eyes; the whites of which stood out in a visually pleasant contrast to his smooth, brown skin. He smiled frequently, and his new set of ivory adult teeth, which looked so large for his petite face, gleamed in the sunshine. Many thought he looked like me, but I thought he had a stronger resemblance to Donny and my mother. His stalky little body with short broad legs was more like Rondo's physique than my long, skinny frame, although I surmised this would likely change as he grew and lost his chubbiness.

Mika also tried to help us do our work. He looked delightful as he diligently picked up spoiled citrus from the ground with his stout little fingers and brought them to us to sift through for productive seeds.

"Douglas is sweet also," continued Delta. I took this as a consolation compliment of sympathy. It was a need on her part to offer some kind of condolence to the fact that she may have been giving Mika higher status. I was sensitive to it, and it was disheartening. I knew she did not say it because she believe, as part of her most steadfast values, that Douglas was as praiseworthy as Mika. She simply made the accolade to appease my sentiments. As invaluable as the comment might have been, her intentions of making me feel better were noble but misplaced.

Regardless of Delta's sensitivity or lack thereof, I appreciated the love that Delta and Donny appeared to have for my children. They would often offer to take them for the day. They enjoyed the children's company, and I enjoyed the freedom.

Whenever they took the children, I would hurry and tend to my chores and then climb up on a remote rock face with my word papers. I would spend my time reading through the passages. Sometimes, I would take a writing instrument that I had obtained from Germa, one of the salvage expedition leaders. I would try to copy the letter forms that I saw on the paper. I relished in the activity and never took this brief time alone for granted.

I tried to stay out of contact with other people when I pursued the word papers for I knew it would be defined as idolatry. If someone did happen to cross my path, I would simply shove the papers in my satchel and tell them I was just resting. As I learned more from the papers, I became a little less guarded and would sometimes share a passage or two with Delta.

> *Lo, children are a heritage of the Lord;*
> *And the fruit of the womb is His reward.*

I smiled and looked up from my paper to meet Delta's glance. "And how are you feeling, Delta?" I asked as I saw her shift in discomfort from her squatting position. Her arms and legs were swollen. She had removed the ankle bracelets that her mother had given her. Her feet were reddened and veins protruded extending up her calves. Her belly extended in an oval swell, which forced her salvage cloth to form pleats in the front. She had lost the plumpness in her face that she had when she was younger. Her features now appeared more sculpted and woman like.

"My back gives me pain, and I have significant leg cramps. I'm told this is nothing unusual."

The questioning tone in her answer made me think she thought that there was likely a connection between her limp and the discomfort. However, I had been well-conditioned not to bring up this past evil with her.

As close as I felt to Delta, I continued to abide by the instruction. I never asked her questions about her mother or about the beating that left her maimed. I was as concerned as the elders that initiating dialogue about events we have no control over may only arouse demons.

Delta was also very effective at avoiding these memories and never spoke of them. She made it clear she wished not to think of them, she wished they didn't exist and avoiding it seemed the best way of denying they existed. So I felt no benefit in trying to arouse any pain in my dear friend. Besides, at this moment, I was suddenly overcome with a need to vomit. So much so that I barely had chance to rise and clear the area where we had our seeds carefully sorted.

Delta looked at me uneasily. "Do you need something for discomfort?" she asked hesitantly. She was always uncomfortable with the prospect of someone becoming sick, which likely stemmed from the days of her youth spent with Violet. She looked back in hindsight at this time. She wondered if her mother's illness might have been better managed if she had received more medicine early on.

"I'm all right," I replied, not wanting to dwell on it.

"I have some herbs in the hut," she continued. "They might ease the pain. They are said to reduce tumours when heated on the reactor metal."

"I don't have any growths Delta," I responded. "I'm fine."

Delta looked at me. She just glared and said nothing. She had developed this way of staring that made one uneasy.

"Delta, believe me," I reassured.

We were able to end that discussion without further discourse. Unfortunately, when I had a similar episode on my next visit, she was more aggressive in her pursuit. We had just sat down to begin mending cloth when I had an uncontrollable urge to throw up again. I went to a nearby bush and projected at the ground.

I composed myself and wiped my face, checking my salvage cloth for any remnants of the purge. I took a small mouthful of mountain water to cleanse my mouth of the taste by swishing the liquid about and spitting it on the ground. I returned to our sewing area and attempted to sit down without acknowledging what had occurred. Delta, of course had other ideas.

"Letsi, you need to, at least, try some medicine." Delta was unusually direct in her address. It must have had something to do with Donny being close by. He seemed to give her a different perspective on confidence.

"Delta, I told you before, I'm not sick."

"So many good people are lost because of that attitude. To ignore the fact that you are vomiting will not make it go away. You need to face it. We must confront our illnesses to overcome them." She paused as though she was considering another approach. She continued to speak but in a softer manner. "I don't wish to lose a friend. Nor does Donny wish to lose a sister. And, certainly, your children should not be denied a mother."

As her words continued, they became more of a scolding than a discussion. It reminded me too much of my upbringing, especially with Donny standing in the background listening but contributing nothing.

"The medicine will not shorten your life if it turns out you do not have a cancer or a parasite. However, it could prolong you days if you do. It can't hurt you to consider the treatment as a precaution."

"Delta! Stop!" I blurted out. "I'm not sick. I'm pregnant."

16

The Stalites appeared to be finished talking as they rose from the circle formed around the fire. There was one last fairly long glance from Neil, and then the whole party vanished into the wall. I remained seated and continued to be warmly transfixed by the glowing reactor metal. I had no idea why they left, if or when they were returning, or what they expected from me.

Yet the warm glow from the reactor metal reflecting off the gleaming walls in the cave had eased my tension to the point that I was no longer worried or in fear of the unknown. The light and shadows shimmered over the sides of the enclosure like happy spirits dancing in the evening on a starry night in the mountains.

I decided to recline and take advantage of my peace and solitude to get some rest. When I closed my eyes, however, my ears began to alert to the various noises echoing throughout the dome. There was a constant pitter-patter of small rodents or large insects that were apparently scurrying about on the floor. And I could hear drips of water dropping from the ceiling to the ground in *tings* and *plops*.

I pondered over whether the coal black nothingness I envisioned was a blessing or a hindrance. Should I open my eyes and distract my hearing? Or might I witness ugly little creatures and the tiny parasitic biota taking advantage of the darkness to engage in their many mysterious rituals? My anxiety did not last for long, however. It became overpowered by fatigue, which served to benefit me from my small-creepy-creature phobia, and I drifted off into a slumber.

The ghouls were attacking Alexandra again. Alexandra was crying for help. My parents were there too. They were physically holding me back from my attempt to rescue her.

"It's just as well, Letsi," my Mother remarked in slow motion. "She is just an anomaly."

Simultaneously, my father was beating me with a switch for not extricating Alexandra. The intensity of the dream had left me vulnerable to the scrutiny of Neil who woke me. His gaze was equally intense and exceedingly extended. I returned the look, although it was probably more from being startled and frightened both from my dream and from the reality that awoke me.

My stare had been a sign of body language meant to say, "Help me. I am afraid.' But the intensity of the stare was probably misinterpreted by Neil. I had been aware of the danger of looking "the look." It was a particular characteristic I had been ascribed with. "Letsi has such an intense stare. What is she so mad about? Why is she so serious?" I had often heard comments about the intensity of my facial expression from other mountain people.

"Don't give me that look," My father would say when I stared him down in the midst of one of his demeaning reprimands. This usually preceded a smack that sent me flying across the dwelling. In a later moment as my mother explained to me how it was my fault for receiving a beating, she would often make the comment that it was the defiant way I stared at my father that had begot my punishment.

I didn't look defiant on purpose. I was usually unaware that I had such forceful facial expression. On the other hand, the look did serve to get me some sense of attention without having to market myself in other methods such as eloquent speeches, which I was certainly not blessed with the ability to produce.

It was that *look* that assisted me in my lobby for the opportunity to go on a salvage expedition after Alexandra's death. My intense stare assisted me when I sat at council with the elders who were reviewing the many reasons why I would not be a suitable candidate for such a trip. In spite of the fact I said very little, even when the council, which included my father, made remarks such as: "It is not likely that Letsi would be a suitable candidate. She is far too emotional. Recall the outburst she exhibited when her anomalous child died."

I just stared and looked at them in contempt. How could they consider that beautiful little girl a mutant? How could any reaction be deemed unacceptable at such a time? They made me sick. Perhaps they read these thoughts in my eyes.

I'm sure that the way I looked at them made them foresee that I would go on this expedition if I chose to, no matter what they decided. They saw in me the look of a woman who was mature and enlightened but also hardened and determined. Life's experiences and hardships seem to tear us down and rebuild us with a stronger and thicker foundation that is more difficult to break or penetrate.

On the other hand, an intense look could be misinterpreted in other ways. I had been told by Anex on occasion not to look too intensely at men or they would take the meaning as an offering of submission, regardless of the intent of the stare. This was especially true if they noticed a hint of passion in your eyes.

The eyes, like our words, however intense, are open to false impression and interpretation. And in the case of Neil, I had really only stared out of a perplexed state I felt from my nightmare about Alexandra. I hoped that he had not regarded it as something else for I was by no means on their side in this conflict.

"I have brought you food," he spoke softly. It seemed to break my trance. The aroma focused my senses. There was a distinct scent of warmed oil mixed with some type of fragrant herb that seemed to clear the nostrils and invite itself down the passages of my airways.

It aroused my palate. I was starving. It certainly put me in the proper condition to consume this mystery. It appeared to be a blend of fungus and unrecognizable invertebrates, seasoned with cuisine that was clearly herbs and oil, but unfamiliar or unrecognizable to my taste buds.

The mountain people rarely feasted on such products. Although, when hunting for rodents, small mammals, and reptiles was unsuccessful for any length of time, the people did begin to sun-dry slugs and amphibians as our bodies would insist we take in some type of protein. It's hard to say if we were repulsed by the look or the taste and texture of such creatures. Regardless, we certainly didn't fancy them.

Here, however, I devoured the offering rapidly. Mainly, it was because of my hunger, and, also, the preparation of these foods seemed to entice my appetite. The cooking appeared to enhance the flavour. The mountain people didn't cook food. We were restricted to sun-dried morsels. We did not have the quantity of reactor metal available to indulge ourselves.

Reactor metal was as scarce at home as mountain water was here. We limited our use of metal to extracting remedies and other medical pursuits. I wondered what it would be like to eat fruit cooked by reactor metal. I also wondered what a blend of dried fruit might do to enrich the composition of what I was feasting upon. A hint of sweetness added to this blend of oil, herbs, and protein would likely enhance the morsels, I thought.

My feeding frenzy had left me unaware that Neil was still there watching me. When I did finally realize this, I was only slightly uncomfortable. Neil began to ask me questions about my home, my family, my history, and my belief in God. As I revealed this knowledge to him, he reciprocated with information about himself.

Neil, like most Stalites, I gathered, did not have a spouse. He had one little girl that he was responsible for, but that child had died several years ago of some type of virus. As well as a leader among the Stalites, he was also an accomplished horticulturalist. He had developed a method of growing edible fungus by planting it in the most appropriate soil and utilizing the heat from the reactor metal as a source of energy for the plants to grow. Within one day, he claimed that he could fill his particular cavern with food to feed over half of the Stalite population for a week.

When I was finished eating, he offered to show me the plot. I was very intrigued, both by the prospect of new edible vegetation that might be produced in the mountain caves of my homeland, and I was also intrigued by his enthusiasm for this venture.

It was a delicate journey to his garden cave. My body was long and paltry but gangly in relation to Neil's shorter frame. He was able to slide with much greater ease and grace through the caverns, archways, and entrances. He also knew his way along the floor which made the trek far smoother. He was very attentive, offering me assistance and guidance along the way.

Despite the looming danger at the bottom of any given fissure within the cave, I was calm and comfortable on the path. I had even afforded myself some sense of accomplishment for undertaking the diverting enterprise. I knew I was entering a new frontier that neither the Moraines nor any other mountain person had ever forgone. Had other mountain travelers ever been presented with this new technology, they would have shared it with the people. As for the Moraines, they simply could not have squeezed through the tiny fissure that posed as the entrance to this cave.

Neil lit up the lair with his reactor metal when we reached the entrance. It was astonishing. There was a vast array of dark-hued fungi throughout the enclosure. Neil began to introduce his work in a technical jargon that only becomes accustomed after extensive work on a project.

I related this to my years and time working on drying and cooking techniques and word papers. I knew that, generally, when I spoke to others about my work, only bits of it had made any imprint on them as they could only relate superficially for they had not actually done the work.

It was like so many things that make us lose our sense of worth. Others cannot validate us because they are generally unqualified to evaluate us. They have not experienced our path. They have only their own experience and expertise to use as a value tool. And, sometimes, the paths of experience do not merge and remain foreign. That, perhaps, is the true meaning of our solitude and the roots of our inherent loneliness. We really do need to validate ourselves.

These and other thoughts went through my mind as Neil continued to brief me on his procedures. While I could only absorb the surface of his intense work, I did come away with knowledge of how to begin a garden in a cave, how to choose species, how to cultivate them, and methods of cooking them. The knowledge set off a dream of possibilities that might allow me to transport some of this wisdom back to practical applications in the mountains.

I listened intently as Neil spoke. "At first, we were selecting out the red striped strain as they are known to possess a deadly toxin. However, in the area where we discarded these mushrooms, the spores took off and developed into a huge mass. We wondered if there might be a strain amongst them that was not toxic.

We began to sample the plants in very small doses. We made record of any visible attributes on those that made us somewhat sick and compared them to those that had no negative effects on us. For those that did not make us sick, we increased our consumption slowly and recorded the attributes. Within a very short time, we were able to conclude that there was a small crease at the base of the edible red stripes and we began to select for them."

"How fascinating!" I verbalized, sincerely enthused. "An anomalous strain that appeared to have the most productive value."

"No, it is not an anomalous strain," Neil responded. "It is merely a different adaptation to the environment. It is the variety of adaptations within the plant's gene pool that increases its chance for survival. While the poison it produced was a hazardous inconvenience for us, for the plant, it made us hesitate to ingest it. The hesitation increased its chance to live as a species.

When we view the whole plant, the whole species in fact, as sacred and not just what appears to be in our best interest from gazing at the surface, we are able to have a much more holistic approach to our horticulture. You see, we did not attempt to eradicate the species after it caused illness to our people. Instead, we allowed it to continue to flourish. We simply picked and ate the subtype of this genus that did not cause us sickness."

"By picking the edible fungus and leaving the poisonous strain to flourish, do you not end up with a surplus of toxic plants eventually?" I questioned Neil, who responded in delight to my enthusiastic interest.

"Yes, but the domination is only temporary. All things seek balance. The plant has to expend extensive energy producing and maintaining the poison in its system. This process deprives the spores of energy that could be used for growth, repairs, and reproduction. Defense mechanisms are costly. Thus, when the plants are plentiful and do not appear to be under assault, the poisonous strains diminish in number and the edible plants flourish. And that is how the cycle continues."

He was incredibly eloquent in his execution of this topic. He had brought a sense of art and spirituality to his food-growing technology. He had developed it into a profound metaphor for life. His soft smooth voice assisted to produce an even more acute protrusion of wisdom supporting his philosophy. I was fixated on the knowledge that I was soaking up like moss holding water.

I had not noticed before that Neil stood before me totally nude in this illuminated garden. His body was painted with plant dyes and white mud mixed with oil. But he sported no salvage cloth.

The walls of the Stalite caves appeared to be a superior shield against the sun's rays. And the Stalites rarely ventured outside their walls. They did not excavate and relied directly on trade with the Moraines for any outside goods. Salvage cloth was not among them. They blanketed themselves with the cave walls.

Neil's frame was small and delicate in appearance. Beneath the paint, there were patches of bone white skin. The Stalites were even fairer than the Moraines. In the green-tinged light, I could see that his silk hair flowed regally down his back. His eyes now appeared blue in colour, and they widened with fervor when he spoke. As I became more accustomed to his polite mannerisms and articulate language, the nakedness of his frail body reclined in my image of him. It was all so elating and exotic.

17

I waddled over to Delta's dwelling to offer her some fruit and nuts. The delivery of her little girl had been a grueling experience for her. I had assisted Anex and Lardes in the procedure, although my swollen belly made it difficult to crouch down and get up quickly. The anguish and pain in Delta's screams had induced Anex to offer her some herbal relief.

It was rare among mountain women to get any medicinal assistance during childbirth as it was a concern that it might cause the baby harm. But, in this case, Anex surmised that the risk was necessary as Delta appeared to be losing consciousness from the pain. She seemed despondent at the end and was not reacting to Anex's command.

"Take a deep breath and push," directed Anex.

"I can't!" came a listless response.

Anex took a moment to check on the baby's position. I wiped the blood and fecal matter from the site as she moved her fingers about in the birthing canal. Delta moaned in discomfort. Anex appeared to be trying to pry open her pelvic bone. I began to pray. There was less else I could contribute. I asked that Delta no longer suffer. Her cries began to fade along with her strength deep into the night.

As I brought dirty water out of the dwelling to dump, I noticed Donny sitting there on a stump. He looked uncharacteristically fretful. I returned a concerned look at him and reentered the dwelling. Delta looked half-dead. The colour was fading from her skin.

Anex slapped her face hard in an attempt to revive her. It was enough for Delta to give one last fighting push. Fortunately, this was adequate enough to move the baby down the canal enough for Anex to reach it and pull it out. She handed the baby to Lardes to tend to Delta.

With me assisting, Anex attended to the gaping wound between Delta's legs. We patted down the torn skin, and blood continued to flow out of the mass of tissue. In the background, we could hear the faint cries of the newborn as we applied light pressure to the wound. The bleeding subsisted somewhat, but Anex asserted that the cut was too deep and unstable, and it would require stitching.

"My eyes are failing me, and they cannot guide my hands, Letsi," Anex remarked, somewhat frustrated. "Where is Denu? Why has she not arrived?"

"She is off in the mountains picking herbs. They are probably having trouble locating her," Lardes replied as she wiped bits of white and red debris from the newborn.

As soon as Delta had gone into labour, the most experienced midwives were sent for. Anex was by far the most experienced, but her ill health put her at a disadvantage when it came to tending to the meticulous needs of a mother post delivery who had a deep tear in her pelvis.

The tear needed mending like that of any deep flesh wound. And this could be better adhered to by a healing specialist. Denu was our leading healer of course. But she also possessed skills and knowledge at mending wounds.

Unfortunately, neither Denu nor any other mender appeared to be available at this time. Most of us had been tending to the harvest quite a distance from the village when Delta began her pains. The fruits were in abundance and needed to be collected quickly before they rotted or dried on the branches.

When Delta first began her pains, there were only a scattered few somewhat frail elders in the village, Anex being one of them. Me and a couple of other extensively pregnant women were also left behind tending to a group of overly active toddlers who might wander off a cliff if they had been brought up with the group of harvesters under minimal supervision.

Anex had already been with Delta that morning as she was feeling ill for a time before the birth. I had wandered over to her dwelling with a couple of toddlers leaving the others under the care of two other expectant mothers.

When I arrived at their dwelling, Delta looked bad, and Anex looked alarmed. Immediately, she sent me for help. Lardes was the only one able to return from the harvest. The others promised to send Denu as soon as they located her.

Obviously, they had not had the resources to find anyone to come and assist in the birth of this baby at this time. At the time of both Mika and Douglas's delivery, I had been blessed with the assistance of Anex and my Auntie Dana. And my labour was relatively easy. Delta had birthed this baby with a relatively limited group of attendants. Lardes had only assisted in one other birth, and I never had.

We were grateful for Anex's superior knowledge and experience, but, now with this gaping wound still hemorrhaging in Delta's pelvis and Anex expressing apprehension about mending the cut, we became quite alarmed.

"Letsi," commanded Anex. "You will have to stitch her."

"Me? I have no skill or knowledge in this."

"I will guide you," Anex replied, with a clear hint of dissuasion in her voice.

Apprehensively, I followed her command. There did not seem to be much choice. Delta would surely die without some intervention. Anex presented me with a small needle, far more delicate than the ones I had used for sewing salvage cloth. She pulled a long hair out of her head at the root and, slowly and painfully, unwound it from her dreads. She passed it to me, and I obediently threaded the needle.

Under Anex's intense instruction, I wove the needle through fragments of ruptured flesh. Delta moaned and whimpered as the needle penetrated into her open tissue. As I gathered the pieces of torn skin and attempted to assemble them in a similar pattern to the way it was before their rupture, the blood flow began to slow. I prayed that my amateur efforts at mending would be enough to keep Delta alive. Anex gently patted the repaired tissue and scrutinized it. I looked up at Delta who had slipped off into unconsciousness.

"She is no longer awake," I pointed out to Anex with a clear tremble of alarm in my voice.

"That may be a good thing," Anex responded. "The bleeding is reduced. She should rest to replenish herself."

We turned our attention to Lardes and the baby. She held her naked on top of a small white piece of cloth. Anex gazed down upon her. She tilted her head from side to side and lifted her arms and legs.

"There is no bruising upon this baby. It seems all the trauma was endured by the mother," Anex testified.

We all looked down at the baby. She looked like a little brown ball all scrunched up. She crinkled her nose. I smiled and looked up at Lardes. Lardes was weeping silently. Tears rolled steadily down her face.

I wondered about Lardes at that moment. She spoke very little, and it was generally always guarded. This was the first time I saw any hint of emotion from her. I wondered what it would have been like to grow up with such a heinous brother like Thomas. She had no children of her own.

Delta never spoke ill of Lardes, but there did not seem to be a close bond between them. Yet here was Lardes clearly overwhelmed with the miracle and horror of birth. This woman would surely be a grandmother to this little girl. Delta was very lucky.

We all exhaled with a thankful sigh, following the birth of Delta's little girl. However, Delta's loss of blood had left her very weak. According to Anex, she was exceptionally fragile and in need of monitoring. I volunteered to check on her regularly as I spent so much time at Donny and Delta's anyway.

A week or so after the birth of her baby, I entered the dwelling where Delta lay on her mattress. Donny was tending to the newborn. I gave the baby a kiss and smiled. Donny's gaze was affixed on his little spawn. He was amazed.

"How are you doing, Mom?" I questioned Delta with a smile, as I offered her some water and fruit. She devoured the offering quickly without answering, which indicated to me that she was recovering.

Let me check your wound. I parted the cloth between her legs. The tear of the flesh looked profoundly swollen, puffed out in hues of blue, black, and purple, with striations of white and green pus. I cleaned it with freshly boiled salvage cloth. It was amazing that any woman survived this trauma for a life erupts from a woman's body like a ruptured pod, dispersing its product.

Women do survive this though, although Delta's healing was retarded by the extent of the rupture. Delta winced as I put on the clay-herb-berry paste to combat infection. Donny handed her the baby who she affixed to her breast. Delta smiled and looked up at me.

"Soon, this will be you again, Letsi."

"Yes. It will be a welcome event. This is a heavy load," I answered, putting a hand on my belly. I agreed with Delta, but I doubted my delivery would be as traumatic as hers. Neither the birth of Douglas or Mika had caused me near as much agony as Delta's experience. And my rupture was relatively quick to heal. I was up and walking days after the birth. Now, as I neared the event of childbirth, my motion was slow, but I had not been ill, and I had not felt any cramping. It seemed the probability for me to have a quick recovery would proceed the delivery of the child I was carrying. Still, the thought of childbirth was a fearful subject as one never knew what fate one had in store during this intense procedure.

"Do you think it is a boy or a girl?" questioned Delta.

"It must be a girl. It must." When I had my boys, I hadn't really given much thought to the gender. But, now, I longed to have an offspring that shared the common bond of womanhood with me.

And, thus, shortly after that time, I birthed a beautiful little girl. So my wants and wishes were accommodated for that brief time. I had relatively little discomfort in the delivery. The baby was within the normal range of size and appeared to have the regular infant reflexes. Her cries signified a healthy child. The baby suckled well, and I recovered quickly. At that time, I was a thankful mother.

"She is beautiful Letsi," Anex commented on her postpartum visit. She had not assisted in the birth of this baby although she attended the event. She was visibly weak, just from the short walk from her dwelling to mine. Delta and I were engaged in seed sorting. Delta was no longer in severe pain and able to travel with her little Shenal. I compared Delta's daughter to my own little infant who I had named Alexandra.

"Her skin seems unusually light though. And her hair is so fair," I commented as she lay on a cloth next to Shenal. Shenal was small but her skin had darkened up significantly in a couple of months. Her hair was a clump of tiny black curls on her round little head. You could already see signs of Donny in her expressions as she smiled at Anex who had looked down into her eyes and made a face. She was a stark contrast to my tiny offspring who had only a light covering of white fuzz on her head and skin that looked ashen alongside of Delta's little girl.

"She's still young, Letsi," offered Delta.

Anex said nothing as years of disappointment had taken away any need for her to engage in optimistic projections. I replied with nothing also. My positive focus of hopes and prayers for the future had ended with Douglas whom both Rondo and I had invested so much time and energy in for very little apparent return, both from the community and from our own self-fulfillment. Douglas was certainly not the only cause of my despair though. He was just an easy target. His was only the most marketable and easiest analogy to point toward.

"What is the point of having a child like Douglas?" I questioned myself. These were very private thoughts, however. I never shared them with anyone, not because I feared how people might perceive me but simply because I felt their answers would be more mundane than those I had already perceived in my head. Answers like "God has a purpose for everything." were no longer adequate. They did not provide enough solace for the pain, the hardship, the discomfort.

The question extended far beyond Douglas of course. It had become life in general. Why was there so much hardship? Pain? It seemed so meaningless, purposeless, and futile.

Alexandra's birth had injected a spiritual sense of purpose and hope into the hypothesis.

But noticing the lack of pigmentation in her skin was just another of life's painful observations. I still hoped that she would indeed darken up, but I would not allude myself that such a hope was a certain reality.

On the good side, there was no one coming for official visitations. There appeared to be no suspicion that Alexandra's light skin was an anomaly because her milestones were not delayed.

By the time Alexandra was two, she had become a novelty. She was radiant. Her hair cloaked over her shoulders in a soft golden wave. It was so unlike the dark wire coils adorning the rest of our heads. And her deep blue eyes that matched the sky on the most tranquil of noon suns simply did not exist anywhere else as an attribute of our people. This was a stark contrast from my black eyes and Rondo's dark brown ones.

Occasionally, a Mountain Person had a green tint to their eyes, always in a blend of dark brown. But none was comparable to Alexandra's. There was no mixing of colour. Alexandra's eyes were sky blue, her hair glistening gold, her skin pasty white.

She was a very different-looking person. Despite the lack of reference to draw from, as her appearance was so dissimilar, I knew she was beautiful. I saw traces of myself and Rondo in her as well, even though her features were so removed from ours. The way she crinkled her nose was like Rondo when he was carrying a heavy load from the orchards. Her smile was similar to my mothers. Her walk reminded me of Donny. Yet her aberrance was so pronounced. I wondered if she was really a spirit being sent in the form of my child to visit with us for a time.

There were also concerns over her sunburns. We were all in danger of the sun's rays with any prolonged exposure. And we often had small burns on our faces and hands from spending too long sorting, harvesting, or other necessary duties without paying attention to the level of shade that protected us.

But Alexandra could endure no time in the sun. Any time she left the dwelling, despite being covered in triple layered salvage cloth, any exposed area would scorch promptly. The ulcerating wounds not only left Alexandra with sores that were in danger of infection, but they also tended to make her sick as well. It appeared to take extensive energy from her immune system to repair damage done by these burns. She would lie on her mattress for days after a burn and beg me for water.

By the time she was two and a half, we had begun to take major precautions with Alexandra. I rarely permitted her to leave the dwelling. When we were in the orchards, I stuck sticks in the ground around her corralling her under a shady tree. I would even construct a tent of salvage cloth around her at times. I would bind the cloth to her skin to make certain it would not fall off. I would also apply clay to her body and on her hands and face as an attempt to deflect the harmful rays. Rondo had begun to double thatch the dwelling and pack it with mud to minimize the sun's penetration.

Both Rondo and I were keenly alert to her needs. When she suffered, it was as though we were also burning from the pain the sun had inflicted upon her. It allowed us to draw closer to one another as we handled the urgency of the condition.

The challenge was difficult, and we had no history to pull from for a reference. No one could recall having a child who looked that way or who was that sensitive to the sun. We had myths to refer to of people that were burnt up because of their evilness and impurity. They generally were described as very-light-skinned people, lighter than the Moraines. But the impression we had of them was that they were ugly and mean and greedy. Alexandra did not fit this description for she was beautiful and sweet and kind.

People were enthralled with Alexandra. Her beauty was gripping. Her voice and her utilization of language were equally captivating for such a young child. It was these redeeming attributes that arrested any suggestion that she was anomalous despite her clear abnormality. At least, nothing was ever suggested officially, and no gossip ever reached my ears to that effect. It wasn't until years later that I even heard the slightest of callous remarks about her. And even then, I believe few thought of her as anything but beautiful.

Douglas loved Alexandra deeply. It was one of the clearest expressions that he had ever conveyed. Once, he had cut his foot on a sharp-edged rock in the mountain stream. He compulsively picked at it and refused to keep it bound. We constantly reprimanded him trying various strategies to get him to discontinue this behaviour as it was impairing the healing of his wound. We had physically restrained him, verbally corrected him, hit him, and yelled at him in a typical struggle to try and prevent him from continuing to pick at the scab. All of our attempts had been futile that was standard in our efforts to show Douglas something. We became exhausted in the battle long before him.

In some aspects, I guess Douglas displayed classic mountain people behaviour. He resisted change and resisted imposed values. But unlike the rest of us, Douglas could not be reasoned with verbally. We could not present our reasons for wanting him to discontinue behaviour; nor could he present his explanation to us for why he disagreed with us. There was so little exchange. He sometimes reminded me of a crying infant that cannot be consoled because they cannot say what they want, and you cannot interpret their cries accurately.

As well as our encumbrance, Douglas had been our teacher. He had not only taught us patience, he also taught us how significant talking could be. We learned, in a forceful way, how much power was contained in the ability to talk. With verbal communication, the one who talked the best got the most attention.

All of the elders and most of the people of high status among the mountain people were good speakers. I thought of myself in comparison to my father. His expressive language and ability to recite mountain people doctrine was impressive. Words tended to flow from his mouth with a perfect pitch and tone in just the right measure of authority.

I, in comparison, rarely spoke and tended to listen to myself when I spoke. I listened, analyzed, and criticized what I said. I hated the way I sounded, the things I said, and the lack of command and sophistication in my presentation.

Yet I fancied myself just as wise as any of our wise people. Their words, however eloquent, seemed so pointless to me most of the time. I could not see the point of our struggle, which was what most of their words focused on. Most of the dogma they presented was about our need to labour in order for the mountain people to become stronger in number. What was the point of this? I wondered. Why must we struggle to propagate our species?—so that we would have more mountain people struggling and suffering? It all seemed so aimless.

However, I never vocalized this in such terms as I could not articulate it very well. And, furthermore, it was also so drastically negative that it seemed even more pointless than the words of the elders and the leaders. How could it help to articulate such dismal thoughts?

I found myself stuck in a loop when I began to philosophize about communication as it pertained to Douglas. It was fruitless to try to explain things to him because he did not seem to understand. And it frustrated me to know that I could not find out why he insisted on picking at that scab on his foot. Alexandra, on the other hand, was able to win him over. She explained to him the importance of taking care of your wound properly, or the wound would become infected.

"Douglas, you muth top picking dat 'cab," she scolded as she went over to examine his sore. "Here! Put thum of deese erbs on your cut."

She handed him some of the herbs she was accustomed to using for her own pervasive lesions.

Amazingly, Douglas ceased picking and placed the herbs on his laceration.

"Here, now put dis coth round yo' leg to hold the 'erbs in," Alexandra instructed with her clear and sophisticated vocabulary for a three-year-old.

Douglas obeyed with no protest whatsoever. Alexandra then tied the cloth to his leg as he was yet to know how to tie, and she was advanced in the process from constantly putting bandages on herself. It amazed us. He had barely let us look at his fester, let alone touch it. Yet here was this tiny, pasty white, articulate child tending to it like a qualified medical elder.

Perhaps it was all the visual clues that Alexandra possessed that made Douglas understand as he had constantly been witness to her grueling punishment with sores and bandages. Perhaps it was the suffering that gave Alexandra authority to tend to his wounds. Perhaps it was her beauty or the way she elicited the cute response with her speech, looks, and mannerisms.

Douglas clearly loved her, and he smiled at her often. Perhaps it was all of these things and a bit to do with the timing that this event occurred. At the very least, we recognized a power of love within Alexandra. And it wrenched our hearts whenever she was ill.

The mountain people had not deemed Alexandra an anomaly. There was no president for it. Anomalies were generally mentally challenged or possessed physical deformities. Alexandra was clearly a bright child, more articulate for her age than others. And her physical challenge was not due to being a cripple. Her beauty, radiance, and intellect were a serious challenge for the dogma of our definition of anomaly. And none appeared to wish to challenge it. Unlike others who were defined mutant in our society, Alexandra had the ability to defend her own self as she could answer questions and challenge their decisions.

The questions and thoughts of the very young could often be challenging. No one seemed to want to risk looking bad in front of a young child. Besides, she was still very young, and there was no need for the elders and the leaders to interfere with her or us at such an early time. Perhaps the steadfast love and hope that her parents had for her would heal her of her condition. That was the hope.

18

Neil escorted me to a section outside of his garden cave. There, he instructed me to wait until he returned with the others. He cautioned me before he left not to move around in the cavern as the floor was dangerous to maneuver in. The cavern had a polished look to it, and there were large round rock formations throughout the enclosure. It was as though the rocks had been melted and they bubbled over into these massive conglomerates; the way sap from the trees would ooze out of the trunk at noon and harden in drops on the outer bark as the day grew cooler.

Neil returned rather quickly with the same party that I was introduced to in the meeting place. Vanel had brought me an offering of food. Again, it was a compilation of fungus, insects, and oils garnished with herbs. This meal also seemed to possess some type of rodent protein in it. I consumed the food set on a small piece of bark while the Stalites sat around me. They too pulled out small plates and began to eat.

When we had finished, I felt quite thirsty as I had not had a drink for quite a while. I pulled a small flask from my satchel and poured a small caplet of mountain water to distribute among the five of us. They drank sparingly and passed the vessel on to the next person. They were clearly pleased with the taste.

"Where do you get *your* water from?" I questioned.

"There are small springs throughout the hills." Alan stood up slowly and shuffled towards a wall in the cave. He raised his hands shakily to the rock in a cupping motion. He shambled slowly to my side where he put his cupped hands in my face. He had retrieved a handful of liquid directly off the rock. I put my lips to his hands and slurped up the water. It had a palatable taste. It seemed a bit musty but not dirty or toxic.

I thought to myself, "These people seem to have all they need here in these caves." They had food, water, shelter, and defense from the Moraines and the sun. Perhaps it was the secret to their self-contained mannerisms. I was intrigued to learn more about them.

"We have talked about it, and we have concluded that you are suitable to help us resolve our dilemma," stated Tonaldo. Her grey silky hair was pulled back in a bun, and her sparing wrinkles looked like small slivers on her painted face.

I found myself flattered. I starved for approval. When someone spoke kindly of me, it was an overwhelmingly pleasant astonishment. I would surmise that most people feel like that when they are given an unexpected vote of approval. And to hear this from a stranger from an alien world was immense. I felt that a comment coming from these people was genuine as they had no biased or hidden agenda to profit from by making this affirmation.

It took me a few seconds to ground myself after hearing it for it truly was only a moment of adulation in my mind. I thought what they were confirming, by making this statement, was that they would continue the negotiations with the Moraines if I mediated. It turned out to be much more.

19

With the death of Alexandra, the world changed from a struggling labourious journey dotted with brief locations of interest to a morose despondent desolate retreat amidst a pool of stagnant rot. I didn't have the energy to die or to exist. I did have duties, however, that I continued to perform robotically. I mended the dwelling, sewed the salvage cloth of Douglas, Mika, and Rondo, fed the children, and harvested and sun-dried the fruit.

Surprisingly, the first month was the easiest or less grim than what was to come. People came to visit often, and their feelings were sincere. Sorrow and sympathy are rarely false in times of ultimate tragedy. And I was in such severe shock that I felt more numbness than sorrow.

People actually assisted me with tending to the children, even with Douglas. I rarely slept, and when I did, I was subject to the realistic nightmare of Alexandra's painful death.

Many mountain people had died in agony, and unearthly moans and groans had been intermittent throughout the village since its conception. My mother's wails and murmurs had been agonizing enough, but

Alexandra's were torturous. The soft whimpers were just as dreadful as her periodic screams.

I begged God to transfer all of the pain and agony to me and set this beautiful child free. The Oneness set her free in death I guess and left me with the pain and agony of my loss in my dreams. God had answered my prayer in trickster irony.

My fatigue due to depression, shock, and insomnia left me with little recollection of daily events. I barely recalled Mika or Douglas during this time and have no recollection of Rondo. This first month was my preference, however, in relation to the months to follow.

The next phase of my grief was arduous. I hated everything. Nothing was appeasing, nothing. I had no thoughts that lingered. There was nothing, nothingness, like prayer. Is that what reaching Oneness is really like? Emptiness? I suppose the hate was skewing the impression—hate and the nightmares.

I longed for poor little Alexandra, sitting in the dwelling, smiling at me, pleased to be sorting the dried goods, pleased to be my little helper, asking questions about the cliffs of the mountains where one could marvel at the Poison Sea, and, on a very calm day, etch out a mirage of the Moraines' land, questions about things she was forbidden from seeing, but had begun to wonder about at the age of four.

I wondered now if the ravens had carried her remains high enough into the sky so that her spirit would view all she had missed in her restricted earthly years. Confined to the dwelling in her illness, I could only describe these sites to her. Perhaps now she could see them. My description and her imagination were her happiness as she lay weak and ridden with sores in her last days, so inquisitive and eager to know despite it all.

She inspired me. Perhaps that is why I hated God when, a few months later, the plagues ravished her little body and left her in such torturous pain that she no longer asked questions. Why was there a need for her to suffer like that?

The next few months after her death, I functioned. I did what was necessary for Mika and Douglas as they needed me. They were older, but they would suffer more without me. That is what I told myself. That was the only life force directing me. I submitted to Rondo, as I had been well trained to do so, but I felt less than ever.

I noticed Rondo holding on to me longer as if he was clinging to life, hanging from the edge of an emotional cliff. He too was grieving. But I could not focus on him. I could not focus on myself. I was unaware of myself. I noticed, sometimes, when I would prepare food for the children, I would gorge on the morsels as if I hadn't eaten for days, and I likely hadn't. It made me think that perhaps no one was tending to me the way I was tending to my tasks. At least, I did not notice anyone.

I believed that no one was aware of my pain or was completely apathetic to it. When I would encounter people, they seemed to speak to me about trivial things as if there was room for trivia amidst my grief. I began to tell myself that no one understood or cared, and it gave me license to withdraw even more. I hated myself for my despondent nature and how that might be affecting my remaining children. I hated my selfishness and my self-pity.

There was one small solace in this time of anguish. I had my small collection of word papers to browse through. I read through them trying to decipher and interpret them. I noted that the time I pondered over them, I was lost to my pain. For the brief time that I read and thought about those passages, there was a peaceful nothingness, so peaceful that I felt guilty; and my pain and self-loathing increased when I would be whisked back into the linear reality.

> *Then from the bowels of absolute peace—of nothingness and despondency—enters the jolt of the still barbed force of reality, gouging*

with its egregious, obstinate data, carving the spirit—constricting the apathy.

But I would have let the papers burn in the noon sun without hesitation if I could have Alexandra back. Instead, I tossed them from a cliff into a gorge. And then I told myself what a coward I was to not follow them.

Despite my detachment from people, on some level, it seemed I did acknowledge a kindness and gentleness among them in the way they related to me. I doubted it was a genuine caring, but it felt softer and less judgmental than I had sensed before. Maybe, my senses were not a result of exterior emissions but rather my projections of self-loathing. Perhaps it was the apathy or perpetual sadness that emitted from me that forced kindness to gravitate towards me in hopes of achieving a balance. I found myself taking advantage of it too. I found myself asking for things, almost demanding.

"This salvage cloth is worthless. Look how easy it tears," I lashed out at Germa. He had come to trade items he had salvaged on his last expedition.

"It was all we managed to retrieve," Germa responded, somewhat annoyed with my tone. He was a tall, thin man with a thick, curly beard that matched a trimmed ball of hair on his head. He was the leader of the salvage expedition and generally approached with a level of respect because of the goods he brought to the mountain people.

It was uncharacteristic of us to complain to him. We generally showed gratitude to excavators as we recognized the risk it took to execute such a journey to retrieve these goods. Germa responded somewhat indifferently to my complaint. "You had best take it though. We may not be going on a venture for a long time."

"Why is that?" I questioned.

"We do not have enough interest. Those who have gone on expeditions before are too old, and no young people seem to have time or inclination."

"I have interest. Take me on your next expedition," I boldly requested. Gumption had never been an extraverted quality for me, and my abruptness was astonishing to myself. I was equally surprised at Germa's reaction as I expected a blatant dismissal of my request for it seemed atypical in my mind. In contrast, Germa looked at me and appeared to ponder the request as legitimate. He tilted his head down almost to his shoulder and scratched the dense hair on his chin.

"Who will tend to your children?" he questioned.

"My brother and his wife will help Rondo. I will pay them with the material I retrieve." I was quick to answer. I had thought of this many times. In my longing for this adventure, I had exercised the details in my imagination. At one time, I had spent many hours going over the details of what it would be like to go on an excavation. I had the answer to many particulars.

At this time, it meant very little that my one-time longing might be coming true. I had lost too much that really mattered to care about my dreams and longings for adventure. However, my years of yearning had left me well-prepared for the questions Germa posed.

We discussed this and several issues necessary to execute such a trek. It rescued me momentarily from the reality of my grief. The focus was on obstacles and strengths for me as a candidate. Germa's line of questioning was not that of a judgmental bias. Instead of reasons why I couldn't go, we focused on how I could go. I briefly felt ratified.

It was only a fleeting endorsement though. Once others were brought into the discussion, the more regimented, stagnant, and adapt characteristic responses were employed. I was a woman, with children, and I was still of childbearing age. As well, my children were still of the age of nurture. Furthermore, my mental state was questionable.

Ironically, it was my mental health that would be used as a quality in favour of me attending a salvage expedition. The rationale was simple. I would be in this state whether on a trek or not. Moreover, there was some support for me to make a venture among the community because of my grief. Some saw the venture as a healing journey.

"My children will be tended to by Delta and Donny in my absence. As well, their father, Rondo, will provide for their sustenance and care for them when he is not engaged in chores." I had rehearsed this speech somewhat with Germa before I attended the council. Like many of the activities in the home of the mountain people, the council of elders and leaders had to give their approval to anyone venturing on a salvage expedition.

Germa certainly had influence in the decision as the people knew they were dependent on entrepreneurs such as him. However, he was still required to act in accordance of the doctrine. And, thus, he had to follow traditional protocol when initiating a new mission.

"You have one anomalous child, do you not?" questioned Denu. I loathed to answer. I felt that, in a way, it suggested that I conceded to my son's status. However, Germa and I had previously discussed these things; and, thus, I was prepared for the question. I had expressed my distaste and rage towards Germa when he expressed the claim.

"What makes my son any more anomalous than any other mountain person? Has he ever really hurt anyone? Has he forced anyone into acts they would not choose for themselves? Who has the right to judge him in this way? It makes me sick."

"Easy," replied Germa. "It is not I who makes these assertions. But if you go before the council speaking as you do now, they will surely forbid you from attending a salvage expedition. They will see you as irrational and unable to handle the challenges that lie on a difficult trek across the unstable territory we will have to cover."

"How can anyone make such a connection? My son's encumbrance has no connection to my ability to hike in the mountains."

"No," returned Germa. "But emotions can have a direct effect on our actions. Surely you know that. The council will surmise that if you are preoccupied with anger . . . or sorrow, it can interfere with your concentration. If you are deep in thought about an emotional situation, you might not be aware of a boulder falling above you. Or you might not notice that the crevice where you are securing your foot is filled with loose debris."

I found myself listening to his point. I wanted to tell him I didn't care if I was killed on this journey, but, instead, I just looked at him and tried to fight off the fluid swelling in my eyes. He paused in his address. I swallowed the mass that had conglomerated in my throat, and I spoke through the cloud of anguish that encircled me.

"My son's affliction has little connection to my ability to focus. I have managed to function just fine all this time. What makes my emotions so significant anyhow? Many have perished on this journey by a rock, a fall, or a landslide. Was it their emotional state that caused the fatality?"

I knew I had strayed from the point. I knew that Germa was not suggesting that all accidents could be prevented by stoic emotion. What he meant was that a stable focused thinker, with limited affecting baggage, would help to appease the mountain gods.

Furthermore, I knew he was not as concerned about my personal demons or how I had learned to cope. His concentration was on the journey and doing his utmost to ensure its success. It had become clear to me over the short period I had dealt with Germa that he had a strong vocational passion about his trade as an excavator. He planned well for his journey. He did not take any detail for granted, from the questions put forth by the council to the supplies he would need in his satchel. My emotional state was one of the details he needed to address.

"Letsi," Germa stated in a matter-of-fact tone. "Your words suggest a fighting spirit. Perhaps they could help on a journey. Perhaps they will cause reckless actions. I cannot say or judge. But the council will judge you as irrational unless you are able to reply to their questions in a predictable mannerism."

It was clear that Germa did not pass judgment on me. Correspondingly, he did not judge the actions of the elders. It seemed he did not feel qualified to do so. His only area of expertise seemed to be on having successful salvage expeditions, and he had had many. This was the path he knew about. The rest were just formalities and protocol of preparations.

It might be viewed as a form of humility, tolerance, and acceptance. Or it could be thought of as indifference. There is a dualistic nature to all that we do. For me, however, his internal motivation was fairly irrelevant. It was his actions that appeased me.

Somewhere amidst my despondency marked with brief moments of anger and despair, I knew I still longed to go on this journey. And so I was able to leave behind my feelings of defensiveness and slip back into my coma of bleakness. It was the perfect baseline to adhere to questions posed by the council.

And, thus, when I was confronted with questions about my proclaimed less-than-perfect offspring, I rebutted with limited emotion.

"Rondo has cared for him from birth and is quite capable of tending to him alone for this short period. He often takes him in the orchards and up in the mountains hunting and fetching water. Also, my brother Donny has volunteered to spend extra time with Douglas. He has always been a good uncle to him."

I looked at my father, who was a member of council, and thought back on how he referred to the attention Donny paid to Douglas as "wasted" time. My father spent little time with his grandchildren. He had only visited Alexandra a couple of times and never when she was very ill. It seemed he had chosen to avoid painful situations.

Yucca, who was now the most senior mountain person, looked frail as she spoke.

"We are not concerned about your physical ability to do this task. But we are concerned about your mental condition. You have recently suffered a painful loss. Is your state of grief such that you could endure a journey such as this successfully?"

This was the hardest to answer of course, even though I had been through it with Germa and knew it was coming. Not because of the pain involved with Alexandra, but because the answer I gave was a conjecture. The loss had killed me. I had no idea if I was strong enough to go on this venture. Nor did I care. Whenever I thought of Alexandra, I'd just as soon be carried off in a mudslide, inhaling massive quantities of mud and water until my lungs burst. When I thought of my loss, I was ambivalent to the world. When I was not thinking of her, I felt little but operated. I looked for escape.

At one time, I longed to go on this quest as a vocation. I no longer had desire to go on a salvage expedition. Now, it meant little to me, other than escape. Newness or something different might occupy more of my senses and thus distract me from myself. My response to the council on my mental state would not address any authentic issues or feelings. They would simply be rehearsed statements, ones rehearsed with Germa as the director.

"My loss was great. But the people's loss shall be even greater if more eager people, such as I, do not participate in the salvage journeys. I know this, and that is my strongest preparation."

It made me sick to say this. It erased any sense of joy at being approved for the mission. It was a lie. But it served the purpose. I was approved for the excavation. Preparations were made for us to engage in the trip early the next morning. We set off to assemble food and water and ensure our families would be stable. I spent the majority of the time explaining to Mika what I would be doing. Or, more accurately, I answered his many questions.

"Is it dangerous?"

"A little, but I will be very careful."

"Where will you sleep?"

"I will sleep in a lean-to or a cave on the way there and one on the way back."

"Can I go on an expedition someday?"

"Someday. Someday, you will probably lead an expedition."

"Why do you want to go, Mom?"

"I want to get some good supplies instead of having to trade for not so good ones . . . And I want to see what it's like there."

"Are you going to come back?"

This question surprised me. Mika was almost at the age of puberty. It seemed a question juvenile to his age. I surmised that his true question was more difficult to express. What he most likely wanted to know was why I was leaving. Why had I left? Where was I gone? In my grief, Mika had been abandoned, and only a shell remained to care for him.

"I hope so," I answered with a meager smile. But I really didn't. I didn't hope at all. I looked at Mika. He was turning into a handsome young man. His skin was a smooth, dark brown. His hair was a mass of neatly laid dreads that flowed back from his face to reveal a pair of striking dark eyes. He seemed to have developed "the look."

Usually, there was a twinkle in his eyes that brought out the attractiveness of his features. But as he stared at me, there appeared to me more sadness. It occurred to me that he was still grieving too. He had lost a dear sister. And, now, it seemed he was losing a mother.

I reached for him and held him as tightly as I could. I kissed his cheek and rested my head in his neck. I knew I could cry uncontrollably at this time if I just let the tears begin to flow. I could have done this, and it would have been perfectly acceptable. Mika held me tightly, and I sucked the tears back up into my sinuses. I looked at him with water in my eyes.

Tears began to stream down his reddened cheeks. I prayed to think of something wise to say at this moment. With nothing enlightening coming to mind, I prayed that the statement I was about to make would indeed help Mika cope with my absence in mind and body. "I love you Mika. You are strong, and you are the glue of this family. Just continue being you. I will always be in your heart no matter where I am."

My talk with Delta and Donny was much more mechanical. We dealt with practical issues.

"Mika must be harassed a bit to do any chores. He likes to wander off with his friends. We let him as much as possible, but he needs to help too. It is hard to direct Douglas to do any tasks, but he can carry heavy loads and will do so if he is in a proper frame of mind. With me gone and Rondo away, he may be agitated and unable to assist.

He usually has a bowel movement in the morning. So if you let him run around in limited salvage cloth from the waist down, at this time, he may relieve himself without making too much mess. He usually holds his salvage cloth out when he urinates, but you will likely have to change him a couple of times a day.

He still walks slowly, so he is easy to catch. Just ignore his loud protests. You may have to hide your cache of food because Douglas sometimes finds it and will eat until none remains. Rondo will have him most of the time though, so it shouldn't be too bad. And Mika makes a very good babysitter by the way." I paused after this as I recognized I was rambling.

Donny and Delta knew Mika and Douglas well. They had cared for them for years. They had been especially helpful in Alexandra's final days. They were very close to the boys. They did not need this paltry instruction. They just smiled and nodded while I spoke. They likely recognized the anxiousness in my utterances and attributed them to my anticipation of the salvage expedition and my guilt over leaving the boys.

Donny had his usual compliant persona. He seemed small, physically, in comparison to Rondo. He had a sadness in his eyes that I could relate to. His expression and the way he held his head down were similar to mine.

Delta, on the other hand, seemed perky and needed to speak more. She liked to speak of anything but sadness. They had grieved over Alexandra's loss too. It had likely robbed them of some of the joy they had for their own beautiful daughter.

It was to our delight when little Shenal wandered in on us to request some assistance with her salvage cloth that had come unwound at the back. Her shiny, dark brown, spiral curls dropped next to her large round eyes as she pushed her head forward in order for her mother to fasten the clothing at the back of her neck. Her cuteness was unbearable, but I fixated on it, as did Donny.

While Shenal had her mother's shape, she had her father's face. Shenal's expression brought back memories of Donny and me in a time when he was my babysitter. He would coach me along to walk to the mountain stream so he could fetch water. I would follow sheepishly, afraid of everything I saw. Donny would take my hand with the intent of moving me along faster. I would hold tight to his fingers and turn my head from side to side marveling at my first introduction to the community and my homeland.

I wanted to go back to that place, to that time when the world seemed more intoxicating, innocent, disquieting, curious, and safe. I wanted to be that age, that mind-set. I remembered how Alexandra brought me back there, full of questions about a world around her, outside the dwelling to which she was confined. Her amazement and contentment in having the secondhand version of this world through my eyes was humbling.

The stories were told by me and, sometimes, Rondo and Mika. Even Douglas seemed to offer her some insight into the world outside. We described the brown and grey mountains in the sunset, towering over the village like giant guardians of the people. We would explain how the mountain streams would bubble over in foam and mist at the bottom of a small waterfall.

Douglas even brought her a stick one day. He would sometimes bring us objects, and we ached to know why. We were sure he was trying to tell us something. When he brought Alexandra the stick and insisted she put it in her hand, she took it eagerly. She did not need Douglas to explain because she was of the same spirit world that he inhabited. She told us it was a magic stick with special powers that she needed. We wept overwhelmingly. When she died, we wrapped the magic stick up with her body.

She marveled in all our expressions. And Rondo's brief descriptions of the mountain streams elated her. The words themselves could initiate excitement in her.

She never complained about her restrictions. She would cry and curse about her pain but never about the fact that she could not go out to play. The vicarious stories were plenty for her beautiful, active imagination. I could find no reason why such a heavenly child would have to suffer like that.

As I stared at pretty little Shenal, I found myself falling into that familiar loop of longing for Alexandra then cursing the fact she was taken from me and then hating myself for being so selfish. I knew I would not be able to hide these emotions from Delta or Donny, so I excused myself quickly.

I had bouts of overwhelming sorrow on several occasions since Alexandra's death. But they had reduced exponentially with time. In particular, since I had focused on this salvage expedition, there had been very few crying fits, hidden away in the bush or a dwelling. And the ones I did experience, during this time, were minimal in intensity.

But, now, I found myself amidst a vigorous, uncontrollable bout of grief. I exited the dwelling quickly and headed up a familiar path toward the Poison Sea. I moved quickly and focused on putting one foot in front of the other. I kept my head down as I often had when I didn't want anyone to see the state I was in.

Putting my head down had been a refuge of invisibility for me. If I didn't see the people, they couldn't see me. It had been my technique for the times I was brought home by my mother or father as they hit me or berated me for some childhood misdemeanor or the days when I first was brought to Rondo and the shame and embarrassment of what was occurring that made me feel so small and worthless. Now, as I walked with my head down, my face convulsed as the tears streamed down my face. I grasped for air with my lungs as my breath was devoured by my walking pace and my anguish.

I made it to the top of a ridge, far from the village, far from the main trail. I slumped over a rock and sobbed uncontrollably. It was painful. Not a physical wound, yet the pain was physical. Unbearable! The crying, noted for its cleansing qualities, was not fulfilling this purpose. I screamed, and the cries were lost into the horizon of the Poison Sea. I cursed the Oneness. I took a rock and began to beat my head until I bled.

Eventually, the outburst brought on fatigue and the crying began to decease. I was only whimpering now, and I had no thought of anything. It became deathly quiet. The grief seemed to desist, but the pain continued. I could hear demons laughing at me. The anguish!

I rose and looked down at the jagged peaks below. They called to me. I closed my eyes. A sense of calmness overcame me. I felt I had found the answer. I prayed that Mika and Donny would be cared for. I heard the demons say, "Do it!"

My heels were on the ledge. But my toes dangled off. I felt serene and tranquil. I leaned forward.

"Letsi!" Delta cried in a deafening scream.

It broke my trance. And I turned to face the terror in her eyes.

20

As I kissed Mika and Douglas goodbye and began my journey, imprints were made in my psyche. Douglas looked puzzled but genuinely aware. I wondered how he perceived events like these. He had attempted to run and follow me but halted when Donny called him back. Would he miss me dreadfully when I was gone?

He certainly protested loudly and violently on the couple of occasions I had left him with my father. Those were desperate times of course. Like when I had to rescue Mika from a boulder in the midst of the deep flowing mountain stream. Mika's friends had come to get me. I sent one of them over to fetch my father while I ran for Mika in the mountains. There, I found him hanging on to a rock in the centre of the stream, afraid the current would sweep him away.

When I returned to my dwelling with Mika, Douglas ran to me and clung to my arm. My father proclaimed to me that Douglas had not adhered to him at all, and it was likely because of my poor parenting skills.

Another time was when both Mika and I were too ill to tend to Douglas. That time seemed less traumatic, and it almost seemed as if Douglas and my father had enjoyed their time together in some ways.

Both times I had asked for my father's assistance, Rondo was on a hunting expedition. And, now, Rondo was off hunting as I parted for this excavation trek. Rondo was frequently absent for many things, and I was accustomed to that. However, it was Mika's sweet acquiesces that was something new as I left on this journey. He was certainly there to see me off. He smiled and waved as I prepared to leave. Thankfully, I could not see sadness in his eyes.

In contrast, I was distressed by Delta's haunting and all-knowing fixed look. She was keenly aware of my instability. Occasionally, the odd mountain person had been put on observation by the elders and leaders out of concern for their own safety. Violet was watched closely when Chris and Delta had been taken from her.

My Aunt Dana had spent a fortnight at her lodging to console her and keep her from harming herself. It was Dana that first expressed a concern for Violet's physical as opposed to mental health. Had Delta revealed the situation she saw me in the previous night, I would likely be restricted from attending this expedition.

I believe that would certainly have been counterproductive, however. The excavation journey had been my only glimmer of life force at this time, not because I was fulfilling a lifetime goal but because I was diverting my attention from the depths of despair. The tediousness of the planning and the physicality of the trek were distracting me from thinking. Thinking made me very sad. Furthermore, I would not be alone at any time. I would incidentally be under closer supervision on the journey than had I stayed home in my own dwelling.

I made these arguments to myself, but they were really for those who might consider prohibiting me on the trip. I was not concerned whether

I was better off here or on the venture. I just felt a small inclination to go. Perhaps I might meet my fate on a cliff along route or in a mudslide.

Right now, I felt fine. I was still disillusioned with life, but I was aware of it. It was a stark contrast from the night before. Had Delta not awakened me from my stupor that night, I would certainly be on a different path today.

Delta had not lectured me or scolded me when she found me on the mountain. She just wept. Sometimes, I wonder if there is a set amount of sadness in the system. For at that time, I no longer felt the despair. It was as if Delta had taken all the sadness, and there was none left for me.

I sat at the edge of the cliff where, moments before, I was poised to leap, and I looked at the ground. Delta's mourn was a low, howling whimper, as if she were trying to repress it. I felt drawn to comfort her. I moved beside her and put my arm around her. She leaned against me. I realized then that it was not only Mika and Douglas I would be abandoning but Delta too and maybe others. I had to find a way to grieve and breathe.

Today, my soul seemed to be focused on my once great passion for learning of the world beyond. It was the only remote and very slight interest I had in life. As I walked away, the image of those people closest to me compressed and then vanished from sight as the distance between us increased. I felt a slight longing for them instantly, and I was glad for the engaged emotion. Any change from despondency was welcomed.

I felt somewhat charged for the trek, and I saw no increased risk in the venture. There were three of us on this pursuit. Our main goal would be to retrieve more salvage cloth, but we also had some leeway to consider salvaging other paraphernalia that might be of use to us technologically. The other members were both male, Germa, who was a little older than Donny, and Stephin, my childhood friend.

Despite our closeness in childhood, I had not had much to do with Stephin since I had been sent off to live with Rondo. He had had a very fruitful life since our youth and had turned out to be a strikingly handsome young man. When he smiled at me as we set off, I could still see that twinkle in his mischievous eye that I had remembered from our youth.

We did not talk much or reminisce however for this adventure was a first for both of us, and we felt a need to concentrate on the journey. Furthermore, my social skills were inept at this point, and I had no interest in developing them. And, likewise, Stephin did not know what the boundaries would be on our relationship on this expedition.

The trek was long but it didn't feel strenuous. Perhaps I was drawing energy from the euphoria of my self-defined "freedom." And perhaps the journey there would be far easier than the return. It was hard to tell. Usually, the trip back seems quicker on any journey. However, in this case, our loads would be more burdensome, laden with excavated material. Thus, it would likely impede our pace returning.

There were treacherous points along route such as a jagged ledge along one of the faces we ventured that descended into a grating of dagger-like notches down its incline. As mountain people, we prided ourselves on our skills in climbing and balancing. From a very early age, we had to develop these skills. Much of our orchard was on a fairly steep bank. And, before work, our actual playground was a steep facing of course. It is where we had to exist. We subsisted within the trees in the midst of the west facing.

I could not think of anyone who had slipped and fell among the mountain people during their toils in the orchards or even on one of these excavation ventures. It was nothing I really thought about as a skill until Anex mentioned traveling with the Moraines. It was only then that

I had a dissimilar reference point to attribute a hierarchy to my skill and place the mountain people at the top.

"The Moraines are very cautious when climbing the Stalite Hills," began Anex on one of her few visits before the death of Alexandra. "They seem very nervous about high places. And their hills are not even very high compared to the mountains here. They say they have lost many people who have slipped and fell in the cracks and small canyons of those hills."

Alexandra listened intently to Anex's description and closed her eyes amidst a burst of envisioning combined with pain.

The ledge that we were now walking along on my first salvage expedition was certainly not the narrowest. It was at least a foot-length wide. But it reminded me of Anex's words.

"We have been given a gift that other peoples like the Moraines and even the Stalites do not seem to possess. We are sure footed on the ledges and peaks of our mountains like the mountain beasts with hoofs that used to roam this domain in a long ago time."

We were sure footed on this excavation trek, but, timewise, we maintained a slow cautious pace. The journey was dreary, and we were exposed to the sun for long periods. We wrapped ourselves in excess salvage cloth to deflect the direct rays, but the extra layers elevated our temperature and left us quite fatigued.

We would rest at several caves and crevices along route that provided shelter from the rays and a damp coolness that soothed our bodies. There, we consumed rationed amounts of food and water. It took approximately one day of travel time to get to the pass where we would begin our search. But we had to camp for the night when the sky darkened. The path posed so many hazardous passages that it was far too dangerous to attempt to move forward in the night.

Germa had talked to us about some of the difficult areas and some techniques they had used in past treks to venture forward. He spoke of some places where the trail was impassable. On past journeys, they had had to construct small bridges in order to continue. These links, however, were not the most trustworthy. There was very little wood and vegetation in the most difficult areas. And thus, building material was scarce.

Germa also mentioned that, sometimes, well into the expedition, his past excavators would have to take out ropes from their packs and lasso a rock on the other side of a canyon. Then they would swing across and climb up the facing. Fortunately, we had not encountered this level of difficulty so far.

However, nothing in this environment seemed dependable. Because of the constantly shifting sand and gravel and the threat of floods, the trek there may not even resemble the passage home. So far, however, our path had been relatively stable.

Germa was the scout as he was the only one of the three of us who had been on previous journeys. Stephin and I were clearly rookies. It was nice to be with Stephin after all these years, even though we spoke very little. Stephin had fathered three healthy children by different mothers in his youth. It had given him elevated status among the people, and it automatically qualified him to membership on excavations and other risk-taking ventures.

Despite not having the opportunity of speaking with him for such a long time, I did not feel compelled to talk to him, even when I was becoming comfortable on our pathway. Our focus seemed to be on the journey. It did require concentration for the difficult trek, but, beyond this, we seemed to be associating our journey with a personal fulfillment; thus, our thoughts were generally on our own spirituality. We paced along steadily, methodically.

We welcomed the darkness at the end of our day's hike. The heavy layers of salvage cloth had become very cumbersome with accumulated sweat from our bodies, and we were glad for the opportunity of shedding the inner layer and spreading it out over a rock to dry.

We soon stopped, and German directed us to a small cave on the north side of the cliff we were ascending. We stretched out our excess cloth in the form of a blanket using out satchels for pillows. We covered ourselves and lay on the hard rock surface. We shivered a bit as our overheated bodies adjusted to the drop in temperature.

The situation seemed surreal. I was beginning to fall into a different state of being. I hoped it was just my fatigue and unfamiliarity with the environment that was making me feel impassive. I prayed it was not the beginnings of another depressive bout. I curled up in my blanket and fell asleep without a word to either Germa or Stephin.

We rose early the next morning. It took a few moments for our senses to orient us to this unknown territory. A sinuous fog surged over the facing of the rock, clouding it with a soft blanket of mist. We chewed on some dried rodent meat and ground berries.

There was a small indent in the cave that contained a bowlful of trapped water. We took turns scooping our hands into the puddle and slurping the liquid into our mouths. It had a stale, musty taste but served to quench our thirst. We saved our small flasks of mountain water that we carried in our satchels. The flasks would only be used in case of emergency. We bundled up with our cloth and headed out of the cave and down the hill toward a large deposit of beige sand stretching across a wide valley as though it was joining two mountains in the range with granite glue.

Partway across the remnants of this long ago delta that made up the majority of the pass we were pacing through, Germa stopped the procession. It certainly would have escaped the untrained eye of both

Stephin and I, but there, in the sand, was a small leaflet of paper. It was light brown, almost the same colour as the sand; but its camouflage was given away by the light breeze that was causing it to flutter slightly.

Germa instructed us to tread very lightly as we closed in on the area where the artifact was spotted. Germa brushed the sand and gravel from the leaflet to reveal more paper. He immediately took out his small metal spade and began to trowel away the sediment. He motioned us to follow his lead. We slowly started pushing the sand away in the area to reveal more and more leaflets and books.

The word papers always caught my imagination. As a child, in teaching time, I always lusted for more to read and decipher. We had minimal word papers because they were not considered a priority. There scarcity made them a gem of sorts, which, I guess, fuelled my curiosity for more.

Germa seemed indifferent to the papers and hurriedly discarded them by placing them in a huge pile aside from the area he was excavating. I tried to appear to follow his lead but, at the same time, make a quick browse and sort some of the books and word papers in a separate pile. I hoped to review them quickly and salvage those that were of interest to me.

Germa had made it clear that we must excavate quickly and find practical artifacts for our community. These included cloth, tools, and metals. Papers and ornaments ranked well below this. Germa insisted we focus our energy on digging deeper and wider and spend little time marveling at the impractical relics from these ancient people.

Luckily, we quickly reached a deposit of cloth, which took the focus from any distractions I might have exhibited in the time I had spent sorting the word papers. We sifted through the variety of colours and textures, searching for the best quality and types most suited for protection from the sun. Germa instructed us to sort for the largest intact articles that suited that criterion. We looked for long, flowing garments and blankets, light in weight yet thick in depth. Light colours were preferred.

We also spent minimal time reflecting on the articles we were sifting through and those we deemed not salvage material. For instance, we spent little time wondering about whom the tiny little baby suit was for that I placed in the discard heap, little time wondering how all of this extravagant stitching with intricate beadwork was created, little time wondering what was the purpose of a small figurine created in the image of a young, light-coloured woman with no genitals.

We were efficient though. Within an hour we had rummaged through the salvage spot and retrieved enough to fill our pack loads to excess capacity. We were then permitted a short probe through the remaining debris that had surfaced in our initial dig.

I tried to distance myself from the shock and startle of foraging among the bones and fragments of people. There were some bones at the salvage site that were surely not animals, especially the skull fragments. I had been told that there were the remains of ancient people at the salvage sites, and it was usually a frightening or, at very least, a disturbing encounter. It was particularly disturbing when the remains were intact.

I stumbled across one such corpse. It was the darkened skeleton of what appeared to be a woman. She had a shawl of loosely stitched thread over her protruding scapula, and she still contained some remnants of hair. It was most difficult to despond from.

It was common knowledge that there were body remnants in the salvage areas. It was one of the reasons there were so many restrictions on venturing on the expeditions. We really didn't know why these people were here or who they were. They appeared to have died without a proper burial or passing ceremony for there was so much debris surrounding their bones and such an accumulation of remains in some sites. Anex talked of once finding several skulls at one excavation site but no other bones. It was a great mystery.

We had taken care to discuss their existence, however. While we couldn't answer the question of how they died, we did ponder why they were there and where they had come from. It also seemed very strange that the excavators would so often come across their frames intact, while the remains of the mountain people would wither to dust in such a short time once we passed. Several mountain people who had been lost for days and found dead in the mountains were far more decomposed in that short time than some of the remains found on salvage expeditions.

We didn't know why this was so, but we had some theories. One was that they had likely been preserved because the sediment in the area was wet. Of course, the sediment on this particular excavation was quite dry so that left cause for dispute. Another idea was that their bodies were intoxicated with some petrifying compounds. This was quite a popular theory as it supported that fact that these ancients were inherently evil and that they supported a lifestyle that promoted the use of toxins in their body that matched the spiritual toxins in their soul. Another less popular but more moderate and contemplative thought was that the types of metals they were located with somehow retarded decay.

One theory that was not accepted, however, was that they had just died recently and there were other people still alive somewhere in these mountains. We would not entertain the idea that there were other people adapted to the mountains. This somehow conflicted with our doctrine of living in the only habitat suitable for people. We prided ourselves at being the only ones capable of surviving in these mountains as it was part of our ultimate purpose.

There was certainly some support for the theory of metal retarding decay, however. The corpse that I had uncovered had an assortment of metal-like substance surrounding it. There was some bluish-coloured bendable wire, which resembled the bundles that Anex was famous for retrieving. I collected a few of them noting the excess weight.

I then noticed another bendable metal. Yet this one was in the form of a thin shiny sheet rolled up on a cylinder. It was extremely light in comparison to the wire. I crammed the cylinder into the sliver of space that remained in my salvage bag with a few word papers. I slung it over my back and secured the head strap in place.

With Germa's signal, we quickly began the trek home. A sense of urgency over took us. It was as if we were in a forbidden world disturbing the elements. And the powers of the mighty mountains might strike down upon us if we tallied in this place too long. If we were not swift enough, we might wake the giant responsible for all the natural disasters in this constantly changing environment. We paced along quickly and softly.

As the sky darkened, we felt our energy drain. It was as if we were fuelled solely by solar power, and, as the sun receded, it appeared to pull away all of our kinesis. It forced us to pause, and we rescinded into a small lean-to made haphazardly in haste from a few branches off a couple of brush bushes. We used our huge pack loads for wall supports. We huddled together in the darkness and closed our eyes.

I dozed briefly but was awakened by the detection of a hand on my outer thigh. The whole trip was certainly new territory for me, but I had not anticipated any type of union advancement by the men on this journey. This was never discussed. We were certainly nestled closely as we bedded down, but that was because of the cramped quarters of our lean-to. I was so exhausted that I had no forethought that our pause in journey would be other than rest. But this hand on my thigh was clearly not a casual slump. It was undoubtedly a gesture of contact—contact, connection, desire.

I had never considered sexual activity with either of these men. My focus was clearly on the venture. The opportunity to leave the mountain was the source of my lust. It was an all-consuming desire in years before Alexandra died. Now, it was a past dream unfolding in fate. In my days of dreaming of adventure, however, union was not on the agenda.

Now, the thought of entering into another nuptial, even if brief, seemed asinine. The affiliation with Rondo, which I was placed into at such an early age, had been the catalyst for my ambition to venture on this salvage. I wished to escape relations, not seek them out.

Yet, someone was clearly touching me. Stephin and I had been so close in our youth but had never engaged in any touching activity. We never had the opportunity. Before we were old enough to even entertain such thoughts, I had been whisked away by duty.

Stephin became a young suitor a couple of years later. He impregnated one girl a few years younger than us named Jeena. Conception occurred very early on with his first encounter. Both Stephin and Jeena had not joined in a family union other than to bear a child. The council had concluded that they were too young and too ill-equipped. It was intended that once Stephin was able to build a dwelling and provide adequate sustenance and likewise that Jeena, the childhood mother, was mature enough to maintain the home, the three might rejoin as a family.

However, Jeena was tightly guarded by her parents, and Stephin saw very little of her during her pregnancy. Following the delivery of a healthy little baby boy, Jeena still remained at home with her parents. They were more than willing to tend to her and the baby. And Jeena's loyalty and security drew her to stay. On the other hand, Stephin had desires and opportunities to dwell more extensively with other girls, and he took advantage of that privilege.

Stephin proved to contain fertile seed. Two more girls bore his children in the next two years. It gained him quick status among the people. He did try to provide for all of his children, but his elevated status gave him liberties with these duties and more freedom to pursue other ventures. He was not only considered a prime suitor but at liberty to choose tasks and duties to pursue.

It was not that he was in a position of complete immunity to the labours that our people had to undergo in order to simply maintain basic sustenance. However, his success as a biological father at such an early age freed him somewhat of the responsibility of tending to these children and gave him clout to choose more adventurous labours. People would often give him some offerings of food and tools as they saw it as a gesture of good fortune for themselves.

The girls whom he impregnated were not given as much freedom, of course, as they had to carry the offspring for a much more significant period other than a mere sexual encounter. Even with assistance from their parents, these young girls still had a much more regimented set of duties to conduct.

Stephin, on the other hand, worked in the orchid for a while and spent most of his time hunting rodents in the mountains where we played together as children. Intermittent with this, he had sex with as many girls and women as was offered to him.

Perhaps this extensive experience had anointed him with the boldness to make a move on me. Certainly, our current situation did as well. While clearly fatigued and focused on the salvage mission, we were nevertheless three adults, two males, one female, compacted into fairly close sleeping quarters. And although we were very fatigued from our journey, the actual process of an excavation had sent a surge of adrenalin throughout the system.

Spontaneous sexual unions were certainly not forbidden outside our residual lodging, but it was not common. We toiled and laboured for such a considerable period of the day, just to maintain sustenance, that we generally had little energy to pursue casual unions. We were in limited contact with the opposite sex once we reached puberty. Girls spent most of their time bearing and tending to offspring, and, by the time they reached adulthood, many mountain people were ill. My mother was a typical example.

The most promiscuous of behaviours were those exhibited by Stephin as a prime stud suitor. His behaviour was encouraged and requested. This gesture of his hand on my thigh was best described as irregular, irregular and unconventionally arousing.

I was just becoming comfortable with Rondo's advances but had never entertained thoughts of having another man touch me. Stephin was someone I felt I knew well, and this seemed to ease any tension I might have. I knew too that his behaviour would be supported by council and elders. His act would be considered a positive gesture for the survival of the people. Stephin had the fortunate position of having a libido that was considered a sacred virtue that all should be willing to embrace.

I allowed him to keep his hand on my thigh, and he took my lack of rejection to be an invitation for advancement. He slid his hand quietly and smoothly along my side, up my arm, to my neck. His hands touched my hair. Stephin slid his hand silently to other parts of my anatomy and pressed against me.

As the motion continued, so did the noise level, and thus Germa began to stir. It took him very little time to realize what was taking place. Before he could react, however, I looked at him, lunged forward, and pressed my lips fixedly on his. The three of us engaged in this activity and pursued things completely foreign to me and likely unfamiliar to both of them. Our sleep was minimized.

While the encounter was relatively dramatic, it was somewhat brief, and we quickly fell into a slumber following it. I dreamed of Douglas when I finally catnapped. He was standing on the top of the mountain peak where Alexandra's remains where cast to the Oneness.

"Douglas! What are you doing up here?" I questioned.

To my astonishment Douglas replied. "Look," he stated in a monotone voice. "It's Alexandra. She reached the Oneness."

I smiled in incredulity. "I'm so happy he understands." I looked up to the sky to peruse the heavens for signs of my baby. I saw nothing. I gazed at Douglas seeking guidance. He had turned away and put his head down in a solemn gesture. He shook his head back and forth as if disappointed about something.

"It is not our time to know," he uttered.

I stared back to the sky searching for meaning or direction. There was something moving down from a great altitude. It was an indistinguishable speck in the beginning. But, as the entity approached, it looked like a black cloud. I strained to make out what this aerial phenomenon was. It was clear these were some type of flying creatures that differed greatly from birds.

As they flew toward me, I could see features on their faces. Their eyes were glossy, dark red with tears of blood pouring from them. Their skin was a tint of green and grey. Deep grooves and scars occurred in masses over their heads. And, as they screamed in a piercingly high pitch, their teeth were exposed exhibiting small, brown spikes embedded in drooping blood red gums. Chunks of mangled flesh hung from their mouths.

They swooped down towards us extending their black webbed-winged arms. They stuck out the claws in their feet and dived toward Douglas. They ripped at his flesh, tearing the larynx from his throat. I stood in horror but could not move. I attempted to go forward but my body was frozen. A second creature advanced in Douglas's direction as he stood motionless holding the flesh of his throat as blood gushed from his wound. I tried to fight my immobility by, first, screaming. I willed open my mouth. I sense the urgency. "I must!" I uttered. "I must!" I shrieked.

I ran toward Douglas who now was on the other side of a bottomless canyon. I lunged forward and took flight. I grabbed one of the creatures by the black webbed wings and flung him toward a second creature. On contact, they both shattered like heat cracked rocks and their remains sprinkled to the depths of the canyon. I ran to Douglas. He stood up and looked down at me. I thought he might be smiling.

I looked again and there was Stephin standing before. "Letsi," he said softly. "It's time to go."

Our focus in the early morning was on the trek home as we knew survival was the priority. We had little food and water and a day's journey regardless of supplies. Occasionally, we glanced at one another with eyes searching for the meaning of our activity in the dark, but we did not speak of it.

Our journey back was gruesome and met with major challenges. Besides hunger, thirst, and fatigue, I lost my footing once and nearly slipped down a rock face. And Stephin had to dodge a large boulder that rained down from an overhanging cliff just missing his head as it fell to the rocky valley below. Also, behind us in the distance, we could hear the rumblings and see darkness. The mountain gods had made their presence known with a mass of black clouds and thunderous roars. It hurried us along even faster.

I feared at any moment that one of the flying creatures from my dream would pierce through the dark sky and mount an attack against us. I was frightened and I felt a desperate longing for my home. It was so good to feel.

Late that evening, we arrived in the village careworn. We ambled off in different directions to our homes. Both Germa and Stephin lived with women who had bore one of their children, and they, like me, pined for their dwellings. We had a longing for the comfortable and the familiar. That which I longed to escape had now become my desire.

I entered my dwelling noiselessly and slid unto my mattress in silence. Rondo stirred and turned to look at me. He half-smiled and quietly questioned me about my trip.

"Were you successful at finding things?" he whispered.

"Yes, it was a productive excavation."

My fatigue served to relax me, and I spoke briefly about the trek. I drifted off into sleep amidst a sentence.

In the morning, I was greeted by Mika's happy shrills calling my name, "Mom," as he hugged me. Douglas too was clearly excited as he wandered about the dwelling occasionally touching my side. Rondo had left the quarters but, soon, returned with some breakfast for us. We ate, and I spent most of my time answering Mika's query.

"What did you find over there?"

"Many things, I have cloth, word leaflets, bendable metal, and some other interesting things. I'll show you as soon as I finish eating." I smiled in the pleasure of his inquisitiveness.

Douglas sat close to me intently eating his fruit and occasionally resting his head on my shoulder. The juices drooled from his mouth and spilled down his neck onto his clothing.

Rondo sat quietly, intently gazing at me. We rarely questioned each other about our actions, although I sensed he was quite intrigued. I appreciated his timid nature and his limited communication skills at this time as I feared what I might say about the trip. I knew I had not betrayed Rondo. But I knew it was better left not discussed.

The men, with whom I had compromised, had become the focus of my thought. It had taken away from the primary purpose of the trip. As always though, our most carnal and primary desires often overpower our intellectual purpose. Or maybe it is just a matter of balance. Nevertheless, the shift of balance in my mind was on my intimate encounter with Stephin and Germa.

In contrast, what I spoke of was the trek and the artifacts I salvaged. It seemed to keep the focus on any apparent uneasy feelings I might be experiencing as a result of the adventure. I also was in somewhat of an altered state. This numbness had been my custom since a very early age. All that which is new, exotic, uncomfortable, or uneasy in any way must generally be processed while we are on a plain of numbness.

The numbness, the trancelike state, serves as an evasion of reality. It wasn't as though I was totally preoccupied with the activity. It was just that I had no one to dialogue with about the ordeal. I did not think it appropriate to talk to anyone, not even those who had participated.

On a positive front, however, the distraction was not leaving me despondent. I seemed to want to be engaged with my family. I seemed to want to share with them.

I presented the salvage cloth to Rondo and Mika to rummage through and choose. The discussion was on the cloth with comments coming mainly from Mika about the variety of colours.

"Mommy this red one is so soft. You would look beautiful in it," he proclaimed, and Rondo smiled. "Mommy may I have this green one? The girls will just love me in it."

I had to laugh. His cocky nature was becoming a feature of his sense of humour. It was so tranquil and freeing to sit and relish in his joy. It was somewhat contagious. Rondo examined the products choosing a couple for himself and putting several aside for Douglas.

We choose several pieces for the family and Donny and Delta who had helped with the children in my absence. The remaining cloth was folded and placed in the corner of the dwelling to be used for barter.

I presented Rondo, Douglas, and Mika with small gem beads that I carried in the pocket of my clothing. We were all adorned with some such jewels. Jewels and shells on various locations of our body were a great luxury.

I proceeded to empty the contents of my packsack. First, I carefully placed the word pages in a small basket in the corner of the dwelling which contained other such papers. Then I took out the bendable metal strings and divided them into piles for my personal use and for barter. Last, I pulled out the roll of bendable metal sheets.

"That looks unusual," commented Rondo.

"Indeed," I replied as I unrolled a small sample. It glistened and shimmered from the reflection of the sun. It sparkled similarly to the shimmer of sunrays on beads of water in the mountain streams.

That night, when Rondo and I engaged in union, I welcomed his advance and responded to it reciprocally.

21

We were headed to the location where Lauren died. It was quite close to our meeting place but a fairly treacherous journey. The Stalites did not like to venture out of the caves as they were particularly sensitive to the sun. They wore little or no clothing within the cave and possessed very little salvage cloth.

Neil, being the youngest in the meeting party, was appointed to escort me to the location on a different route than the elderly Stalites. According to the Stalites, it was a necessary detour for me as I was not petite enough to contort through the small crevices in the core of the caves. Furthermore, it was a particularly untrustworthy path that required prior knowledge of the fissures and gaps that could swallow an unsuspecting novice. For these reasons, it was compulsory for me to journey on the outside of the hills and reenter at another location.

I was asked to lend some of my cloth to Neil for the journey. While on the inside, I was clearly a follower. The walls were difficult to hang on to because of their smooth texture that perspired musty water on many slates. It was slippery to pass through, and I felt unsure of my footing in this maze of ridges and holes.

The darkness dimly illuminated by a reactor metal torch was an added hindrance. I could not distinguish between shadows and holes in the floor. Thus, I was significantly dependent on Neil to direct me. Neil was patient and meticulous about navigating me through the labyrinth of tunnels and caves.

However, once we exited the caves and began our trek on the outside path, I took the lead under Neil's guidance. He knew the direction, but was not as confident as to the safest pathway. He was not as sure footed on the outside as the rays of the sun seemed to agitate him. With something to grip on to and an ability to see the trail, I was in command of the corridor. It was not a long trek, but it took awhile as we maintained a particularly slow pace.

The rocks and the cliffs were smoother and gentler than the mountains of my home, but they were not an easy path for someone who was not accustomed to the smooth sides of these slight mountains. Within the caves, the Stalites tended to feel their way with precision. But, on the outside, their senses were distracted by the refined slopes of the taupe Stalite Hills, softly offsetting the bright indigo sky.

The scenery abruptly commanded our attention with the foliage strategically positioned around the mounts contrasting a bright green hue intermittently throughout, as if authorized by the power of the sun illuminating the chlorophyll in their system. The contrast of green to brown promenaded the difference between inert matter and life matter. The colours of the world were visually imposing and forced us to take notice.

The air was much dryer than in the cave. And we felt the warmth entering down into our throat and being cooled by our inside flesh. On the outside, we had to acknowledge the many physical interruptions that competed with our mental and spiritual faculties. Thus, on the outside, the Stalites had to accustom themselves to the increased sensory input.

This had served to obstruct Neil's sense of orientation. I, on the other hand, was relatively well adapted to the outside. I felt a sense of strength and "neededness" in being able to assist Neil.

"Here, take my arm."

Neil responded by grabbing tightly to my bicep. We moved along the outside of the soft hills. There was no worn path and very little ridge to anchor our feet on. Compounding this was the slippery slope that contained a light dusting of beige sand over the smooth stone. Our feet slipped down on the sharper inclines. Neil was anxious on our short trek across the outside of his habitat. He began to slow as we reached a slight gully on the eastern side of the fourth hill we climbed.

"This is the summit." Neil sighed with relief. "We enter here."

We squeezed through a meager cleft in the mountain and inched our way along a narrow ledge. There was still ample light on this entrance layer of the dwarfed mountain, and the site was spectacular. The caves were adorned with hanging cones, cones created from solidified drips of mud. They were magnificently shiny and polished looking. It was as if someone had taken the rock formation on the outside of the hills and rubbed them with abrasive salvage cloth until all of the sediment and erosive pours were removed, leaving an opaque, gemlike configuration.

They were not astutely shiny like the veins of quartz we would find in our mountains but rather a pastel-buffed incandescence. The hues were equally magnificent with blends of mauve and dark red, and soft pinks speckled with crimson and maroon. And the majority of the backdrop of hanging cones varied in shades of brown from light beige to dark bronze and sienna. The different tones were so distinct yet so flawlessly presented in a collective.

With Neil now in command, we slithered our way down a sharp incline inside the chamber. I could see a central fire of reactor metal emitting its emerald rays. It grew as I descended into what seemed to be vortex in shape. We joined the circle and united in its serenity.

As my eyes became accustomed to the darkness, I was able to distinguish the form of the particular enclosure we occupied. It angled outward as it rose above where we were seated. The space looked like the inside of a large upside down cone. The walls of the arena were garnished with solidified drips and small shelflike ridges, which appeared to be seats. There were cones protruding from the ground as well as the ceiling. The plateau on which we were located was a large surface with very few visible faults where one might fall to their death. The area in this hidden cave was colossal. And the high ceiling with its massive hanging gems were tremendous.

We sat on the circumference of the ring and calmed ourselves by the rays of the reactor metal in the centre. I was content to rest and marvel at the sight of the metal reflecting off the burnish cones. It was an amazingly appeasing spectacle to the soul. I had almost drifted off to sleep in the midst of the peacefulness when Tonaldo began to speak.

"Lauren was not killed in this place but off to the side in that tunnel." Tonaldo pointed to a small crevice to the left of me. "The story of how this happened is long and sorrowful."

The Stalites all seemed very uncomfortable at this point, which alarmed me somewhat. They had seemed so serene and methodical up until then. At least, I had not noticed any sense of heightened negative emotion in their mannerism prior to this.

On the other hand, I was just becoming familiar with their emotional presentations. So perhaps I was misinterpreting the language of their mannerisms altogether. Regardless, there was clearly something troubling them as Tonaldo regrouped to present her narrative.

"The people of the caves are dying. We are not bearing enough children. There are now only three children below the age of fertility. And those of child-producing age have not conceived for several years."

I thought about this statement as Tonaldo prepared to continue. It was a striking opening remark. I had not given this any consideration in my time observing and recording mental data on these people. But then I wondered; how small was their population? I had only encountered a handful of Stalite adults and no children in my brief meeting with them. Where were the rest of them? I now began to speculate.

"We have tried many things to increase our fertility: herb combinations, increased activity, special attention to cycles, elaborate ceremony . . ." Tonaldo paused. "All have had minimal success. The mountain water and trade with the mountain people and the Moraines have been of assistance in increasing our health and longevity but not our birthrates." Tonaldo concluded her statement and then there was a pause in the address.

It was a disheartening topic and one that took time to present. The Stalites' health seemed a positive note. I remember the medicinal herbs that Anex had returned with on her travels to the home of the Stalites. She commented on their absence of illness. It was such herbs that had reduced my mother's discomfort and many other mountain people's pain. However, it was not known whether these herbs could reduce the cancers and other illness of our people as the quantity was too small. During my brief tour with Neil, I had begun to wonder if we might cultivate them in some of the cracks and hollows of our mountains to have a more reliable supply.

Tonaldo continued, "As a last resort, we chose to seek outside seed. We hoped that the mixing of our blood with the *others* might provide us with new genetic tools to flourish in our sacred home. For this, we looked to the Moraines as they are the only other people that resemble us as a species.

It was not a preferred option. But we were a desperate people. We knew that we had many differences with the Moraines, but we felt we must try. It was a slow discussion among our people. It took us a fair amount of time to even become at ease with the prospect of uniting with these people who seemed to have very few spiritual qualities.

We first felt that we must challenge our thinking about the Moraines. We knew we had a general aversion to the Moraines because of many past conflicts. But we also thought that most of the conflict was surrounding certain issues such as trade and territorialism. We decided to challenge our thinking to look for the positive aspects that the Moraines possessed."

For the first time on my journey across the Poison Sea, I felt a compelling need to question what was being suggested. "Does it not compromise your values and principles to try and convince yourself that your enemy is virtuous?"

"The enemy is not the person," responded Alan in slow, orderly speech. "The enemy is that vice that one might possess that conflicts with our ethos."

"We do not see the Moraines as our enemy," clarified Neil. "We see some of their behaviour as our enemy."

"While the Moraines do possess distinctions that we do not desire, they also have many positive elements," continued Tonaldo. "They are strong and hardworking. They are able to function outside the caves. They have incredible ingenuity at inventing and building unique technologies. These were powers that could help our people."

"On the other hand," interjected Vanel, "we knew that they had violent tendencies that could hurt us."

Tonaldo continued, "This caused us great concern, and we spent many hours contemplating the possibilities. We concluded, with much reluctance, that we would try to reason with the Moraines and present our proposal but only if we could find a willing proponent among our young women.

Several of our women volunteered to be bred with a Moraine. Lauren was chosen for several reasons. She was the largest of the girls and she had engaged in union with Stalite men. It had been over a year of continued contact, yet she had not conceived. This had become the situation for most of the women. In fact, no woman among our people has conceived in many years. The youngest children among us are several years old.

Lauren ventured forth. She was willing to undergo this union to help the Stalite people. Still, we were quite apprehensive about the engagement and discussed all of the possible consequences we could think of before we accepted Lauren's sacrifice. Despite being presented with all of the risks, she did not relinquish her vow.

Lauren was a beautiful girl with long soft hair and glistening eyes. She was a well-selected candidate. She was one of the tallest Stalite people with fairly wide hips. Lauren longed to have a child for herself as well as our people. Once she expressed her solid conviction, we chose to focus on selecting a Moraine to approach. We did not approach any Moraine leadership unit on the matter but rather went directly to those who had direct trade with us."

I wondered what the Moraine leadership process was. Was it similar to the elders and council of our people? Their system seemed somewhat less structured and regimented than both ours and the Stalites'. At least this is what I concluded from the limited observations I had made.

They seemed to have a more liberal agenda with additional individual freedoms. Even their habitat seemed more open and varied. Moraines lived sporadically inland from the Poison Sea along route to the Stalite caves. Their dwellings and surroundings seemed very individualistic.

The flora and fauna varied as much along route as did the homes. It was in contrast to the village dwellings of my home.

I had quickly judged that the Moraines had more freedoms, simply based on their living structure. Thus, I did not question why Tonaldo stated that they had not gone to any head council with their proposal as it seemed appropriate to approach the traders directly.

"We know very few Moraines. Our contact with them is minimal. We do trade with them at their request, but we have little contact with the outside and thus with very few Moraines other than the traders.

There were some Moraines we had exchanged with on a recurring basis. One was Suz and her party. She approached us from the west, close to the Ravine Mouth. Another trading group was Sollele and his entourage. They would link with us from the direction of their homes in the south east.

The home of Sollele is close to the cave in which we are now in. We believe it was some Moraines from his party whom have been pounding on the hills, trying to extract reactor metal. We thought that if we approached Sollele with the proposition, in exchange for large quantities of metal, his people might halt their desecration of our sacred hills.

Sollele had done extensive trading with our people, and we had been in close contact with him for several years. He was quiet when among us, as well as young and viral. Physically, he was not as robust as the Moraines that occupy the Ravine Mouth."

I knew of this. Anex had mentioned that in her observations. "The Moraines are huge, but some seem noticeably smaller further inland, close to the Stalite caves."

Tonaldo continued. "We did not know him well, but what we observed seemed somewhat suitable."

Tonaldo bowed her head and continued, "We pursued Sollele to join in union with Lauren. We approached it as a first time union and thus eligible for a Union Ceremony."

They seemed to recognize my ignorance about a Union Ceremony and began to describe it.

"When a young Stalite woman begins to menstruate, men will approach the other women expressing an interest in uniting with the young woman," explained Vanel. "The elder women of our people will discuss the men's requests with the young woman. After the senior women have counseled the girl, she will choose one or more of those men to join in ceremony with her. They will court briefly and then the ceremony is prepared."

Vanel continued, "There was a brief courtship between Lauren and Sollele. Lauren was humble and hesitant when in Sollele's presence, but he interpreted it as shy. He saw it as an expression of coquetting. It heightened his infatuation towards her. As his desire increased, his listening sense declined. He no longer could hear the necessary instructions for the ceremony. We were deeply concerned about his inattentiveness to these important details."

Vanel paused, appearing to grapple for words to continue. Tonaldo interjected.

"We suggested to Lauren that perhaps the prospect should be aborted. But she disagreed. She was committed to the union."

Vanel continued, "At the time of the ceremony, those of us observing felt guarded against Sollele's demeanor. He seemed overwhelmed with the process. He did not seem able to exhibit control. As the ceremony advanced, Sollele was clearly abandoned of faculty. When he was presented with Lauren, he seized her and thrust himself into her. She screamed in pain. His size combined with his force, was clearly injuring her, and she cried and tried to break free. Alas, his strength was overpowering. In fact, several of our men could not detach him from his victim. One of our men grabbed his arm in an attempt to break his trance. Sollele threw him to the rock wall and he fractured his skull.

Several other men rushed to Lauren's aid, and they, too, were hurled away. In his climax, Sollele's force loss brawn, and Lauren was able to free herself from his clasp. Her tormented cries echoed in the cavern as she fled from the ceremony site to an adjoining crevice."

"Unfortunately, the site to which she escaped was unstable," continued Tonaldo. "It was a forbidden cave. It was considered leakage."

My puzzled look indicated to them that they needed to explain further.

"The unstable caves are a great source of water for our people, but we learned long ago that the water had to be retrieved from outside the entrance," inserted Neil. "Within these crevices, the walls are not stable. Jagged cones of rock often fall from the ceiling of such a cave with little notice. We have learned which ones to avoid."

"Lauren was not thinking clearly. Or she would not have entered such a place," continued Vanel. "The stability of this site had been further compounded by the pounding of the Moraines in that area."

"Regrettably, we did not focus on Lauren's whereabouts immediately," added Tonaldo. "Our attention was focused on Sollele, whom we attempted to subdue. The three remaining men of our flock with any warriorlike qualities had managed to restrain Sollele briefly by striking him in the head with a large boulder and then holding him to the ground. Others at the ceremony began to gather small rocks as weapons to use against this perpetrator. Sollele struggled free, however, and ran from the cave. We have not seen him since."

Neil continued, "I went to the site where Lauren had fled. Blood amassed her entire body. From her waist down, it appeared the blood source was from a torn and desecrated pelvis. From the waist up, her chest cavity had been punctured by a knifelike cone which had apparently fallen from the roof of the cave."

The anguish!

22

Often, when our desires are accomplished, two things happen. Our desires become obsessions as we seek to re-experience that sense of Oneness we achieved in the accomplishment of our goals. Or we are unfulfilled by these desires, and the achievement is a disappointment.

I felt neither. For me, most of my dreams and wants became reality when they were no longer my desires. Thus was the case for my excavation treks. I longed to travel on such a journey for so many years prior; but when the opportunity commenced, the longing had ceased. There was no gratification in my first excavation. There was no gratification in my salvaging paraphernalia. There was no gratification in the experience with Germa and Stephin.

There were, however, some sparks of satisfaction and contentment in the excitement that Mika displayed for his presents and for his inquisitiveness about my adventures. I had decided that if I was going to exist, it would be for Mika and Douglas. I suppose I had customarily been righteous in my consideration of them. But I had not been considering them as of late. I had not been considering anything. The pain of my broken heart following the death of Alexandra had been so pervasive, I could not feel. I wondered if this is why my mother seemed so apathetic at times. Was it simply the pain took precedence over all else?

I decided after my first excavation trek that I would rely on my detached skills as opposed to my detached feelings. I had, of course, been engaged in activities of caring and nurturing almost exclusively post puberty. It should be possible to coast into these activities simply from extensive practice.

Thus, this is how I continued. I continued to do all that I had done prior to Alexandra's death, relying on rote memory. And if I was blessed to experience brief moments of fulfillment through the joys my children expressed, I would acknowledge this as an accomplishment.

I tended to my chores, attended to Douglas, told stories to Mika and answered his questions, submitted to Rondo, and made brief social visits with those where I felt most comfortable. Thus, other than my immersing myself in domestic bliss, I generally only went to Delta and Donny's. But even those were brief meetings. Other than tending to my own household, I generally only left when I needed assistance or when Delta requested my help.

I no longer could bear to engage in conversation, talking or listening, particularly in casual conversation. I made every effort to restrict the chance of being placed in situations where I would be required to talk or, worse, listen. And thus, my visits at Delta and Donny's home were now intentionally brief.

On one occasion, when I was at Delta's dwelling upon her request, Chris was also present. Delta had invited me and Chris to help her dry the fish and birds that Donny had recently retrieved. He had apparently been very lucky on his hunting and fishing excursion. As a result, Delta was burdened with a surplus of meat that needed to be prepared quickly to dry before it spoiled. She had summoned me, through Mika, to assist her. In return, she would give us a share of the product.

"Hello, Letsi!" Chris presented himself at Delta's home.

"Well hello, Chris!" I countered, in a somewhat surprised tone.

It had been a long time since I had crossed paths with Chris, perhaps since before Mika was born. We had met briefly at the stream on the mountain once. It was just a chance encounter, and our conversation was brief and superficial: the flow of the stream, the colour of the sky, and similar ritualistic topics. It was an awkward meeting for some odd reason.

He had been such a close friend in my youth. Or so I had thought. Yet, when we met on the mountain, it was as if we were strangers. As I reflected on this, I realized that we really had drifted apart. The time in our youth was temporary, as is all else. It appeared that it could only be looked on now as a memory.

Instead, when we met, both were clearly preoccupied with our own individual circumstances, circumstances far too involved to explain in a chance meeting on a path. Our lives had had several hardships with limited enlightenment in the years since our childhood. I certainly was not at a point to understand all that had happened in mine as I was still living it. One cannot explain, let alone understand, without time to reflect.

For me, talking about my life to Chris at that point would have been a mish mash of anecdotes, open to too many misinterpretations. Likely, the same was true for Chris. Thus, it was a short conversation when we crossed paths on the mountain.

As we passed stating it was nice to see each other, I reflected on our youth together and surmised, I hadn't really known him well then either. I mean, I really did not know much about his thoughts, his dreams, or his desires. I only knew of his stories. Those, of course, were most entertaining. Perhaps his captivating stories had really been a mask to himself. The only thing I knew about Chris was that he had once been very descriptive and imaginative. I wondered if he still possessed this creativity. Or had it been siphoned away by the funnel of life's disappointments.

Delta, on the other hand, I knew well. I knew she was extremely uncomfortable to talk about anything personal. She would not mask her discomfort by avoiding subjects or fabricating a more comfortable version of events, but she would try to make uncomfortable topics as brief as possible.

Even when she said nothing, she said much. I loved this about Delta. I loved that she did not draw out any uncomfortable topics yarning on them endlessly. Uncomfortable topics were dealt with through brief verbalizations and plenty of time to reflect. Chris could be described as a creative speaker, but Delta was a practical one. Indeed, Chris and Delta seemed quite different for twins.

However, while I may not have known Chris very well, Delta surely did. She had talked about him, regularly, particularly since the birth of Shenal.

"Chris used to hide like that and peek out when he thought we were in trouble," Delta commented one day when Shenal had spilt some seeds from a basket and then ran to a nearby shrub to conceal herself. "Shenal get over here and pick up these seeds!" she added.

Shenal cautiously reappeared and began to put the seeds in the basket.

Chris has not fathered any children. Following his break up with Katrinka, I had heard that he had paired with many girls but had not been successful. I knew no other details. And Delta did not express much more about it.

It was nice to see him though, this morning at Delta's. I pondered about my reaction to seeing him. Anything I felt that differed from indifference was a novelty now. Not only was it a feeling but a pleasant feeling. Perhaps it was the clear sky and the calm mountain air that morning and the memory of Chris in my childhood that somehow synapsed a sense of connectedness within me.

The three of us sat and engaged in slothful dialogue as we defeathered tiny birds and gutted small fish. It was necessary even with the smallest of creatures to ensure the intestines were removed before drying. It was believed that the digestive tract accumulated most of the cancerous substances and the most deadly of viruses. I wondered where the theory came from. It had been a law among the people, and so there was a slice of mandatory divinity attached to it. But I had never thought of challenging it as a necessity until this very moment.

"It is imperative that we restrain from eating the animals as much as possible despite our hunger. The animals are infested with the evils of the past, which plague our people. Only in the most malnourished state should we ingest these food sources, and then we must take precautions to only consume the thoroughly dried muscle tissue." My father's words echoed in my mind.

"Have either of you ever ate other than the muscle of these animals?" I questioned the twins.

Both twins shook in a negative motion. Chris, however, seemed compelled to recite an added anecdote.

"That's what happened to Germa. He was up in the mountains and came across some baby vultures in a nest in a tree. He climbed to the top to get them but fell as he shifted down with the nest in hand. He bumped his head on the fall. And that is likely why he did not clean them properly. He probably wasn't thinking clearly." Chris continued, "He is on his deathbed now."

I did not even stop to question Chris's ownership of the facts. I was startled about the character in his story. I was unaware that Germa was ill. I had been so self-absorbed with my own self-proclaimed tragedy that I was not in tune to the suffering of others.

"When did this happen?" I asked.

"A few days ago," Delta replied.

"Yes," added Chris. "He is said to be dreadfully ill. There is a green tint to his skin like that of the olive berry leaves. He still has a bump on his head, and he is throwing up. He can no longer walk."

As Chris continued to take liberties with what he really knew as fact and what was clearly reality, I began to sort through the comprehension and repercussions that could ensue as a result of Germa's affliction. If he was, in fact, fatally ill, it would be a major blow to the salvage expeditions. He was the only experienced explorer left executing them.

Stephin was the next in seniority, and his knowledge level was much reduced. And then there was me and two others that had attended one expedition each. I felt overwhelmingly compelled to find out the actual level of impediment Germa was experiencing as opposed to the virtual account verbalized by Chris.

Following the task of drying Delta's protein and briefly commenting on how nice it was to see Chris again, I offered him an insincere invite to my dwelling sometime. Then I quickly gathered my share of meat and headed home.

"It looks like a fair amount," Rondo commented as I placed the meat out on the rocks surrounding our dwelling and sparsely oiled and herbed them.

"Indeed," I answered, but my mind was elsewhere. "Delta stated that Germa is quite ill."

I paused to look at Rondo shift his eyes toward me but not directly at me.

"If this is so, there is no one left with any real experience at leading excavations."

Rondo said nothing more. He knew where the conversation was leading. He was aware of my preoccupation with travel. We had never talked about it, yet he was aware. We talked of little, yet he seemed to understand so much. Or perhaps this was just my judgment. Perhaps he understood nothing. Perhaps his silence afforded him a perception of wisdom he did not possess.

Either way, he said nothing so I continued to present my procedure plan. I planned to visit Germa to see the extent of his illness. If it was as severe as Chris had suggested, I would attempt to ask him what he would propose for the future of the salvage expeditions.

While things were likely still registering with Rondo, I set off to the other side of the compound to see Germa. It was funny how the numbness served to help me on my engagement. I was barely troubled by the scowls of Germa's woman or of her neighbours as I approached.

"I heard that Germa is not well," I said to Luara, his companion.

She nodded in response.

"May I see him?" I asked in a voice as polite and firm as I could present.

"If you wish," she responded despondently.

I invested little effort in interpreting her response as I was preoccupied with concerns about salvaging and the decline in direction it would take without Germa. Often, it is in reflection that we torture ourselves with interpreting and cracking the codes of what was "really" meant. In reflection, however, I do not think she thought much about my visit at all. I knew very little about Luara as she lived in a distant section of the dwellings.

Luara was several years my senior and had two healthy children, one of which was Germa's. Luara had likely been quite wealthy from the standard of most of our people. Germa had salvaged extensively and likely traded for many food sources. Luara was likely considered blessed.

I think that was a fortunate thing for me. Because Luara was probably envied by most people, she would not feel threatened by my visit in any way. If anything, she probably either viewed me as a spoiled foul seed intruding on her property. Or perhaps, at best, she would feel sorry for me as I was not as worthy as she. I was not worthy enough to have her wealth or her success in childbearing.

My only initial concern in approaching her was that she might forbid me from meeting with Germa. I feared she might interfere, because she either did not perceive me as acceptable material for visitation or because she was aware of the intimate encounter that occurred between Germa, Stephin, and I on our last salvage expedition. I would not expect that she would feel threatened by it if she knew. But I suspect she may not have accepted me into her dwelling had she known.

However, I was jolted from my introspection by Germa's state when I entered the dwelling. His face was swollen with a grey shade to it. His eyes were puffy and the limited sclera that could be seen was a grayish yellow rather than white. He would not be recognizable if he were not lying in his own dwelling. Beyond this, the smell emitting from him was putrid. The stench of the dwelling reeked of the vilest vomit and feces. I wondered how coherent he might be.

I greeted him in a semicasual tone, stuttering my words somewhat. "H-Hello, Germa."

He lifted a shaky hand in my direction. He weakly drew his fingers and thumb in a somewhat pointed position. I had seen many sick and dying people make this motion. I wondered what significance this common gesture of the sick and dying actually meant.

Germa mumbled the word "water," and I reached for his capsule and raised it to his lips. I sat and observed him for a period. He said nothing in his semiconscious state. Occasionally, he moaned. Luara went in and out of the dwelling attending to small tasks. She brought in a small sample of herbs and berries commenting that Germa would not likely be able to ingest them.

My stay was brief and nonproductive for the purpose of the salvage expedition. However, I did make acquaintance with Luara. When I left the dwelling, I looked at Luara with genuine concern and respect. It would be difficult to watch a man die like this. His body was slowly being devoured by bacteria, transforming him into a congealing mass. It was likely arduous for her. I told her that I would come back with some salvage cloth with her permission. Germa was clearly in need of constant cleaning. She seemed grateful for the extra material.

Germa's situation became a preoccupation in my head for the next moments of time. I felt compelled to help him or to do something. I could only think good thoughts about this man and remember his positive effect on my life. Surprisingly, the memories of intimacy that I recalled most deeply were not that of our physical encounter. I have come to believe that physical intimacy does not resonate as strongly with women as it does with men. And thus, I felt far more grateful for his patience in walking me through the interrogation process I underwent with the council prior to our excavation trek.

Although I knew he had done it for the purpose of his mission, he did not cast judgment over my thoughts and beliefs. Prior to approaching the council, he had coached me extensively until I was able to respond to their unacceptable questioning in a calm manner. He had taught me a mature acceptable way of displaying outrage.

The next morning, I rushed about tending to some required tasks about my dwelling and then quickly assembled an herb concoction that might alleviate Germa's discomfort. We generally placed the herb bundles in a small wood vessel or on a rock with an indented surface and let the sun leech out the ingredients. Unfortunately, we felt that many of the key elements were likely dried up or leaked out of the vessels.

I often wondered if there was a better way of recovering some of these ingredients. It was then that I noticed the bendable metal role I had retrieved in the corner of my dwelling. I unrolled a small sheet and formed it into a basin like container and placed the herbs in it. Within minutes in the sun, the herbs were baking. The oil was not evaporating but rather accumulating in a ripple in the basin.

I poked a small hole in the bottom of the sheet and placed a small capsule underneath it. The oil slowly dripped into the container. I filled two capsules with the scant bit of herbs I was processing. It was clearly an effective way of retrieving medicinal oils. From then on, the bendable metal sheets were viewed as a more significant commodity to retrieve on salvage expeditions.

I went back several times to visit the dying explorer and found myself developing a friendship with Luara. Germa was generally incoherent but occasionally uttered my name when I entered the dwelling.

I learned that Luara was somewhat taxed by the burden of caring for him. She had moved herself and the children to the storage unit that Germa had constructed to store salvage equipment and materials. The toxic smells expelling from the sleep dwelling were not only nauseating but a considered a health risk as well. Luara had a sister who helped tend to him and Germa's sister was available occasionally, but, mainly, Luara was burdened with the task herself. She seemed to appreciate the menial effort of support I had offered.

By the third visit to Germa and Luara's, I had brought both Mika and Douglas with me. Mika ran off to find friends as soon as he had carried the supplies. Douglas just sat rocking back and forth at the dwelling door rubbing his nose and pulling on his hair.

Luara's children looked at Douglas as he made his unusual motions. I immediately felt defensive and prepared to leave. To my surprise, Luara told her children to offer Douglas some of the fruit she had on her bark plate. And to my delight, Douglas accepted the offering. Douglas rose to run around, and Luara instructed her children to follow him. No one had ever done such a thing. I was moved by the gesture, so profoundly that I had trouble not bursting into tears.

It aroused an ember of hope from within me, hope that people could care about one another, and there was some meaning in it all. My hope was that the people could see that all life was valued just by existing.

When someone is sick, however, the definition of hope and denial become blurred.

I tried to be cautious about it. I had not felt a sense of meaning in anything with the exception of brief periods post childbirth. I had, at this point, attributed these feelings to chemicals in my system. The same hormonal composition that made the pain of childbirth bearable likely also heightened an appreciation for the good things in life.

What is unfortunate is that this feeling does not last. I had remembered reading on a word paper once, "Desire leads to suffering." I certainly desired to be enlightened, to have some meaning for all the difficulty we encountered, and the lack of answers I discerned had caused me great pain. And hence, I tried hard just to appreciate the feeling of "acceptance" that Luara had extended while it lasted.

Luara made me feel accepted for those few visits I had with her. She did not go out of her way to extend any level of generosity as a host. It was simply her mannerism around Douglas that exuded warmth. The fact that she included him with her instructions to the other children was a major expression of enclosure that I had not had the opportunity of taking for granted as some may have.

The greatest gift she gave me was that she did not offer me pity for the burden of caring for Douglas. She simply acknowledged him as existing. Pity was such a loathsome judgmental comparative. People self elevated their status by self promoting themselves through pitying others.

"She is so unfortunate. I am so lucky not to be her." It was by far the most insulting compliment one could receive.

Luara gave off no such vibe and certainly did not speak in this mannerism. Perhaps it was her preoccupation with tending to Germa as well as caring for her youngsters that left little time for such judgments. She seemed not only to appreciate the minimal assistance I had offered, but also my company.

It seemed she was feeling somewhat alone in her plight. It seemed she was given goods and sympathy from many people, but, as for the actual time invested, most people appeared to be staying away. Germa's offensive state was likely keeping people at a distance. Most of Luara and Germa's immediate family appeared to avoid spending time with Luara as Germa became sicker. Likely, it was both the stench Germa emitted and the fear of contagious toxins that caused people to shun her and her children, not only the virus, but also the bad luck as well.

The mountain people were known to avoid others experiencing hardship. Mountain people believed that there were evil spirits and ghouls inhabiting the darkness around the homes of people who were dying. The longer the person suffered, the stronger the demons became.

As a child, I was often instructed not to play around certain dwellings because someone inside was very sick. In turn, I had experienced this shunning first hand when Alexandra was dying. I was not only completely distraught over her suffering, but I was very sad for my son Mika, whom I knew was being shunned by others during this period.

The most honouring and noble of Luara's mannerisms was that she was able to extend hospitality to me in spite of her own enormous grief. It truly humbled me.

I hadn't really considered the plight of others in my self-pitying state. I had not empathized with the suffering of others. I had not opened my soul to the calling of our common human dilemma. I had selfishly not even considered that I might be able to alleviate the suffering of others if I chose to grow beyond my own self pity. The whole brief experience with Luara had been enlightening.

Germa's plight did not last much longer; but I did make a point of visiting every day for the next week he lived. He seemed to recognize me. Luara told me that he mentioned me a couple of times. I looked at her and wondered if she knew of our intimate encounter. I thought either she did not or was not that concerned about it.

I wondered what it might be like if I found out Rondo was intimate with other women. I decided I likely would feel somewhat indifferent. I would not feel excluded by a sexual act but maybe the emotional sharing I seemed to crave. If I found out he had held someone when they were grieving the loss of their child the way he had not held me when Alexandra died, this would likely be very painful. But as for the act of attempted procreation, I would not see that as a major betrayal. He was free to do as he wished.

When Germa passed, he was in clear agony. He could not digest any herbs to reduce the pain and cried out, moaning, screaming, and gurgling. After his passing, several people were there to help Luara reassemble her dwelling.

The entire hut was torn down and tossed over the peaks of the mountains into the west canyon. A new house was then constructed. People left many offerings which would surely help her adjust to the hardship of providing for herself and her children alone. I limited my association with Luara during this time, partly as I felt that it was more appropriate for her to be in the company of her longtime acquaintances and partly because I felt that I would feel rejected from a perceived lack of acceptance with all these other people close by.

Shortly thereafter though, I did approach the council for permission to head a salvage expedition. I was confident in my presentation to the council but not optimistic that they would approve my request.

"You have only been on one expedition. Do you think your visits with a dying man have been enough to prepare you to run an expedition?" questioned Yucca. With the death of Ernest, she had become the chief councilor. I surmised from her health status, that she would likely succumb to death soon, and my father might be one of a few candidates for her position.

"Germa has taught me much. I feel prepared for this adventure," I answered.

The questioning shifted a bit with Denu's query. "I have heard that you are making some advances extracting oil from our medicinal herbs. What is this method you are using?"

"I use my bendable metal sheets to dry the plant. I can shape the metal into a cone and then the oils are contained and drip through the bottom." I took out a small sample of bendable metal and demonstrated my procedure. I could see that many of them were amazed by the process. They had never seen this shiny malleable material before. They could not help but marvel at it.

"I hope to retrieve more bendable sheets on our next trek."

The session lasted for several such questions, and then I was excused. Shortly afterwards, they announced that I may attend the next expedition, but Stephin would be heading the journey.

The decision was disappointing but expected. I knew Stephin had been chosen because he had been on more expeditions and because he was a man, but I was disappointed because I felt I could have done a better job as the leader.

I had known Stephin well as a child. And it had always been I who initiated the adventures and the strategies in our play. Stephin tended to follow. This was my premise for assessing myself superior to him.

On the other hand, I thought perhaps this was not a broad enough basis to make a judgment on Stephin. We tend to assess people's future performance by what we remember of their past shortcomings. However, it is often not fair or accurate. Besides, I thought to myself, trying to be convincing, if Stephin is still more of a follower, he will be more likely to listen to my suggestions and take my advice. And in that way, I would have much decision power on this venture.

Regardless, the expedition was headed by Stephin, and the rest of the party consisted of me and a younger man named Barone. I knew nothing of him other than he was a distant relative of Germa. Needless to say, our expedition was far less efficient than those run by Germa. We walked for the first day following no particular direction. We camped overnight briefly and continued in a scattered direction the next morning.

As expected, Stephin was more than happy to take both mine and Barone's suggestions about directions. Even with that, however, our lack of experience shone through and we were close to becoming frustrated as we wandered in this desert environment, wondering what on earth we should be looking for in our search. It was only our fatigue the prevented us from expressing our anger and agitation towards each other.

Fortunately, we eventually stumbled upon a small excavation site that presented some salvage cloth but mainly various metal sheets and rusted metal objects. There were some word papers and drawing papers that consisted of lists and numbers. We also uncovered some apparent tools, of which could be useful as cutting utensils. We concentrated on filling our bags with cloth and bendable metal wires. Overall, it was not a particularly productive haul, but it would be measured acceptable to our people.

I spoke very little to Barone or Stephin. I had not seen Stephin since our last trek. We did not speak of our intimate encounter, nor did he attempt to initiate a second such rendezvous. I was very guarded against it. My focus in this trip was to do an adequate job.

I knew that those who partook of this journey had become dependent on other experience to guide them. With the death of Germa, the experience was gone. There was a very low level of knowledge contained within the memories of our brief experience with Germa. Thus, we directed all our energy at trying to find an acceptable site. Although it was a small find in comparison to the quest with Germa, we did scrape up some useful material. However, it had taken far more energy to do so, and we knew we had to focus our physicality securing our way home.

Our expedition while not great was satisfactory. Hence, we felt moderately satisfied but far from elated when compared to the excavation journey we partook of with Germa. We began our trek home with a feeling of moderation in our souls. Perhaps the limited excitement of our journey had left us somewhat content and we had no interest in expressing excitement. Thus, perhaps another reason Stephin and I never spoke of our intimate encounter.

Also, we had made the hazardous and reckless decision to continue forth in the dark for some time. This was against our better judgment and certainly would have been forbidden if Germa was alive. While it was Barone's suggestion, both Stephin and I were novice and foolish enough to agree to it. It was not long into our night, however, that we realized our error.

As Stephin inched his way ahead on the narrow path, he fell down a rock face where there was no place to secure a foot hold. As he slid rapidly down the dropping facing, he blindly sought to wedge his hand into a crack or crevice to prevent his fall. In the darkness, he could only manage to jam his index finger into a small crack. It twisted and snapped but managed to stop his slide. With no light, we listened for his cries of pain to assess his position. We dropped a rope toward the sound and anchored the other end around both our waists.

"Grab on to the rope!" I yelled down from a secure position on the ledge. Barone anchored me from behind, and we let the rope dangle swinging back and forth with my outstretched arm. The rope touched his shoulder and he was able to grab it with his free arm, but it moaned in pain the entire time.

We ascertained that he could not wrap the rope around his waist because he was dangling in mid air hanging from the small crevice where his finger was painfully secured. Instead, he wound the cord several times around his free arm. We pulled quickly as we knew he was not well fastened to the rope. After the second tug, Stephin let out a troublesome cry.

"My finger is stuck," he cried. "It will not dislodge."

From that cry everything seemed to happen so quickly. The rope began to slip and we knew it was unraveling from his fragile grip. We knew that he would lose hold of the rope if we did not get him up immediately. Quickly we tugged and heaved on the rope. We heard a thug and a snap. Then Stephin screamed deliriously. I located his cry and felt for him below the ledge. I grabbed onto his hair as I lay flat on the path.

"Help me. I cannot pull him up alone." Stephin tried to grab onto my hands that were tangled in a grip about his hair. Barone crawled over top of me grabbing Stephin's arm and attempted to hoist him up. I was able to clutch him under his armpit. We tugged and inched him onto the ledge. With once forceful tug by Barone and myself, we seemed to dislodge his wedge hand because he lunged upward and onto to the ledge.

In doing so he let out a haunting wail. We grabbed at his body latching onto to any part of his salvage cloth and pulled vigorously. Without light, we worked blindly to get him to safety the entire time; he howled in agony.

"My hand!" cried Stephin when he pulled him to rest against the wall of the Mountain. We knew it was bleeding but we could not see exactly how or where it was cut. I took some salvage cloth from my bag and wound it around the damaged hand. I put my arm around him and he leaned against me whimpering like a child. Barone eased up against the rock facing, and, before long, exhaustion had served to lull us into a deep slumber as we slouched against the facing.

Early, as dawn approached, the sun god sent tiny rays shooting about the earth to torment the living back into consciousness. As the rays began to pierce into our thoughts, we recounted the night's adventure in our mind. I looked down at Stephin who was slumped over on my shoulder and then to Barone who appeared concerned as to the Stephin's wellbeing.

We directed our attention to his hand wrapped randomly with swaddles of cloth. Our stirring roused Stephin who let out a slight groan as he moved and raised his arm. Slowly we unwound the dressing. It was a mass of black crusty blood. When we reached the last layer, we slowly eased it off the wound to prevent bleeding.

As we slowly unraveled the blood hardened cloth, dark red blood began to trickle and ooze from his hand down his arm. I lightly dapped at the blood to get a better look at his injury. His hand was mangled and clearly distorted. Yet within moments we could clearly see that a part of Stephin's hand was missing. The smallest digit on his left hand was apparently wedged in tightly to the rock facing from which he had dangled the night before and had endured immeasurable trauma. It appeared it had been pulled from its socket when we hoisted him up the incline. Now, he was left with a missing baby finger.

Barone and I looked at each other and could do nothing but laugh. Perhaps it was the fatigue or just a stress release but we both burst into an unruly laughter.

"It looks like you have lost your 'pinky,' Stephin," I proclaimed. But Stephin was in no position to join in our humour. The pain of his bruised and swollen hand was still significant, even if the loss of this little finger might be considered inconsequential. Stephin still had to endure the pain and the increased energy it would take to make his way home.

Once home he would also have to fight off infection and endure dressing changes. He would also have to bear the brunt of other's amusement over his misfortune. The site where he met his adversity would now forever be referred to as "Pinky Mountain." And it would be said with a smile.

We made it home successfully that day. It was a hot disorienting trek in the sun. The path was regulated, but it did pose some dangers. There were a few high areas where Barone almost slipped, a couple of small washouts in a valleylike area, and a dry thunderstorm that appeared to be chasing us out of the salvage area. Perhaps it was the mountain gods that we had awakened the night before.

When we reached the peaks of our homeland, it was dark. We had only the light of the moon to guide us on this fairly familiar path. Stephin looked directly at me as he posed this question. Under the limited illumination, his eyes looked pensive, and I could not interpret the gaze.

"Shall we plan for another expedition?" he asked before we parted for our homes.

"Indeed," I answered. "In four full moons?"

"I shall get back to you."

The three of us turned from each other in the direction of our huts. The moon pierced all-knowing rays in my direction as it rose above the horizon.

Stephin's hand healed eventually, and, in due course, he was able to find a place for the humour that others found in his misfortune. At a much later date, Stephin was known to make light of his missing finger. "If only I had lost a thumb. Perhaps then I would be given greater status. A thumb is considered noble. 'Thumb Mountain' would be a far greater title."

23

Our trio organized three more salvage searches over that year. Stephin appeared to be taking charge. We worked well together in a collective spirit. Stephin worked very cooperatively with me, accepting all of my suggestions, clearly valuing my input. And Barone had settled into the role of follower.

Stephin had likely lost his libido significantly over this year and thus was focused on other things. He never approached me in an intimate manner again. And I certainly made no motion to invite him to. The period to which men seemed to be fixated on union was apparently only for very young men. I had learned that from Rondo, whose appetite had ceased somewhat.

So men who have fathered children and are beginning to seek out more work-oriented activities are said to be approaching eldership. The absence of lust makes one wiser and more industrious, I guess. At least, it seems that way among the men.

As for me, submission had been mandatory. Thus, I rarely considered my desires toward others. Not just to the act of intercourse but to all life ways. My life had been dictated. And, yes, it had freed me of some responsibility. I had not had the opportunity of choosing whether to bear children; thus, I had not had the opportunity of blaming myself completely for Alexandra's suffering. I did not choose to have her and thus had not chosen her fate. I blamed myself anyway. But the people did not. They pitied me but did not blame me.

Pity was, by far, a worse judgment of course. They felt that this thing had happened because I was less fortunate than them. Less fortunate is generally equated with a lesser person. Pity, I found, had one consolation quality, however. I realized then that this was part of the reason I was permitted to become an explorer. My imperfections, or my "lesserness," made me more expendable. It was easier to grant dangerous tasks to women who had so many spoiled seed. It was not seen as the greatest loss.

Indeed, the interest in the bendable metal paper was considered a development on my part as well. But I believe my uselessness as a child bearer was the chief attribute that granted me the permission to explore. Had I not been a pitiful failure at bearing children, there may have been more opposition to my exploring.

Not that I had any great support or respect for these ventures, but I would have never been considered for the trek across the Poison Sea to the Stalite caves at such a young age if I had bore several healthy children. I still had years to go before my fruit would dry up. I still bled regularly. And I was still relatively healthy. Yet my success as a mother was not sufficient. And thus, I was considered a strong contributor but expendable.

There was one consolation to my impasse, however. My father seemed to have recognized some of my successes in a public directive. It was the closest thing to a compliment I believe I ever received from him.

"You have accomplished much," resonated my father's comment when I was asked to cross the Poison Sea. The words did resonate like a resin, a thick burdensome tar that clung firmly to its position until it was discovered and actualized, and its potency was unleashed.

You have accomplished much.

24

I sat mulling over the horrific details of Lauren's death. Tonaldo was clearing tears from her face. The others had their heads bowed in solemn dolour.

Despite the emotional shock of the incident, I was able to rationalize the events in my mind. There were clearly so many implications in Lauren's death. It was a simply a false projectile placing the blame solely on the Moraines. There were so many components that blurred reason. Survival could be construed as greed, depending on your perspective, or risk-taking with poor judgment.

Lauren had been sacrificed to a false god.

"Your loss is great. And now that you have presented me the heinous traits of this grievous event, I am overwhelmed." I hesitated to continue. "However, I feel I must also talk to Sollele."

The Stalites raised their heads.

They paused and looked amongst each other. I am sure they must have expected me to make such a request, but I sensed a feeling of disappointment among them. Regardless, the Stalites were willing to accommodate my meeting with Sollele and passed on my message to

Suz, Jaffy, and Daniel. Thus, I did not have to expend the energy to travel back to the original meeting place. Instead, a Stalite messenger retreated to the meeting place, and I advanced to search out Sollele. Neil escorted me to the end of the south escarpment.

"If you continue along this ridge for a brief period, you will come to a few dwellings. Ask for Sollele. Someone will guide you to him. Here! Take these."

Neil handed me some small reactor metal pebbles.

"These should give you some barter leverage. Be cautious of these people. They are known for spontaneous aggression."

I was grateful for his offering and advice. I had not thought out exactly what I was going to do when I met Sollele or how I would meet with him at all. I thought I would certainly need items to trade. Despite the fact I was an exotic stranger traveling in a place none of my people had gone before, I did not think the Moraines would be willing to assist me with no gain to their own livelihood. Before I left the cave site, Neil took my hand in an apparent display of affection and respect. I reciprocated by looking at him and bowing my head forward. I then turned and began my journey.

The path was an easy trail for a mountain person. I was within sight of the Moraine dwellings almost immediately. And the trek was generally downhill. As I declined the ridge amidst the olive-coloured shrubbery, two robust figures emerged among some small fruit trees at the base of the hills.

As I shortened the distance between us, I could see that they were men of less stature than Daniel or Jaffy. They were still burlier than a Stalite or mountain person but clearly slighter than the Moraines living closer to the Poison Sea. I walked slowly in their direction. I could see that one man wore a shredded cloth that was belted around his waist. The belt supported large rod shaped tools, likely used for hunting or harvesting the grass from which they made their grassbake products. He also sported a bandana around the cloth draping down from his head to his shoulders. Thick light brown hair extended beyond the head wrap flowing down to his waist in length.

The other man was even smaller. He was covered in a cloak of layered cloth. The cloth was bright orange and yellow in colour, and the contrast of colour against his pale skin made him appear a deathlike pale. He had on a second layer of green cloth that protruded from the sleeves of the orange material. The material looked similar to the smooth salvage cloth that Daniel had given me following the episode with the rachnals, but the clothing was far more beaten and worn.

Both men covered their faces with a rough looking material I could only faintly make out in the distance between us. Only their eyes protruded from the layers of cloth.

"I am looking for a man called Sollele," I stated as soon as I was within speaking distance.

The two men glanced at one another. I could not interpret their gazes beneath the ragged salvage cloth covering their faces. The deep heavy set lines in their weatherworn eyes did not reveal any particular age but rather a story of pain, hardship, and fatigue. I recalled Anex's description of the inland Moraines.

"They are smaller in stature than those along the coast of the Poison Sea but still thicker than the mountain people. Their life is apparently harder than those to the north. The dirty water is scarcer and the sun more pronounced. The vegetation is fair, and they have more direct trading with the Stalites, but the few I saw at a distance certainly looked less healthy than the Moraines in my entourage. The Moraines I traveled with briefly discussed them when we saw them on the south ridge of the Stalite caves. They cautioned against them, stating they were known to attack and rob any who came in proximity to their territory," continued

Anex as she hoisted herself up slowly to a semiprone position. She was visibly weak but apparently not in that much pain.

"I only saw them at a distance, however," Anex proceeded. Anex did not see me often at this time. If we happened to meet as I passed close to her dwelling, she would call me in. I would concede out of respect, but I generally preferred not to visit and often hurried by her shelter in hopes that she would not see me. She was a reminder of too many things I did not support. I did not support counseling those that had children with problems. It seemed too condescending.

Although she has been generous in her words and often helpful in my times of need, it was always an unequal relation where she was the superior. And so, even though I valued much of what she said, there was always a disconnection in our discourse because one side of the conversation was always perceived as the greater, and thus there was never a balance.

It was always assumed that I be the listener and she the speaker. The roles, it seemed, had been set in stone and irreversible or interchangeable. The limits on this arrangement limited our relationship in general, and the limits were synonymous with a barrier set in stone.

Nevertheless, Anex had shared a wisdom that I longed for, and that was adventure. For that, the least I could do was show respect to her and visit her in her dying days. She asked me questions about my children.

I felt awkward responding. I still felt judged by this woman. I expected her to follow my remarks with some words of advice. I kept my answers very superficial. I did not want to open myself to her. I was so very guarded. She may have only wanted to show love to me. But I remained reserved. She smiled at my answers and made no gesture to correct me. She said very little. She seemed in great need of rest. It seemed as though she just wanted company.

On our sparing visits, I found myself waiting anxiously for one of her relatives to enter the dwelling so I could leave. I later reflected on this as very callous behaviour. I was too busy to bother with her and I didn't feel I owed her much. For me, it was a revelation in retrospect. I was just as capable of being cold and detached as anyone else I had judged for displaying a similar vice. I was no different, certainly no better and maybe even worse.

Anex may have only seen the Southern Moraines at a distance. I, on the other hand, was very close. I remained on the ridge some ways up the incline. I felt I had enough distance between us to retreat if they appeared hostile toward me. I had every confidence that I could move faster up the hill than them.

"I will give you each one small reactor metal and a jugglet of mountain water if you bring him to me," I added.

The two leered towards me presenting their deep-set epicanthic eyes. Their skin appeared darker than the Ravine Moraines, but it could have been from the brown dust covering them. This powdery substance was littered along this side of the Stalite Hills.

"Give us the metal and the water, and then we may consider finding this man you look for," replied one of the two as they both started to move in my direction.

"I shall give you the metal now, and, on completion of this task, I shall give you the water," I called out as I retreated on the ledge.

As soon as I backed up, the Moraines halted.

"Bring the metal to us then," called out the other man.

I had no intention of getting within arm's length of them.

"I shall leave it at the edge of the ridge if you back up."

Slowly they retreated, and I moved forward cautiously, placing the small pebbles at the base of the ridge and backing up the path quickly. They picked up the offerings and examined them closely, ostensibly marveling at them. It was amazing that these small, seemingly insignificant rocks could illuminate a cave or bake food simply by rubbing them and setting them down.

The Moraines seemed to accept the offering and turned in the direction of their dwellings. Once they were at a distance of minimal visibility, I hid my scant food and water jugglets in the crevices. I then ran down to the base of the hill to look at the fruit in their small orchard. The trees were small, shrublike with an abundance of tiny black green leaves.

Amongst the dark leaves, little figlike spirals were camouflaged. I brushed the mass of tiny aphids from the fruit and picked it from the branch. I peeled it open to reveal soft inner flesh. It had a green colour and a mesh of dark brown seeds. I scraped a sliver of the flesh with my finger nail and raised it to my lips.

"I wouldn't do that unless you want your guts infested by a parasite that will dig its way into every organ of your body," called out one of the Moraines as the other two laughed.

They startled me, and thus any fear I had about encountering them up close was subdued.

"I am Sollele. What is it you want?"

I briefly examined him being cautious not to offend as I stared. His eyes looked pallid, like the sands of the Stalite Hills. He was shorter than me yet broader. He was clearly petite, at least in comparison to Daniel. I assembled my words before I spoke.

"I wish to talk to you about that which occurred with the Stalites."

"We did not cause that death." blurted out one of the other Moraines. "We have had to give up food to those people or suffer the wrath of the shore side Moraines. They have much more than us. Those of us on the sun side of the Stalite Hills are far more hungry. Yet we were forced into paying for this accident. We were blamed because everyone is under sanction. Without the reactor metal, we cannot cook our grassbake or seep the poison out of the fruit you hold. We suffer the most. We need more reactor metal!" His voice began to elevate and increase in volume. I was alarmed.

"Do you have more?" He lunged forward at me and grabbed my arm and shook it. The others neither supported his action nor discouraged it.

"Yes," I answered. "I have another couple of rocks and three jugglets of water. But you must release me to retrieve them."

He released me almost at once. He likely did not do so because he trusted me, but rather he felt I had no option but to give my supplies to them as I could not escape. Once the Moraines saw how quickly I ascended the hill to the location of the jugglets, they soon recognized that they would not be able to catch me if I chose to retreat.

I had already seen the temper of one Moraine in my experience with Daniel. Moreover, Daniel had been somewhat hospitable toward me with the exception of that conflict. In contrast, these Moraines were clearly antagonistic, and I had not even initiated any discord towards them. Knowing how frustrated they got from communicating made me think that they could be even more potentially explosive than I had first considered. I was not about to remain close to them while I attempted to discuss the situation about the Stalites.

I reached down to the cache of supplies and visually presented them to the Moraines from halfway up the incline. As they started to advance, I cautioned them not to.

"Stop there! I will leave this place if you try to force me to give you these supplies."

They took a few steps backward.

"I have come to talk to Sollele, and that is all I want in exchange for these gifts. I will place the jugglets at the base of the hill if you back away."

They retreated immediately. I scurried down the hill with the jugglets and just as swiftly ran halfway back up the incline. They moved forward, grabbed the water, and quickly consumed it.

"I shall throw the rock to you and then I ask that you leave."

I tossed the reactor pebble, and the two jockeyed for it. The larger of the two picked it up. They both walked further into the orchard and out of view. Sollele remained.

The brutal attack on Lauren described by the Stalites was vivid in my memory, and it induced me to keep my distance from Sollele. I began a mental negotiation with myself as to how I should interview this man. How should I get his perspective? How much should I reveal to him about the Stalite version? Furthermore, I wondered how bad his communication skills were. How much of his version would he be able to articulate? In the end, I decided to pose an open-ended question.

"You know why I am here? Do you not?" I hoped that he would volunteer some information about the incident, but he offered nothing. He looked as if the blood was rising inside his eyes. He moved to sit under the shade of an orchard tree and removed the cloth from his face. There was a mass of dust circling his eyes. They highlighted the weatherworn wrinkles in his skin. His mouth and cheeks seemed relatively smooth and youthful. I tried another approach.

"Why do you wear that mask on your face?" I questioned.

He looked to me with more of a sense of calm and answered. "The dust here is bad. We don't like to breathe it."

I pondered his statement and decided to follow his example. I sat on a rock a distance above him and grabbed a small piece of cloth from my satchel and wrapped it around my mouth and nose. He watched, and though Moraines give off few nonverbal cues that I could pick up on, I thought that he was honoured by my gesture. I knew he was somewhat calm now, so I thought I must try to get some information out of him for his own defense. I took off the mask and began to look to him for some answers.

"The Stalites say that you are the prime cause of the grief they are experiencing."

"And why is that? Because I had sex with one of their women? They offered her to me. She wanted it. I did not kill her. Why do they need to blame someone? Why can they not take responsibility for their own weaknesses?"

I was not startled by his response. Nor was I expecting it. I had felt rage and disgust when I listened to the tale of Lauren's gruesome death. But, equally, I longed to believe that Sollele, the man the Stalites had chosen, had made a mistake. That his lust, misinterpretation, and inexperience with the situation had been the major factors that had caused the misfortune. And that he was deeply saddened and remorseful about the entire crisis.

To me, Sollele's response indicated that the Stalites had made a grave error bestowing any honour to this man in the first place. What, I pondered, made them make such a horrid choice? There was no one here but Sollele to answer my questions, so I asked him.

"Why did they choose you for their ceremony? You clearly speak of them with contempt only."

"I speak with contempt for them; they speak with contempt for me. They have no respect for us, and we return the same."

I saw no point in pursuing a discussion with this person who appeared to express such indifference towards the people who had entrusted him with such a sacred commitment. A person to whom he had made love to had died in the process. Yet he was so hostile regarding the encounter. Hostility, I have been told, is generally a cover for deep pain; but it certainly does not make it excusable. I was still trying to rationalize the choice the Stalites had made. And thus, I still felt compelled to hear Sollele's account of the event.

"Would you tell me what happened the night Lauren died?" I called out to Sollele.

He paused and sat on a grey boulder on the side of the path next to the tree. "I had went there on the day they had asked me to attend the ceremony. They told me they would pay with reactor metal and spores. I was given a couple of metals and one small meal when I reached the cave. They also offered me a flask of their musty water. I squeezed through the wall to the area where they wished me to take the girl and injured myself when doing so."

His story was a bit scattered and hard to follow. I assumed that when he went through the entrance I had just come out of, he slipped in a crevice but was caught in the opening. I could see how this could have occurred given his size and the difficulty getting through the narrow opening.

He lifted the salvage cloth from his elbow and revealed a deformity on his lower arm. Clearly, something must have been fractured to leave such an extrusion. I had often heard among my people that the Moraines appear to have a high tolerance for pain. "They are tough." This tended to be a general description of their people.

Those who had witnessed them burned by the sun or injured by an accident on their ship had always commented on the lack of emotion they displayed during their bouts of pain. Even when they were dying they rarely screamed. It was almost like an indifference towards it. That is not to say they never expressed their pain. There were records of them howling during a procedure to treat infection or cut off rotted flesh; but generally they tolerated pain quietly.

"I had seen the girl Lauren on other occasions during trade sessions. She had been formally introduced to me on one such trade, and then I was taken to speak with their council. They asked me if I would consider a union with her. I asked for payment. They offered the rock and food, and I agreed.

I met with them several times, for they liked to talk a lot. Each time they offered me some measly article of trade. During instruction, they talked of many things. They used words like "sacredness" and "preparation." It took them a long time to say things. I'm not sure what they wanted at this time. It seemed that they were making an act of pleasure into an act of labour. They fed me small samples of food at these times. So I endured the boredom of their talk."

Sollele took his mask cloth and wiped his brow. He was perspiring and the dirt around his brow was starting turn to mud and drip into his eyes. He seemed to be more articulate than the other Moraines I had encountered, but his speech indicated a much different thinking process than the Stalites. He had clearly not understood the delicacy of the situation. And he did not seem to possess any respect for the Stalites.

"On the day of our sex, I was brought into that small cave. I could not fit properly. I had to force myself through, and, in doing so, I lunged past the ledge and fell into a crevice. The only thing that prevented my fall to death was that my arm was caught in the entrance crack. The Stalites just looked at me as my feet dangled."

I envisioned Sollele in the cavern held in space with only his wedged broken arm obstructing his fall.

"I managed to arch back one toe and then lever myself onto the ledge. But in doing so, my arm snapped and limply slid through the opening. My escorts realized my discomfort and ushered me along to a large cave lit with reactor metal. They braced my arm and offered me a concoction of spores for my pain. It was strong. It made everything hazy. I thought I was sick from it. It reminded me of the time I had ate some bad meat, and I could not think right. The good thing was I didn't feel pain. I just felt . . ." Sollele started to hesitate the way I had seen Daniel the day I asked him about the grassbake. I knew if he got too frustrated, the conversation would likely be over. I tried to interject in hopes of getting him to continue.

"Confused?"

He looked at me.

"Did you feel confused from the concoction?" I explained.

"Yes," he said somewhat encouraged. "The spores made me confused, but my arm did not hurt." He continued with his story.

"They began the ceremony quickly after my injury was tended to. It seemed . . ."

"Strange?" I suggested.

"Yes, very strange. There were so many people there touching me and each other. Lauren was brought to me. Two of their people were spreading some type of liquid on us. They rubbed it in. I was quickly aroused and wished to take the girl. I was prevented in doing so by those tending her. Others were in the cave. They were engaged in similar actions.

Finally, Lauren was ready to submit. I performed quickly. A few men came and pulled on my arms. I pushed them away in anger as my arm was sore. When I was finished, the girl ran from me screaming. I sat to recuperate.

Next, several of the Stalite men affronted me and began an assault. I fought them off despite the pain in my arm and my drugged state. Then I fled from the site. It is a wonder I did not perish in one of the many floor crevices along route. I did not even know of the girl's death until several days past."

He paused in his account, and I took the opportunity to try and digest what he had just said.

"This whole affair has caused me much grief. My people are angry with me because of the trade halts. I am persecuted by both my people and the Stalites. People do not wish to trade with me. Women are beginning to shun me. I have had to force myself upon some."

It was becoming clear to me that I could no longer remain objective. I hated this man at this time. I had no more patience for him. It was clear that there were some factors that could be used as an excuse for his behaviour. Clearly, his discomfort, unfamiliarity of custom, and intoxication could have limited his rationale and judgment in such a situation.

However, his complete absence of remorse and his self-centred focus was repulsive. A tiny woman died a gruesome death, and he was a contributing attribute. He had been intimate with this girl. And yet he showed no concern for her. He complained about how his life was now so hard. It seemed so selfish. I couldn't understand why the Stalites had chosen him.

I knew why I hated him. His view was so skewed from mine that there was no common link. I could not identify with his position. To me, he was despicable. I could not mediate in this situation. So often, when we are told to work out our differences, it really amounts to avoiding one another.

But I could not avoid this man. I wondered if he was the "Demon Spawn" that was referred to in our doctrine. In many of my talks with Anex, Delta, and Donny, we had often concurred that there was a purpose for everyone. What could be Sollele's? I wondered.

I could not negotiate an open mind about this person at this time. My feelings of detest were too strong. One must acknowledge and deal with one's emotional state before pursuing other levels of intellect. I knew I must end my time with him before I exercised these emotions in a manner that would only complicate things further. Before I did, however, I decided to try one last question.

"Do you feel sorry for what happened to Lauren?"

"I don't know. She is probably better off where she is now, in the Good Place." He paused. "I did not know her well."

It was as if he was talking about a stranger. This lack of sensitivity was too much. I could no longer be patient with him. I felt no sense of objectivity when he spoke. I was angered by his apathy. So I exercised a sense of arrogance in the matter and ended the discussion with him.

"I thank you for your time. I must return to the caves now."

"What! That's it!" he reacted. He did not make secret his surprise with my abruptness. However, he quickly regrouped to focus on himself.

"Give me my food and metal then."

"I have nothing left. It was given to your peers."

"What peers? I am my own man. I gave you information. I must be paid." He began to advance.

"Wait! I have one jugglet of water I can spare. You are welcome to that." I replied as I retreated up the path. I had carried the heavy load of water with me through this entire journey. I had guarded it closely. And I had used and shared it sparingly. While I knew I had not agreed in advance to pay him for his time, it did seem proper as I was leaving him with a judgment of condemnation.

Sollele responded by lunging toward me as fast as he could. I turned to run, but the pivot slowed me. He was swifter than I expected, and he was able to clasp onto a piece of the cloth that covered my legs.

"I expect more. You interrupted my work for your foolishness."

I was able to pull away from his hold as my garment tore. However, he still had a grasp of the ragged edge of the cloth and, with a tug, was able to trip me. I fell to the ground cushioning my face with my hands.

The powdery dust was on the path stirred by the commotion and formed a small cloud.

As Sollele reached forward to grip my legs, I pulled my cloth with all my might and it tore completely. I kicked at his arm. He was left holding a large piece of my clothing. I scrambled up the facing in a half-crawling motion. He was close in line, and I was in fear. He seemed like a bloodthirsty hunter as we referred to people in the mountains who sometimes became obsessed with hunting down live food.

I knew my best hope was to continue scampering up the hill. I did not look behind. Any attempt by me to fight him off would likely end in failure. It was best to run. I was quick up the incline, but I had no assessment of how close he was. I decided to veer off the trail and jump a ridge.

Once off the trail, I needed to focus on the ground as it had been made clear by the Stalites and the Moraines that the ground was not stable. There were sink holes and large fissures throughout the surface; some of which were hidden by the cover of sparse vegetation.

It gave me the clear advantage, however. Sollele stumbled in one of the sinkholes and bumped his head on a rock. With that delay, I was able to acquire enough distance from him to turn and assess the situation. As he raised his head, he disclosed a large gash discharging blood. It appeared to subdue his primordial focus. He sat down by the sink hole and took the piece of cloth he had ripped from my garment. He tore a long swaddle and wound it around the cut on his head. His breathing was rapid and his large chest was heaving.

As his arms were exposed, I saw several large scars on them. I wondered what kind of life he had led that he would receive such wounds. I continued to climb the hill carefully dodging the holes. I was now moving at a much slower pace attempting to catch my breath. I turned to review his condition every once and a while.

"Give me the water then," he grunted in a resigned voice.

"Back down the path, and I will consider it," I countered.

He motioned forward, but I turned quickly and began to withdraw.

"Wait!" he exclaimed. "Very well then."

He slowly turned to step from the mountain facing. He staggered a bit and was cautious with his footing. He turned to look occasionally to see if I was ensuing. His concentration was clearly placed on the route, however. With hindsight, it appeared he recognized the danger of his trek. His wound was clearly an impairment, and he proceeded cautiously. He made it to the bluff that introduced the path and halted.

"Pass it to me then!"

"I shall not," I answered. "You must continue down the path. Then I will follow and place it at the bluff and return up the pathway to the Stalite meeting place."

He reluctantly consented and headed down the mountain slowly, turning every few steps to ensure I was moving forward. I knew that I had escaped, and I certainly owed him nothing. Yet I honoured my agreement. I would not have done so in years earlier. But I no longer sought justice for others. I sought it only for myself.

I waited for him to descend to a fair distance down the hill. Then I placed the small jugglet on the bluff and made my way hastily up the route. He, too, began to scale upward. But I was quick and well out of his reach.

This did not restrict him from yelling obscenities at me. He also grabbed rocks along the ridge and hurled them at me. His strength was clear by the distance the stones traveled, but I was too far away to be hit. He grabbed the small shelled flask. The allure of the clear mountain water caused him to abandon his attack on me. He drank from the flask in a rhythmic motion.

I, in turn, slowed my pace and headed toward the Stalite meeting point. I looked behind me constantly, ensuring he had not decided to pursue me again. I wondered if he was going to clean that wound on his forehead or just leave it covered with my dirty clothing that had been dragging along the earth gathering filth.

I wondered if the Moraines cleaned their wounds with the dirty water of their ravine system. Or did they expose them to the sun long enough for it to burn closed the veins and arteries? As disgusted as I had been by Sollele, I realized I was equally puzzled and intrigued about his behaviour.

I made my way along the ridge to the escarpment and entered the small crevice that I had exited through. I had hoped there would be someone along eventually to escort me further. But I was even more blessed as someone was there waiting on the inside as soon as I entered.

25

Grief is the simplest and most complex of emotions. The sadness seems to be directly proportional to the immediate time spent with the one who has passed, multiplied by the amount of common history you have with one another, minus the animosity or indifference you harbour toward that individual. I think a number equation for grief might look like this:

$G = It\,(Pt - A)$

$G = Grief;\ It = Immediate\ Time;\ Pt = Passed\ time\ of\ Common\ History;\ A = Animosity$

Donny and I used to make equations like that on the occasions we would visit one another. We had always enjoyed the numbers in our learning time, and we seemed to carry that into adulthood. Periodically, we would get our hands on some number papers or sheets from a salvage expedition that contained number riddles. We enjoyed attempting to solve the great mysteries using the methods available in numbers.

Anex fit well into this particular equation. I had once looked up to her as my mentor and closest companion. Yet, at the same time, I resented her counseling and thought of it as condescending. And then, as the children grew older, I spent more time in work and salvaging, rarely sharing a moment with her. Moreover, when Alexandra was suffering, Annex's health was beginning to fail, and she was not in my presence very often.

She had not shared in the grief I experienced over the death of Alexandra, at least not with me directly. Of course, as I think about it, I had not shared in her grief experience over the death of her own son, Scout. I wasn't even born then. And so we had shared some close moments, but we also had differences and many life experiences apart from one another.

Thus, when she passed, I was sad but I was also distanced. My grief was not an aching or yearning. My time with her had phased out slowly over the years. The permanence of it had a minimal jolt for the memories of her were far stronger than her loss. With my mother, the loss was more painful. I missed her. Or rather, I missed the relationship we never had.

The memory of Anex, however, was bestowed in the wisdom she had bequeathed upon me. And so, it would never be lost. It had surfaced time and again when I was on a salvage expedition or a venture, and something she had said would become relevant to the situation. I could hear and see her sharing her wisdom in that moment as if she was still there. And so, when Anex died, I was not distraught but rather honoured that I had had the privilege of knowing her.

Grief is truly a hardship, however. It is not always wisdom we seek from those who are gone. What we long for is the alleviation that they had given us, the alleviation from loneliness or sadness. Many people who have lost someone close will often say, "Now, who will I have to talk to?"

On this topic, Donny had become somewhat of a confidant in our village. Those feeling troubled or forlorn had come to appreciate his quiet gentleness and found it a comfort in times of distress. It was not new for me to seek solace at Donny and Delta's, but it was interesting to see others looking for a similar haven from their woes, grief being one of them.

"What happens when we die?" questioned Barone. He had brought over a chunk of reactor metal for Donny in exchange for some dried meat. His wife had recently died in the agony of a childbirth gone wrong. He was left with a baby that might not live. Another recent mother was attempting to nurse the baby as well as her own. A similar situation had been successful one other time trying this procedure, but it was too early to tell if Barone's infant son would live or go to join his mother.

Donny paused; "No one truly can say, Barone."

"What do you think of the doctrine, Donny?"

"I think it has some merit. It has been handed down through generations. The fact that it has been preserved so long warrants it some recognition." Donny peeled some freshly dried raven jerky from a bendable metal sheet and placed it on Barone's bark slab.

The doctrine spoke of a place after death where the mountain people left their bodies and traveled as a spirit to live in the Oneness. Without their physical body, these spirit people did not have thirst, hunger, or disease.

"If this is a better place, why do we not just kill ourselves so we may go there?" questioned Barone impatiently.

"That truly is the great mystery," Donny replied smiling. "It is said that those who have passed have no physical pain, but I wonder if the spirits, if indeed they exist in this manner, I wonder if they too bear mental, emotional, and spiritual turmoil. And does our suffering affect theirs?"

When we catch a glimpse of divine wisdom, it surges over us with lightning speed. The white light opens and shuts its flood gate in an instant, letting out only an infinitesimal amount of its purity that launches through our being to let us know we must think about what we have heard, or seen, or tasted, or felt. When I heard Donny speak these words, I thought instantly of Alexandra's suffering even in death.

Was I contributing to her suffering with my longing, guilt, fear, self-loathing? Did I need to let her go so her spirit would not be troubled?

26

Vanel was waiting at the meeting spot. I sat down in relief as I fully comprehended my success at eluding Sollele. There was no greeting from Vanel, at least not verbally. She did not ask me of my venture. She looked at me more with curiosity than concern. I felt compelled to fill the void with my own experience.

As soon as I sat down, I found I began to cry. I don't know what caused the outburst, but I am sure it was to do with the encounter with Sollele. I believe the danger of my meeting was just dawning on me. I had been in a very risky and terrifying situation with what could be defined as a murderer and a rapist. The reality of what had occurred was overwhelming me.

What might have happened if he caught me? What could I possibly do to ratify the situation with the Stalites when this man took no responsibility for his actions? How would I explain my judgment to the other Moraines if they asked? How would they react to my conclusions?

I couldn't see any way that this situation was going to be resolved. And I had been terribly frightened by Sollele. I longed to go home. If I was going to die, I wanted to die at home.

Vanel sat beside me and put her weary hand on my shoulder in a motion of comfort. I continued to sob uncontrollably. I knew I must compose myself as I put my face in my hands. I took some deep breaths and began to wipe at the tears. My breath heaved, and I resisted the compulsion to give way to floods of sadness. I tried to think of the task at hand.

I had to relay my conclusions about Sollele to the Stalites. I hoped that perhaps they could just avoid trading with such a group and focus on the Moraines that appeared more moderate. I also knew that the Stalites, in some way, were responsible for the death of Lauren as they had made such a terrible choice for a suitor.

As I began to reason these things, my tears dried, and I was able to converse.

"I had a lurid encounter with Sollele." I paused. "What made you chose this person for an act of procreation?"

Vanel looked at me solemnly. "We are a desperate people. We are dying. The only way we feel we may continue to survive is to mix our seed with those who seem to be more adapt. We can only hope that good qualities will be selected from the parents of the offspring produced.

We knew of his vulgarities. But we also knew that he was one of the most reliable trade partners we had. And thus, we hoped that perhaps his insensitivities could be tamed through the expression of intimacy with a woman for we know of many instances where a woman has soothed the savage soul of a man.

Unfortunately, his behaviour turned out to be the opposite. He was blatantly rude and inconsiderate during the preparation and violently careless and selfish during the ceremony. And, now, he is shamefully unrepentant about the tragedy. Even his own people are judging him harshly."

I began to weep as I uttered the next question with a sense of urgency; "But you had many warning signs about his character. Why did you not stop it before it was too late?"

Vanel looked at me with weary eyes; "We ask ourselves that every day."

She paused for a moment and tried to shift the conversation.

"We did not choose him. There was no choice. He is one of the few *others* that we encounter."

Vanel looked at me with a longing I could not interpret. "You are another." She paused and stared at me for several minutes. Then she turned to the small fire glowing in the centre of the cave as if to gain energy for her thoughts to be expressed.

"The Moraines are clearly barbaric. We are aware of that. We had just hoped to bridge the gap with shared seeds." Vanel looked at me again. Her dull green eyes looked very sad and humble.

"When Lauren died, it was not our intention to obstruct trade between our people and the others. It was our intent to end all trade completely. At the time, we saw Lauren's death as the demise of our people. Yes, the younger Stalites wanted to avenge her death with the termination of Sollele's wretched existence. But those of us who were wiser felt it would be best if we ceased to relate to those on the outside.

We were resigned to our fate. We believed that we would die as a race eventually, and that our sacred knowledge would leave this world with us. We saw no point in sharing our technology or our wisdom with the Moraines as they did not seem to have the qualities necessary to keep this knowledge. And so we believed we would take what we knew to the next world. We had no interest in resolving the conflict. We chose to spend our last years appreciating what we have and remembering what we had.

The Moraines, on the other hand, sought continued trade. They tried to appease us with gifts left at the meeting place. But we were not looking for bribes. What we needed, they could not provide.

On their last entrance into the meeting place, Suz was brought in and remained there overnight, hoping we would come to meet her. Because of her clear resolve and out of deference for this particular Moraine who had always appeared to be respectful towards us, we decided to go and listen to her. She suggested that a mountain person be brought in to try and help us reach an agreement. At first, we saw no point in such an attempt, but we began to think of other possible solutions."

Vanel took a deep breath. There was a wheezing sound in her lungs. "We saw the opportunity to meet with a mountain person as an opportunity for us to procreate. And so, you see, it is you we seek as another possibility of sharing our seed." She paused for a moment allowing me to process her words. "Would you consider adjoining with our people?"

I tried to appear unaffected by her request, but I could not. I had only been half-listening to her lament until that point. Until that point, I was still mulling over the situation with Sollele. It hadn't even occurred to me that the Stalites would have had this in mind with me. I was perplexed and confused by the invitation.

"You have taken me by surprise," I returned. "I did not expect this. What all does it entail?"

Vanel bowed her head in a nodding gesture suggesting to me that she acknowledged my surprise and confusion. "We would ask that you join with one of our people in our Union Ceremony. You would be well prepared. We would accommodate you and tend to your needs and wishes. It would be our hope that the seed you are given will grow to be a child of the Stalites.

"I cannot live among your people. I would surely die before I bore a child. And I have my own family to tend to in my home." This was the first thought that entered my mind as I mused over this unexpected request.

Vanel continued, "Perhaps the seed will germinate in your womb in your home. Perhaps you could return with the child. Perhaps the child may only exist in your world and bring your people joy and wisdom. What we ask of you is only the opportunity to attempt."

"This was not my purpose for coming," I answered as I began to regroup. "The dispute that holds up trade between our people is how my success will be measured by my people. A child of this nature would likely be branded an anomaly in my world. I will be looked upon as the one who wasted a trip crossing the Poison Sea."

"Your purpose will be fulfilled as part of the negotiation. We will resume trade with the Moraines. We would also endow you with extra trade articles that may interest you. We are aware that you must return to your home. But perhaps you will carry one of our children on your journey and in your future. And perhaps we will meet again." Vanel was starting to repeat herself. It seemed they had thought out many possibilities. The possibilities seemed overly optimistic. But I suppose that, in desperate circumstances, we must hold onto hope and sometimes creative optimism.

"What of Sollele?" I questioned.

"He will eventually receive his dues."

I contemplated what this might be. Would they seek revenge if he ventured in their territory? Would he "accidentally" fall in a bottomless crevice? Or would they just wait for him to receive his ultimate fate from the powers beyond? I didn't bother to have the point clarified because I was able to rationalize that as long as they were going to resume trade, no more on this matter would be asked of me. Now, however, I was being asked a much greater request, and I needed time to think about it.

"Your position and request have besieged me. I need a few moments to contemplate what you ask."

27

O soulful babe, weep ye not
To the hills that were forgot
For the world's more full of sorrow than you can understand.

As life goes on, the layers of grief, regrets, and shame metamorphose into a solidified mass. We chip away at it, eroding and releasing some of its conglomerate shape. But it continues to accrue at a rate far exceeding our ability to dislodge it.

When we rise to the top of it, there is always the danger that a painful memory will surface, eroding the foundation sending us crumbling to the depths. There, we may dwell in a dark crevice avoiding the surface, and time becomes our master.

As I got older, I noticed I spent more time wrestling with the demons in my mind than those that existed in my reality. There were many thoughts that reminded me ruthlessly of my past mistakes or those who had wronged me.

At one point, I had yearned to go back in time, to a period just prior to puberty. This seemed to be the time when the difficulty transpired. I calculated this much later in my life. Now, as a grandmother, I was believed to possess some life experience and have discerned some wisdom to make better choices. I wanted to precede to an age just before things appeared to become pivotal, a time when all contemplation and actions would *not* be accompanied by second guessing and afterthoughts. Was this the time when I played with my friends in the Mountains when my worries were not my conscious but the wrath of the adults?

I wondered if I could take the little wisdom I had acquired over my lifespan back with me to this earlier time. Would I be able to make better choices? Would I be able to assert myself more maturely and thus be able to get what I want more? Would I know what I wanted more? Would my youth prejudice the judgment of those around me to the point of disregarding all I said? Would the depression I feel still be in my mind and soul?

Or would going back to childhood with the knowledge I now possess be a disaster? Would I not be able to enjoy discovery because I already knew the answer? Is the revelation and enlightenment in the journey as opposed to being in the outcome? Would I lack the initiative necessary to grow?

I thought at one time that going back to my childhood with the knowledge I have now accrued might give me power. But now, I am not so sure. I am not so sure that power is what I seek.

If I cannot go back to this time, can I use the wisdom I have accumulated to cause the mountains of regret to cease? Certainly, their growth is far more conservative as you get older. When we think of regrets, we usually wallow in self-pity for the mistakes of our youth.

Mika seemed to be so in control as a youngster in this pure time. I wondered if I was imparting any of my plausible wisdom upon him. Or was what I told him just lecture predesigned to make him feel less confident? It seemed as though most tribulation rolled off of him though. It either rolled off him or was absorbed and assimilated. I wondered if he was able to channel the negative into the positive. Or was it just that the negative would manifest in aggression at some unpredictable time?

Mika reminded me of Donny in many aspects. He seemed cool-headed about adversity. He had a leisurely attitude about vitality—leisurely and witty. He took things with a stride of ease and an air of amusement. He was by no means cynical, nor was he irresponsible. But he could not be defined as a serious child. And this he carried into adulthood.

I would sometimes hear him making light of his *ultimate purpose*. "I would like to fulfill my ultimate purpose with Nanco. She looks so good." I once overheard him saying to his friends. They looked on in bewilderment, not knowing whether to interpret his comment with fear or frolic. Mika just smiled, shrugged, and ran off to catch up with Nanco.

Nanco was a very young-looking girl. Although in actuality, she was at least a year older than I was when I was sent to live with Rondo. She was not tall and was quite petite in frame. At a distance, when we would see the older children playing, we would wonder who the little girl was that was hanging around them. Then we would realize it was Nanco who was at least as old as the others if not older.

Nanco had a long narrow face with high cheekbones and eyes that protruded from their sockets. Many of her peers teased her about her "buggy" eyes. Mika thought her eyes were cute with their dark tracing and thick eyelashes. He particularly liked them when her hair was worn down. She often wore her hair pulled back in a bun as did most of us. It was more efficient for work and play. Even for those mountain people who had hair that could be worn down and look presentable, it was a nuisance. As we went about our daily tasks, branches from the orchard or pines would tangle in our hair and leave it nappy and disorderly. However, when Nanco wore her hair back, it narrowed her thin face even more, and her large protruding eyes jutted out further giving her the appearance of being choked.

When her hair was down, however, it thickened up her face, and the wave of her chunky locks blended well with her large eyes and thick lashes. Her eyes did not look bulging when her hair was down. As well, when her hair was down, her light brown skin emitted a shiny smooth complexion.

Mika loved to look at her. But he was first attracted to her fun, easygoing personality. She seemed to appreciate his humour and ground his carefree attitude.

"We must restrict ourselves from our selfish passions, as that is the way of the ancients. Their selfish overindulgence left them soulless and empty until the shells of their carcasses were all that remained," Mika stated mockingly as he stood on a rock pretending he was addressing the people.

He appeared to be doing an impersonation of his grandfather. His friends looked somewhat uncomfortable not knowing whether to interpret his rant as humour or blaspheme. Nanco on the other hand had no problem countering him.

"Well if anyone would know about evil ways, it would be you. You're the most evil of the bunch of us," retorted Nanco. The friends all laughed, and Mika looked at her with a twinkle in his eye.

Three months after Mika ran off with Nanco that day joking about the ultimate purpose, we learned that Nanco was with child and that I was to become a grandmother.

The people were surprised that Nanco was of age. Nobody was aware that she was bleeding, not even her parents and, certainly, not the leaders and council. They were even more surprised that Mika was old enough to father a child. Some remained skeptical.

It was their youth that had people baffled. Both Mika and Nanco *seemed* so young. Many had seen them together walking alone on the paths, but all thought it was innocent. Furthermore, no one had seen them display any type of affection toward each other, let alone catch them in the required level of intimacy it took to create a baby.

I too had been surprised about the situation when Mika came to me and Rondo in the dwelling one night and told us he was going to be a father. At first, we thought surely this was a joke, but it soon became clear it was not.

In hindsight, there may have been some clues. Mika would sometimes bring Nanco to the dwelling when he had to sort seeds. She would help him so the task would be done sooner, and they could free up their time. It was not unusual for the children to help each other with their chores, but it was the way that they spoke to each other that seemed a little peculiar.

"Mika you're putting left-bent ridges in with right-bent ridges. They make much different trees you know."

"I know Nanco, but they both produce about the same amount of fruit don't they," Mika replied.

"Yes but the left ridge is usually very sour. And the right ridge has a sweetness. When you plant them close together, they all end up being sour," Nanco answered matter-of-factly. Mika looked toward me, and I nodded in agreement with Nanco.

Rondo and I had not often corrected Mika as he worked; we did not want to make him feel inadequate. Actually, we had not given him any extensive training in labour. We had both been so preoccupied with our own toils and struggles. As such, we had not paid close attention to how precise a job Mika did as long as he didn't do anything too drastic. As long as he was contributing, we saw this as a quality in itself. We were just thankful to have one child that might perhaps be self-sufficient. He seemed quite comfortable with Nanco's instruction however and did not appear to take it as negative criticism.

"Very well then," he answered to her. And then I'm sure I caught him wink at her. At the time of this conversation it struck me as if the two of them seemed like an elderly couple that had been together for a long time. Of course, I shrugged it off back then; but, now, I realize the message that was trying to get through to me at that moment. Sometimes, we are sent messages that we do not understand until a later moment.

Of course, had I known they were becoming intimate at this time—I questioned what I would have done anyway. From my perspective, Nanco was better off to spend time with someone her own age rather than be whisked off to live with older suitors. So, even if I would have known about Mika and Nanco, I probably would have done nothing.

I surmised that the reason we found them too young to procreate was not just that they appeared physically young, but also that they had a pureness of heart that gave this presentation. Mika did not appear burdened or serious. He kept these qualities of childhood well into his adolescence.

Nanco also seemed young for her young years. She not only looked like a little child, but she also spoke with the voice of a little girl. Her voice was tiny and somewhat high-pitched. She also conversed with such seriousness and conviction. The high pitch voice contrasted with the articulate speech. And thus, the qualities jived and made her appear naive.

Nanco lived with both her parents. They were equally quite surprised when she began to be sick in the morning. They were first alarmed thinking she might be ill. She was their only child. Both her parents had had union with several others but had not produced offspring. When they came together and Nanco was born, they felt it a great blessing.

Nanco was believed to be born early, before her time in the womb was complete. She was a very tiny baby, and it was not expected she would live. When she began to gain weight and grow strong, it was alleged that she had a fighting spirit. She grew as the years went on but was always smaller in stature than her peers.

When Nanco began to develop morning sickness, her parents watched her worryingly close. She tried her best to hide her discomfort, but her parents were overly attentive. They had Denu come to examine her.

Denu, as well as an elder, was a respected healer. She had developed many oils and herbs that alleviate sickness. Sometimes her medicines were believed to have cured people. When Denu was brought to Nanco's home, it was under the belief that Nanco was developing abdominal problems. Her parent's first thought was that Nanco may have underdeveloped bowels and thus was becoming sick from them being stretched as she grew. However, as Denu began to inspect her, noticing the particular swelling of her breasts and stomach, their theory changed.

They began to ask her questions about menstruating and contact with men. Nanco did not reveal whether she knew she was pregnant. But she did indicate that yes, in fact, she had started bleeding a while ago and had kept it a secret. She also confessed to their surprise that she had been with someone, but he might not be considered a man.

While her parents and Denu were digesting the information, she was able to slip out quietly. She hastened to find Mika and told him the predicament. She hurried back home as she knew they would be looking for her.

Mika, in his wisdom, came to us right away to explain what had happened. We were grateful for his comfort in talking to us. It was nice to be prepared when the council approached us, asking how we might contribute to the situation. Without hesitation, we offered to take in

Nanco if need be. We knew that Mika was too young to care for her alone, but we would be willing to help if her parents could not.

Her parents, however, were not interested in our offer. They were more than capable of caring for their daughter. They had watched over in her fragile early years and were quite committed to her long-term care. And it came to be that they had to care for her extensively during this time.

Nanco, like many of the pregnant children, had trouble carrying and bearing the child. It was further compounded by her tiny physique. While her parents knew she was a strong-willed girl, they also knew she had physical limitations. She was sometimes tired or short of breath as a child. She would have to come home from work or play earlier than most children to rest.

During this pregnancy, she seemed to need extra sleep. She spent many extra hours just lying in her dwelling. When she rose, her head would become dizzy if she had exerted herself too much that day. Nanco was not required to do many chores during this period.

As she grew in size, she experienced more discomfort. She would cramp up after walking any distance. And, at times, she was spotting. Her parents prayed and asked for the prayers of others during this time, hoping that she could carry this baby to term and deliver it healthy without losing her life.

Nanco was well-guarded by her parents. Mika was acknowledged but considered too young to care for a wife and child. His apparent immaturity proved to limit his responsibility. Mika was allowed to visit Nanco on occasion. He took the opportunity to do so and helped tend to her and pick up the slack of the chores she was unable to complete. Mika was genuinely concerned for her health.

Now, with his elevated status of prime suitor, he could have went and sought out new girls. But he chose to spend his time with Nanco. And so, in many ways, Mika was far more responsible for his years than many of us.

I envied Nanco. Her parents kept her and wanted her. When Nanco delivered the baby, it was a very fragile procedure. The birth was overseen by one of Nanco's mother's relatives named Perious. Both I and Opheala, Nanco's mother, were present for the delivery. We worked in a subservient capacity to Perious. This was the best situation, as neither Opheala nor I were emotionally equipped at this time to take charge.

Nanco looked so very pale and weak during this delivery that we feared that she would not make it. Her breathing varied from laboured to shallow during the birthing procedure. At times, she appeared to stop breathing, and we could not feel her heart beat. Perious would shake her, and she would then gain consciousness.

We were relieved when the baby finally oozed out but concerned about its tiny size. Nanco fell asleep immediately following the delivery. We left her to rest and tended to the little baby girl. We hoped that Nanco would be able to nurse her.

Because Nanco was so sick, visitation to her was restricted. It served to limit our family's opportunity to see the baby unfortunately. Her parents chaperoned visits closely. It was not to offend the visitors but to make sure that Nanco did not overexert herself.

I went to visit with Mika the day after the birth. Nanco looked extremely delicate. A yellowish pale tinge permeated her skin. The baby was minuet and very hairy. She did not cry and barely moved. Yet I saw traces of Mika and Rondo in this tiny little girl. I picked her up amidst a large bundle of boiled and dried salvage cloth.

"Hello, Mesha."

She stirred slightly. Everyone looked concerned. It was hard to assess who was frailer, Nanco or tiny Mesha. There was clearly a somber demeanor to the entire setting. That included Mika.

Mika was almost as ashen as the mother of his child. He was burdened with the consequences of his actions. As with all men, the consequence was not direct. Men do not have to carry or bear a child. Because their only necessary involvement is an act of pleasure, they do not necessarily have to burden themselves with the later stages that involve both joy and suffering.

In some ways, it was comforting to know that Mika had a conscience. While I did not wish him guilt, I felt his awareness of "the suffering of others as a consequence of our actions" was a beneficial adage. On the other hand, I was very sad for him. He looked devastated.

I passed little Mesha to him wrapped up in the swaddle. He hesitated taking her for fear she would break. He held her as I watched him closely. He smiled at her beauty and her miracle of being. But he was clearly distraught. Nanco looked at him and commented with a weary voice.

"She is beautiful, isn't she, Mika?"

"Yes she is," he answered but his voice shook. I thought it was best that we leave at this point. I was worried that Mika would not be able to maintain himself. He was given strength from Nanco's question. But he clearly wanted to express his worry. I excused us quickly saying we would return tomorrow.

We left the dwelling walking arm in arm. He seemed to be leaning on me as we made our way across the village.

We continued to visit daily for the next few weeks. Each day, both Mesha and Nanco appeared stronger. Nanco appeared to feel everything would be fine and did not know what all the fuss was about. Those of us who had experienced childbirth realized that she was under far more duress and was much weaker than most new mothers. And we knew that little Mesha was much smaller than most babies. We were much more reluctant to suggest that they were progressing healthily. We had lost our sense of pure and naïve hope.

On the other hand, Nanco was more aware of her own body than anyone else. Few thought she would live as an infant, but she did. No one thought she was of age to have a child, but she did. Perhaps no one believed she and the baby were healthy, but, in fact, they were.

Each day her parents loosened the restrictions on her visitations. Rondo went to see his granddaughter and even Douglas peered in at his little niece for a moment.

We visited religiously, and Mesha was now almost a month old. She still struggled, and her mother was very slow to recover. Fortunately, the baby had taken to suckling from Nanco regularly, and this had served to improve the health of both parties. Mesha had gained weight, but she still only looked the size of a small regular baby fresh out of the womb.

Most mothers would be up and about by now, tending to short chores with minimal lifting. But Nanco had only been out of her parent's dwelling once or twice a day to wash herself or to take a short walk to the storage shed. She was still visibly weak. When she walked, her legs looked like brittle malnourished sticks jutting out from her cloth. Her skin was still pale and her face so thin that she resembled a skeleton.

Mika had taken to helping out at her parent's dwelling. It was good for him. It shook part of his guilt and eased his anxiety somewhat. It also gave him opportunity to spend more time with Nanco and Mesha. No longer could he turn to his friends for comfort. As I watched him bringing food into the dwelling for Nanco, I hoped he would not have to sacrifice his good nature and humour to get through this traumatic event.

"That is a good young man you have raised there, Letsi," commented Denu. She startled me from my thoughts. I had not seen her approaching with Perious from behind me. I assumed they had come to check on Mesha and Nanco, and I was surprised when Denu stayed behind to talk to me while Perious entered Nanco's dwelling.

"I think they will be fine," stated Denu. I was still somewhat puzzled as to her reason for addressing me. She had rarely spoken to me directly or indirectly. Even when I had been before the council for approval of salvage expeditions, I don't recall her having said much.

Although Denu was about the age of Anex, she still looked strong, healthy, and young. Her hair had not yet grayed, and she still walked rather briskly without limp or slouch. Because of our difference in size, I had to look down at her while we spoke. This seemed to relax me despite my anxiety as to why she was addressing me.

"I don't know. The baby is so small. And Nanco is nothing but skin and bones," I answered.

"True. But their will is strong. Our spirit can sometimes act as a healing power." I listened respectfully to Denu about this subject. If anyone would know, she would. She had been responsible for treating and healing many of our people. I answered with nothing. Denu did not waste time and began to reveal her true motive for taking up conversation with me.

"The council would like to meet with you," Denu proclaimed.

I was certainly startled.

"What on earth do they want?" I replied in a defensive tone. I had little to do with the council on any official capacity other than to get permission for salvage expeditions. And at this time, I was certainly not planning on venturing out on one. I regarded the council as unacceptably judgmental.

I was no longer shocked or in fear of the doctrine on the ultimate purpose. I knew now that the people do need laws to govern them, and I respected this. However, I thought the laws should be challengeable and not just be accepted on blind faith. The ultimate law, I thought, should always answer the questions: Is it good for the people? Is it good for the person?

I still had many questions about sending children off to procreate and deeming others anomalous. I struggled with the concepts and saw the council as an entity enforcing these oppressive laws upon us. I had trouble seeing them as trying to maintain order so we may flourish as a people.

"They wish to speak to you regarding an urgent matter," responded Denu hesitantly, as if she did not want to discuss it with me at Nanco's parents' dwelling.

I immediately became guarded. What were they up to now? I wondered. Were they thinking of deeming Mesha anomalous? Surely, they didn't expect me to contribute to such as procedure in any way. While I did tolerate the many laws of my people, I had absolutely no inclination to infringe on the rights of others in order to enforce such laws.

Had I given off any indication of such in my brief addresses for the salvage expeditions? I had been respectful of their positions even when I found their comments despicable, especially referring to Alexandra as a possible anomaly. When I thought of this, the laws and the council made me sick. They would be crazy to choose me to become involved in any of their affairs. They certainly could not force me. Surely, I had enough status to refuse such a task.

My mind was racing, and I was becoming agitated.

"What is this urgent matter? I should be entitled to know before I stand before them. I should have some preparation," I answered somewhat defiantly.

Denu put her head down looking somewhat impatient. As I watched her, I felt a sharp pain of fear shake my body as if a mild jolt of lightning from one of the electric storms had shot through my system. Denu had authority, and she exercised it on occasion.

There were many things she could do to make my life more difficult. She could speak against me going on salvage expeditions. She could even recommend I have limited access to visit Mesha. Although I was now too old to blindly obey them, I still feared the council somewhat. Not so much for what they could do to me directly, but because of what they might do to make life difficult for the rest of my family.

"Walk with me," Denu instructed.

I obeyed.

"You may have heard that there has been a halt on trade with the Stalites and the Moraines." she began as we walked toward the site where the council was to meet.

28

I thought about leaving my family behind as I prepared to meet the Moraine ship that was waiting to depart at the meeting site on the banks of the Poison Sea. The infinite number of sand granules glistened as they met at the foot of our colossal geologic formations. Here, I was about to undertake the utmost adventure that a mountain person might ever go on.

And yet all I wished to do was stay behind with my family.

I had listened intently to all the points that the council made in favour of me crossing the sea despite my concern for my family.

"You have been on several excavations, have you not? Your family has been well-tended to in your absence. You have proved you have a strong network surrounding you," put forth Denu.

"Besides, there is really only Douglas to care for now, and you have many who are willing to take on the burden for a short time," reasoned Winnette who bore a striking resemblance to her mother Anex.

"What if I do not return?" I retorted. I was insulted by her reference to Douglas as a burden. Even if it was true, I did not believe it was her place to define him as such. I never referred to her mother, Anex, as a burden when I would take time away from my work schedule to sit with her just so she wouldn't be alone. But I could have said it if I chose to be rude.

The council people seemed to have no qualms about being rude and insensitive. It was almost as if it was a prerequisite for qualifying for a position on council—knowledgeable, superior orator, rude, and insensitive.

Winnette answered swiftly with a stern voice that suggested she was expecting me to be more respectful when I addressed her. "We all might die anytime. When we lose someone, we must regroup and support one another in the time of grief. Your question is a 'what-if' that no one can answer. We do not know our ultimate destiny. We can only deal in this reality. And the reality is that, while you are gone, your son will be tended to."

"But what of my son Mika? He is greatly burdened over the health of his daughter and her mother. He needs support. He is quite vexed."

"There is nothing you can do for him, Letsi. Your staying here is not a direct variable for the health of your granddaughter. And Mika must learn to cope with the suffering of the world as we all do," replied my father in an old, shaky-sounding voice matching the grey in his thinning wiry hair. I frowned as he spoke in his detached voice. You would hardly know it was his grandson and great-granddaughter that he referred to, let alone his daughter he was addressing.

Despite the fact that I hated him for not showing any sign of involvement when he spoke of his own family, I did agree with him to some extent. There was nothing I could do to take away the burden of worry. I could alleviate the work load and make sure Mika took time to eat and sleep. But I could not grant life to Mesha and Nanco. I could not change their destiny.

And, selfishly, I also thought to myself that I wouldn't be able to handle their death very well if they did not make it. It would be too similar to Alexandra's death. To see more young beautiful people die would likely send me into another depression, and then I would be of no help to Mika anyway. So, by going on this trip, I reasoned that the physical distance could allow me enough detachment that if something happened, I would cope better and, consequently, be of more help. Perhaps going away might be a good thing as selfish as it seemed.

Surprisingly, the council began to list the few qualities they believed I possessed that drew them to the conclusion that I should go on this venture.

"You have been on many salvage expeditions and have proved yourself to be a proficient traveler," mentioned Denu.

"You have shown great innovation with the use of the salvage material you have brought back, namely the soft metals," added Winnette. "And Dana tells me you are a great teller of stories from the word papers you have salvaged."

My Auntie Dana and Winnette were still quite close. Although my Auntie Dana rarely spent time with me, it was nice that she spoke well of me in absence.

The accolades that they were bestowing upon me were somewhat flattering. I had spent so much of my life feeling worthless. It was nice that there were those out there who recognized some quality in me. It was nothing I would deem profoundly touching, however. I knew they had discussed my attributes in my absence when they had decided, in my absence, that I would be the one to go on this journey.

I wondered why the people didn't make testimony to those who were down and destitute. I thought that these comments they were bequeathing me with would have been a much greater help when I was very sad and forlorn. They had limited meaning to me when they were just being proclaimed because they wished to use me for a venture.

Of course, my father had to leave me with one additional comment that was supposed to be a compliment. But when I heard it, it felt like anything but one.

"And, now, your one healthy child has produced an offspring at a very young age. He will certainly be a contributing suitor for the future of the people."

I rolled my eyes and tears welled up in them. Their compliments were designed to have me concur and then consent to go on this journey across the Poison Sea. But I only felt sadness. Any accomplishment I had made was overshadowed with the suffering that I incurred in this journey of life.

Though true, I was getting better at appreciating the good that we experience over time. I was beginning to grasp the value of the scarce moments of goodness. But, overall, the proclamations designed to flatter me seemed somewhat empty. Their motive was not sincere enough.

I would store these comments however, and I would remember them in times when I felt I needed to appreciate myself more. I would use these comments for back up. I was teaching myself how to be mentally and emotionally healthy. And feeling good about oneself is a mandatory attribute of mental and emotional health.

While I was not moved to accept their offer of mediator based on their compliments, Denu's final comment did win me over.

"We talk now of your past accolades. What you must look to is your future. Think of what you might accomplish by going there. You could learn of new technologies or new medicines to share with our people. You may be responsible for solving a dispute among other peoples. It would certainly be an honour and bequeath great respect on the mountain people.

The other peoples value us for our mediation skills. That is why they have asked for us several times. If you can help with their negotiations they will assume trade. This would gain respect for you and your family. Not only this," she paused, "but doing good for others will increase your own self respect."

I was certainly being seduced by Denu's arguments. I could not help but admire Denu. If anyone knew about being valued among the people, certainly, she did. I would say that almost all of the medicines used by the mountain people had been either created or improved by this woman. Certainly, she had found the most use for the reactor metal. She was responsible for extracting more potent medicines from traditional plants, and the people were grateful for it. She probably recognized the benefit to trade with these other people more than anyone.

Denu bore more than one child. I was not sure how many as I did not know her story well. She had one living daughter who had a teenage son close to Mika's age. I surmised that Denu had her share of adversity throughout her life. Despite all of the development she had made with the medicine, she had never been on an adventure. Perhaps her path had been discovering particles that limited our suffering. Perhaps that had been her adventure, her escape, and her solace. I thought about the words she spoke.

More status for me and my family could only help our plight, I thought, although it could not really prevent the suffering of things we cannot control. That, unfortunately, is the human dilemma. However, if all went satisfactorily on this journey, it could be helpful to my people and my family. And I did still have a yearning to explore, albeit a now-quieted voice in the back of my head.

Furthermore, what was the alternative? If I did not go on this journey, how would the council react? There were a limited amount of sanctions the council could impose upon me. I had accomplished my ultimate purpose. That was all that was really required of me. The council could not decree to shun me if I chose not to engage in this venture. Yet I knew there were many things they could do.

Just by spreading rumours about my lack of compliance, I could soon be blamed for lack of trade between the peoples. That, in turn, could be interpreted as "lack of resources to combat illness" because of me. And then if someone died, I might be unofficially deemed secondarily responsible. It could create hostility against me and my family. Hence, nothing could be done against me directly, but, indirectly, the consequences could be far worse.

I was being swayed towards their decision.

"Why me?" I asked. "Surely there is a man available."

"There are only a few healthy men that are your age, Letsi. Of these, few have undergone any type of journey. Furthermore, they will be needed for more salvage expeditions," added Randil. Randil was one of the few mountain people to be recognized as a strong labourer and an elder. He was noted for having great endurance.

I thought of Stephin and Barone. They were really the only other experienced journeymen. I'm sure the council had discussed them in length as well. Barone was likely not chosen because he was not a great communicator. His introverted nature had increased since the death of his wife. I wasn't sure why they chose me over Stephin, however. I surmised that they likely saw me as more expendable.

I shrugged in defeat as I looked up at the council.

"When do I go?"

The decision to have me attend this mission was a hurried one. The Moraine vessel had been waiting the entire time. I put together a generous amount of salvage cloth, a fork comb, and a couple of word papers in my satchel. I did not want to make too heavy a load as I knew there would be plenty of mountain water to carry.

Rondo and Douglas were in the dwelling as I prepared to go. I gave Douglas a big hug. He tried to squirm out of it, but I held him firmly telling him I loved him. Douglas was now in a man's body yet still very much a child. He babbled "Mom, Mom, Mom" in a man's deep voice. He was now able to control his eliminating functions, and that was certainly an accomplishment we valued. He was even able to carry water from the streams. I was appreciating more things about Douglas now. In particular, I loved that he bore no judgment on anyone. He seemed to accept fate as it is.

Rondo looked at me and wished me luck. I nodded but wondered to myself why he wasn't the one going on this venture. Why had he never taken the notion to travel? Why had he never even taken the risk to share with me emotionally? Was it just not in his makeup? I knew very little about his dreams. I knew very little about him at all.

I walked from the dwelling and met up with Mika. I embraced him hoping to transfer any strength from me as I could for what he was enduring. I truly wanted to stay and try to help him in any way I could. I wanted to make up for my despondency when he was growing up. This time was lost however, and all I could do was feel guilty about it whenever a crisis occurred.

"When I am in this strange land, I will look for any material that could help Nanco and Mesha," I committed to Mika. He smiled as I walked away.

I had not been to the edge of the Poison Sea since I was a child sneaking among the wind deformed conifers. I had no inclination to return. I hadn't wondered much about the other people for several years since I had ceased to meet regularly with Anex. As I walked down the path and began to taste the sulfur in my throat, it aroused my curiosity about these people, and I began to wonder what type of adventure I was in for.

The Moraines remained in the hull of the vessel until I boarded. It was stated that they would not surface until we were over halfway across the sea. I wrapped layers of cloth around my mouth and nose in an attempt to filter out the toxins from entering my lungs.

I chose to stay on deck because I thought there would be more air to breathe outside than in the stagnant air below in the hull. There was no evidence to suggest whether in the hull or on top of the hull would be my best choice. But I felt better on deck anyway because, from there, I was able to view my homeland and the majestic mountains as we sailed away.

29

It was all too overwhelming. I needed time. So many things had happened. Was this the initial plan? Is this the only reason the Stalites agreed to meet with a mediator? I wondered if they had wanted a woman, or would they have preferred a man to breed with for this encounter. I chose not to ask them at this time. I decided I would approach my own council about it when and if I returned to the mountains. I wanted them to tell me, to be honest, and share their true meaning for sending me. I wanted to know what they discussed behind my back. I wanted to know to my face.

And what of Sollele? He wasn't guilty of murder, rape perhaps. And perhaps he was guilty of being an ingrate. No doubt the Stalites could find a way of making him pay. If he ventured too close to their homeland, he could easily have a mishap in one of the deep crevices. I have no doubt that the Stalites could see to that.

What if the Stalites hadn't found me "acceptable" for their ceremony? Would I have had to return to my homeland a failure? It was all very surreal. I had a major time trying to focus on what was asked of me.

As for their proposal, if I consented, what would I be in store for? Could I renege? It seemed Sollele could not. Vanel was still sitting there and appeared to be aware of my thoughts.

"The ceremony will be constructed to make you as comfortable as possible," she began. "You may stop or change the process at any time. You may have several suitors if you chose or just one. Neil has volunteered to join in union with you if you would prefer the comfort of having made acquaintance with the person."

"It seems you have gone into great preparation for this event without having any expression of interest from me," I rebuffed, somewhat annoyed that these plans had been so much about me without my input. It was all too familiar. My purpose, here as at home, had ultimately been my womb.

"I need more time to think . . . alone," I answered in a somewhat dismissive voice. Vanel bowed her head and exited through an adjacent cavern.

I knew I was sinking into a spiral of disappointment and depression, but I also knew I would have to deal with it quickly. This purpose was indeed disillusionment. I let myself succumb to the flattery I had left home hearing. It had served to motivate me for this trip, but, now, it was a cause of disappointment. The Stalites had no interest in my negotiating skills. I repeated my thoughts allowed.

"Does no one have any interest in my skills besides this one purpose?" I hollered. The words echoed off the cave walls. Somehow, the words I uttered set me free from their meaning. And I began to laugh. I laughed almost to tears. I caught my breath and sat on the solidified drip that was shaped like a chair, a throne perhaps. It brought be back to my childhood. It made me think of the time I was crowned "Queen of the Mountains" by my childhood friends.

I composed myself and began to think about the offer. It seemed it was yet another situation where I had little control. I wondered if our destiny was just a series of obstacles and tasks that we must confront or steer clear of until, finally, we cease to have the energy or the will to continue.

I thought about their offer. It was certainly not the most tragic event I had ever encountered. I was beginning to put a positive spin on the proposal. Thus, I thought I had learned enough coping skills to devise an itinerary to proceed with the Stalites' proposition.

While there were many negatives, on the positive side, if I consented, I would be leaving with the Moraines and Stalites in reconciliation. I would also be returning with extra trade items if I engaged in this activity. Before this proposal, I was aware that I would be returning home with some grassbake and reactor metals; but if I agreed to participate in their ceremony, the amount would likely be doubled or more.

One of the two areas that made me most uneasy about this proposition was using my womb as bargaining leverage. This was not a new concept to me or any of the women of my people. However, I never saw it as a virtue. It was always at a cost that was never fully compensated. The bartering of our reproductive system, no matter what gain in material wealth and social status, always seemed to be at the loss of part of our intellectual status and our soul.

The second area that left me most apprehensive was that I was not comfortable with the act itself. I knew little about the customs of these people, and I knew nothing of their intimate customs or performances. I feared what was in store for me. It was something new and foreign, and it made me feel uncomfortable. Perhaps it was not as uncomfortable as when as a child when I was first sent off to live with a suitor but similar to that. I wondered if during this act, I would revert back to my early days with Rondo.

As strong as the feelings of opposition and apprehension were, I knew that if I did decline the proposal that Vanel had put forth, I would receive nothing. And, in my homeland, it would be perceived that I had failed at my task in this foreign place. Thus, I would lose status, I would still feel frustrated and depressed, and I would have less to offer my family.

So, I surmised, it would be best to submit to their request. But I would do so with my own agenda. As I sat mentally devising a list of counter requests, Neil entered the cave.

"We hope we have not offended you," he recited. "Is there something you are displeased with?"

"There is nothing particular about your people that offends me. It is my purpose or the lack of value that my life seems to be equated with that I find offensive," I responded bluntly. I surprised myself on my openness. I was not concerned that I might sound as if I was "being childish." I felt alleviated to say how I felt, and I did not feel guilty for feeling that way.

Neil looked at me somewhat puzzled. "Do you not place value on bearing children?"

I looked at him and began to explain the ultimate purpose of the mountain people. He listened intently and waited for me to finish.

"You speak of how your people regard bearing children; but what about you personally? How do you feel about having children? Do you not regard them as sacred?"

I did not need much time to think about this. I knew my children were sacred. I knew there was something at work beyond the basic tasks of sustenance that fueled my drive to care for my children. Just to think of them tugged at my soul.

"Yes, I think of children as sacred," I answered. "It is just that I feel that women, and I being one of them, are forced into the act of procreation. Our thoughts and feelings and desires do not seem relevant in the process, only our passive submission."

Neil seemed perplexed with my remark. I surmised that it was because he was a man.

"We do not wish to force you to join in our ceremony," he stated almost indignantly, as if I had somehow offended him.

"But what choice do I have?" I countered. "If I do not, I will go home having failed. It will be a great hardship for my family."

Neil nodded as if he finally understood. He realized then that their request was being presented to me as an ultimatum. He thought for a moment.

"This is what I can offer. I invite you to join in our ceremony. If you accept the invitation, we will resume trade with the Moraines. If at any time during the ceremony you wish to stop the process of union, you may do so. It is your choice."

"Would you still resume trade with the Moraines?"

"Yes, at least for a time that will allow you to return to your home without losing face. We have no dispute with your people, and we do not wish you ill favour. We only ask for your help if you are willing to give it."

I was impressed with his offer. It seemed fair. It relieved me of a great burden, and it empowered me. It inspired me to talk with Neil further and negotiate a possible settlement and solution.

"Very well! I will engage in your ceremony. But I ask for the following additions if the union is complete. As well as resuming trade amongst the peoples, I would like twenty reactor pebbles, four rocks, and samples of your oils, medicinal herbs, and successful spores. In particular, I would like any medicine that you have that may help women recover from childbirth and that will help premature babies develop."

Neil nodded in agreement as I put forth my proposal.

"I also need you to acknowledge my opinion that Sollele, while definitely a negative factor in Lauren's death, was not the primary cause of her fate."

Neil exhibited a clear impetus of consternation on the last point. "We do not support that last statement."

"You need not agree. You just need to accept that that it is my conclusion." I was not concerned with how they dealt with Sollele in the future. But I felt part of the responsibility for Lauren's fatality rested on the decision of the Stalites to invite Sollele into their world in the first place.

He thought for a moment. "I concede. I will present your query to the others, but I believe they will be in agreement." He paused again. "Do you find me acceptable?"

I pondered over his question. "Do you mean for the ceremony?"

"Yes."

"My impression of you is that you are a good man." To myself, I thought my judgment was not based on enough authenticity. It was a first impression. A first impression is not foundation for representation. The front facing of a dwelling is no indication of the frame or overall construction. Nevertheless, it is that first attraction that does elicit romantic desires as void of substance as they may be. And that was all that was likely necessary for such a transaction as was being put forth.

I liked what I knew of Neil. I respected his graciousness and his wisdom. But I had no idea how I felt about him other than this. We did not know each other well. And we came from different places. Physically, I found him small and somewhat frail in appearance. I was not accustomed to this body type. His pale colour was also a foreign site to me, and it seemed sickly.

In addition, I had another concern. I was afraid. I didn't really know what to expect or how I would feel as this is always a vulnerable activity for women. I tried to express my concern to Neil the best I could amidst my uneasiness. While I had imagined Neil in a domestic manner, I had not truly considered an act of union with him. My mental self was free to think and do. But my physical self had physical consequences that impacted on all other realms of my being. I was anxious.

Neil nodded as I expressed my trepidation. He assured me that respect, dignity, and concern for my needs would be met by him and his people. It did little to put me at ease, but I decided to delve into the activity. I felt somewhat consoled because I had the assurance that the ceremony would end if I chose to exercise my prerogative in this manner.

Assuming our talk was finished, Neil unwrapped a bark folder that he had taken from his satchel.

"Here is a small meal for you. I will leave to present your requests and concerns to the advisers. If they are in agreement with your requisition, the maidens will return to prepare you for the ceremony."

Neil gave me one last temperate glance. He held my hand briefly as if to close the negotiations, and then he left through the fissure he entered. I sat and gorged myself on the nourishment he had bestowed upon me. It was again a mixture of spores and some type of sluglike species that slid down my throat. As I devoured the morsels, the spices and oils increased my thirst, and I realized I had very little water left. I had used up most of my rations on Sollele and the other Moraines on the south side of the Stalite Hills.

I scoured the small cave with my eyes in hopes of securing a source of liquid. I noticed small beads of dew molding on the upper cones in the centre of the cave. I reached up to gather the offerings on my finger tips. I licked my fingers vigorously. The taste was stale but served to offset my quench. I stuck my tongue out and circled the cone lapping up whatever drops that clung to my mouth. Water is our most basic primal need. It is our greatest overpowering lust, I thought to myself as I searched for more droplets.

Two women who looked approximately my age entered the dwelling as I was slurping the rock facings.

"This is not the best cave to retrieve liquid from the walls. But it is a relatively safe enclosure," stated one of the women. "Unfortunately, the caves with more ample supply are less stable. Here, let me go and retrieve you a plentiful supply while you sit and have Karin begin to prepare you." The young woman walked out to an adjoining tunnel and put a small wide-mouthed flask in the centre of it. She anchored herself to the large cave by holding on to one of the ridges of a rock nodule that protruded on the left side of the opening of the tunnel.

In her stretched position, her muscles were well-defined over her entire body. She was sleek and thin, but with the limited light of the reactor metal, it was clear that she was not frail. There was great definition to her outline.

The other woman brought me to a small bench-like rock towards the middle of the cave. She spoke in a quiet but solid voice. "I am Karin. And this is Nelma. We are your maidens. We shall prepare you for the ceremony."

Nelma was even smaller than Karin. Her legs were shorter but thicker like logs as opposed to sticks. She had thin, silky, light hair that shone with a bright auburn tinge from the reflection of the reactor metal. She wore it down with no fasteners. It stayed in place though and looked perfectly symmetrical as it shimmered with her movement like the dancing motion of a small wave. She had dark thick eyebrows and eyelashes that contrasted her light green corneas. Her thin round face had a childlike cuteness to it. Her head was painted with a reddish clay mud directed in lines. Blended with this was dark, grey-coloured soot.

As I scanned her body I saw that the paint adorn her from head to foot. Throughout her decoration were some type of symbols in thin geometric shapes created with a soft bluish green dye that I surmised was retrieved from some type of plant.

The mountain people would sometimes cover their face in white clay when they were close to a deposit in the streams. It soothed the skin and protected against the sun. We found it looked visually pleasing against our dark skin, but we did not use it as a regular or ceremonial decoration. It was for practical purposes mainly.

I wanted to know more about the Stalite symbols and their adornment, but it didn't seem appropriate to ask under the circumstances. Furthermore, the women seemed somewhat hastened to prepare me for the ceremony. Nelma and Karin gestured softly toward me in an indication to sit down.

"So the Stalite people have accepted my requests?" I queried.

"Yes," answered Nelma as she handed me a small flask filled with the musty liquid she had retrieved from the tunnel. "They felt they were quite reasonable. The others are now preparing the final essentials for the ceremony. Thus, we must begin to prime you as quickly as possible."

What, I wondered, were these final preparations? It was clear that most preparations had been made even before my arrival in Moraine. Nelma and Karin sat beside me on a ledge and unwrapped and placed a small root weave basket in front of me. Karin took out a small jugglet of oil with a sweet, barklike fragrance and a tiny specimen of grey spore that had been dried. She picked up the spores and handed them to me.

"These will make you feel more relaxed, but will not impede your muscle control. They take a while to take effect, so it is best that you take them now." I complied. I chewed up the spongelike medicine and washed it down with the rest of my mildewed water. Nelma picked up the sweet smelling oil.

"This oil heightens sensation and contains fragrance that enriches reception. We will daub you with it when the others arrive."

Others? What others? This ceremony was certainly going to be foreign to me. I wondered to myself. But said nothing to the Stalite women preferring to have the instruction continue.

Nelma unwrapped a tiny bundle of dark fungi and leaves.

"It is believed that this compound increases both receptivity and fertility. When the others have arrived, we will offer you the preparation to ingest and begin to knead the oil compound into your skin as Vanel and Tonaldo initiate the ceremony with a brief incantation. We will continue with our massage until you make indication to Neil that you are prepared for union with him."

I felt a sense of urgency when they spoke. "How am I to signal Neil?"

"Any act of affection will give him qualification," answered Karin.

I thought to myself that I should have known the answer to this as it is something we tend to communicate without much conscious expression.

"Do you have any additional concerns?" asked Nelma. I could see faint reactor lights through the fissure on the north side of the large cave we were in. I knew now that there was a parade of Stalite people about to enter through the wall.

"What will the other Stalite people be doing here, and how long will they stay?" I inquired as the Stalites began to enter the cave and take places around the circumference. I felt my level of anxiety increasing. I hoped the spores I had been given would soon sedate me.

"They will remain the entire time, and they will be engaged in similar acts," replied Karin. "The ceremony increases the receptivity of all the people." She turned to look at the others entering the cavern. She then bowed toward me. "We are ready to begin the initial preparations for the ceremony. We ask your permission to begin."

Puzzled but intrigued, I nodded. I think the first wave of the sedation was beginning to affect me.

"First, you must take the elixir," directed Nelma.

I ingested the compound slowly commenting on its barklike taste. The maidens ushered me to a flat rock more toward the centre of the enclosure. They slowly began to peel the layers of my salvage cloth off to administer the oil solution. I was somewhat self-conscious about my nudity. However, the fact that everyone else was without cloth limited my embarrassment. And I was beginning to feel a more potent level of drug in my system distracting me from any sense of shame.

The women's touch was gentle and soothing. The oil served to subdue what remained of the insect bite scabs on my extremities. Stalites encircled me at a distance. Neil stepped forward and stood before us. He reached for my hand and began to massage the oil into my arm following the lead of the maidens. My flesh was pacified and my body felt at ease. I closed my eyes to restrict my visual sense and heighten my sense of touch.

Alan and Tonaldo stood upon an upper ledge in the cave and began an incantation:

> *Once, the human race was the parasite of the universe. It plagued the earth like a festering boil. It erupted over the surface like maggots below a thin layer of skin.*

The intoxicant had taken full effect. I felt a little overwhelmed, but the normalcy that everyone else displayed at the encounter calmed me. The maiden's touch became more central to my focus. I opened my eyes and searched for reassurance in their eyes. I looked to Neil who appeared entranced with the proceedings.

Now, those few remaining must seek restitution in humility. Our path must be more harmonious with the macrocosm.

I scanned the enclosure slowly turning my head from side to side. I witnessed the intensity of all those people who appeared to be participating in similar acts with respective partners. I reached out to return the gesture to one of the hands stroking my skin softly. In return, they guided my hand to Neil who began to join in the caressing. Neil advanced as the women retreated. The women searched for partners of their own to engage with. Neil's predilection was far more resolved than the women. My state was accessible and he extended in response. His gestures were commanding yet he asked permission before indulging in any motion as he proceeded. I immersed myself in the activity.

Glimpses of the surrounding ceremony demonstrated several members in several acts of copulation. The coolness of the damp cave served to ease the ascending temperature. Neil and I were on the floor, my body marginally protected from the rough sediment by a sparse laden of cloth. Neil transfixed on me briefly and put his mouth on mine. My body pulsated. An act requiring union can be a very self-centred activity. And just that quick, I was finished and the spell broken. Neil was complete shortly after. I began to notice similar actions around the cave. I held onto to Neil as I perused the scene. Stalites were slowly parting and recovering their composure.

I rose from my spot and reached for my cloth. The compound I had taken was beginning to wear off, but it served to keep me at ease in this setting. I sat leaning against a cone, and Neil rested beside me. I concentrated on the coolness of the rock and where it touched my face. I slumped against it half asleep.

Slowly, all around, the Stalites started to assemble in a more solemn and circular presentation. They appeared to be resting against the cavern walls. Neil said nothing to me but reached for my hand. I accepted the gesture and continued to peruse the cathedral-like enclosure.

I noticed there were three children among the Stalites. They were not young children but certainly prepubescent. I wondered if they had been present during the proceedings. I also speculated as to whether they made up the entire next generation of Stalite people.

In the whole enclosure, there were only about fifty people. I thought of how serious their situation was if this indeed this was their entire population. It was a sobering thought, and I empathized with the Stalites on their plight. I wondered if I might be now carrying seed that could aid their people.

I continued to look around the enclosure. I noted Vanel sitting to one side with another Stalite man that I had not yet met. She was clearly fatigued, likely from her participation in the ceremony. Tonaldo was still sitting on a ridge in an upper layer of the vortex. She appeared to be deep in meditation. I wondered if she had remained there the entire time. She slowly opened her thin eyelids and hobbled to the centre of the cavern. She made a brief statement:

> *Our knowledge of the Sacred Plan is limited by our mortality.*
> *Let us hope we will share our knowledge with future generations.*

The Stalites began to rise and disperse. I looked about me, still feeling numb from the drug and the physical exertion. The numbness helped me to digest all that was around me without feeling beset. Neil rose to his feet and motioned with his hand for me to follow.

"The Moraines are likely at the meeting place as we speak," submitted Neil. "Are you ready to rendezvous?" he asked.

"I need some water first."

I turned to the site where my belongings were and wrapped myself in my cloth. I picked up my satchel and nodded that I was ready to proceed.

Neil grabbed a flask and guided me attentively to a crevice to the side of the vortex. I surmised that this place was similar to the site where Lauren met her fate. There was a sound of dripping water echoing through the walls of the small enclosure.

We slid in cautiously, and he took me to a spot where liquid was slowly trickling down from a fissure. I put my mouth to the spot and suckled the water from the rock as though I was a nursing baby. When I finished, Neil drank as well. As he drank, I looked up to see the miraculous brown and mauve cones hanging delicately from the ceiling of the small cave. I stepped back from underneath them out of respect for their size. I had no interest in angering the gods of the Stalite Hills.

Neil and I filled all my flasks as my mountain water supply was all but gone. I wiped my hands over my face. I wished I was home in my mountain stream, bathing at this moment. We ushered our way back to the opening that would take us on the outside trail on a northern trek. I fastened up my clothing and passed some cloth to Neil.

We moved steadily on the outside holding each other's arm. We did not speak. We reached the point of reentry and began our trail through the maze of inside passages toward the site of our first meeting.

In a chamber located just before the meeting place, the elders and other Stalite people were gathered. Alan handed me a satchel filled with the supplies I had requested. They had also added more water and a small medicine bundle. A small Stalite man, who appeared a little older than I, stepped forward. He introduced himself as Zeela and began to open up the root basket of medicine and explain it to me.

"This bundle is for attachment. If you are pregnant, it helps the tiny baby anchor to your womb. It is believed to reduce the chance of miscarriage. You take one fingernail size portion for a week. And stay in bed if you notice spotting."

There were very few miscarriages amongst my people, and that included the very young mothers. Even Nanco had carried her baby long enough to bear despite having major difficulty doing so. Of course, I wondered if the drug might help her in the future. I hoped it might ease her struggle should she have another child if, in fact, she was still alive when I returned.

"Do you have many miscarriages among your women?" I questioned rather boldly and rudely. But I thought I must ask and ask now. It could likely be my only chance to find out more.

"Yes," answered Zeela. "Only a few women will conceive following a ceremony. And of these, most will not be able to carry the baby to term. Or the baby will be born still."

I felt a wave of understanding hit me hard as if I had been slapped in the head with it.

"When you were asked about working with a mediator among the mountain people, did you request that it be a woman?" I asked.

Zeela hesitated as if this was not his area of expertise. Tonaldo intercepted the question.

"Yes," she answered. "We thought the ceremony might have more chance of success with a woman."

I sighed from the revelation. Now it became clear why the council of my people had been so adamant that I attend this journey. I was only chosen over Stephin or probably any of the other excavators because they had specifically requested it be a woman. I tried not to take time to feel sorry for myself, as I knew that time was limited. I hoped I wouldn't look back on this as a sad event. Instead, I looked for something positive. I was beginning to recognize that I was developing skill at looking for positive points as a response to negative vices. I was starting to be able to differentiate between blind optimism that left one cynical and positive facts which gave cause for hope.

Yes, it was sad that I had been manipulated into attending this journey, not because of any developed skill on my part but more for my ability to produce children. On the other hand, I thought of the Stalite women, and I realized how thoughtless I was. These women recognized the value of what I was able to do, just by being fortunate enough to have a fertile womb.

I knew I would have to revisit my thinking on this subject but not now. Now, I had more pressing issues. I thought about this drug and how it might assist my people and Nanco in particular. I thirsted for more of Zeela's knowledge.

Zeela took another bundle from the basket and set it before me. "These spores are believed to have high concentrations of sacred qualities that help one build up muscle and bone mass. Babies that have taken this spore in our past have gained weight rapidly." As he prescribed his instructions, of course, I was thinking of little Mesha.

Zeela put forth several more concoctions. Some were for pain and discomfort; others were used to reduce the effects of assaults on the body from the cancers and bacteria. I listened intently to his instruction, very absorbed on discerning all the knowledge he was imparting on me. The last bundle he pulled from the basket was a small, reddish green herb.

"This herb has properties that can neutralize some of the effects of the toxins from the Poison Sea. Sometimes, the wind blows the lethal air from the sea to our caves. We have combated resulting illness by using these herbs as such." He took a sliver of the herb and placed it next to a small reactor pebble. He rubbed the pebble until it began to emit heat and light. He placed the small herb fragment on the pebble, and it started to smoke.

"You must inhale the smoke as such." he bowed his head in front of the smoldering herb. "And then you must spread the smoke around your body to act as a screen against the poison. Do this several times on the voyage. Do not wait until you feel ill for by that point, the toxins have entered your body."

I wasn't sure how that herb would work, but I was certainly willing to try anything that would reduce the chance of me falling prey to the demons of the Poison Sea again.

Tonaldo and Alan then stepped forward and placed their weary hands on my stomach.

"We hope that the ceremony will be a success and that we will reunite with you someday with a child that carries our seed." I looked at them both. Water was accumulating in the corners of their dull grey eyes. I bowed my head in a token of respect.

Neil put his hand on my shoulder and then gently whisked me away through the narrow tunnel that led to the Moraine meeting place. Neil stopped just before the entrance.

"We will leave you to go the rest of the way. We have no wish to meet with the Moraines at this time. It is just through that opening. Stay to the left wall until you reach the cave entrance. You will have no trouble in this cave if you stay to the left." He paused to see if I was comfortable to walk on the treacherous floor by myself. I indicated that I trusted in his direction and would have no trouble negotiating the floor of the meeting place.

"We would also ask that you explain to the Moraines that trade will now continue with our peoples. They will know what to do."

I looked at Neil and was at a loss for words. I had a feeling if I made it back to my homeland and had a chance to digest my adventure, I would be grateful to all that he and his people had done for me. We looked at each other and embraced.

"We will think of you. You will be in my thoughts."

I vanished through the wall.

30

Probability versus possibility:

Although the odds were against it, the success of this mission had the potential to be exceptional. I pondered the possibilities as I attempted to defy the odds on my short but critical voyage home across the Poison Sea. I was still riding on the euphoria of the ceremony and *success* of my mediation. Furthermore, reuniting with the Moraines I had met on my journey and presenting them with positive news served to fuel the elation.

My trip back to Moraine's Edge with Jaffy, Suz, and Daniel was swift, as the trip back from somewhere always seems faster than the trip *to* somewhere. But it seemed to fly by even more so as I was intently preoccupied with all that I had seen, learned, and done.

The Moraines were quite pleased as well, now that trade issues were resolved. And they appeared to wish to express their joy to me by being exceedingly obliging. They carried some of my supplies and served me generous portions of their cuisine. After hearing the news of resumed trade at the meeting site, there was a jovial attitude.

And our delight seemed to carry us faster along the trail. Thus, we were able to make it to some of the dwellings along route close to Moraine's Edge before it was completely dark. We did not have to set up camp that night as we were accommodated in a hut that belonged to a relative of Jaffy's. They were happy to put us up for the night after hearing that trade would resume. It was nice to feel joy and to share in the glee of others.

The next day, we set off early with the east rising sun pushing us on from behind. As we progressed, we came in contact with many Moraines tending to their chores. Some apparently engaged in the arduous task of preparing grassbake. They were throwing the grass into the air and letting it fall on a large piece of cloth.

The grassbake seemed to be a major staple of their diet. Yet they were dependent on the reactor metal for its completion. From that perspective, it seemed the Moraines were quite dependent on trading for reactor metal for their own sustenance. No wonder everyone felt more at ease with resumed trade.

In other areas, Moraines were carrying large planks similar to those on the Moraine vessel. A few were up in the trees of their orchards. Most stopped to gaze at us in an affable watch. It was clear that news of resumed trade had preceded us.

Within what seemed a short trek, I began to smell and taste the acrid air approaching from the venomous waters of the Poison Sea. And then I saw the ship off in the distance past the homes that collected on the mouth of the stream that flowed into the soupy water. Upon seeing it, I wanted to pick up the pace for I could not get home fast enough.

But, suddenly, I halted remembering the words of Zeela. "Do not wait until you feel ill for, by that point, the toxins have entered your body." Immediately, I sat down, and I took out a sliver of herb from the bundle along with a reactor pebble and began to smudge it.

The Moraines looked at me curiously but did not interrupt. Daniel, in particular, looked at the small herb sample inquisitively.

"The Stalites claim this can reduce the chance of a toxic reaction," I explained when I had finished the ritual.

Daniel lifted the specimen. "This plant grows in great numbers on the south side of this ravine," he proclaimed. He was quite enthused about his assertion as if he might be able to use this knowledge to improve his own people's health. I did not ask him to expand on his statement for fear it might frustrate him, but I surmised that he was thinking of trying to develop this herb as a medicine.

Daniel had been with me as an escort the entire trip. He had looked after my health, and I was grateful. I wanted to find a way to thank him without insulting him.

"You are a knowledgeable herbalist," I decreed smiling and nodding my head.

Daniel looked at me somewhat confused as he seemed to be trying to digest my comment. Did he not recognize it as I compliment? After a brief moment in thought he seemed to process my words in a positive manner. He nodded his head with an abrupt jerky motion as if he was accepting my words as an act of friendship. Indeed, that was what they were meant to be.

I put my bundle back in the basket, took a drink of water from one of my flasks, and chewed the last of a grassbake morsel I had been saving to ingest just before I got to the boat. I then packed everything up and indicated that I was ready to proceed.

"I shall leave you now," stated Suz. "This is as far as I go."

"Thank you for your guidance," I offered to her. She nodded in acceptance. She made no further comment as though she had no words for parting. She turned and walked eastward back toward her home.

Daniel and Jaffy continued along with me. As we advanced toward the vessel, I could see two very forceful looking Moraines loading the last of the cargo into the hull. I approached apprehensively but full of hope.

I hoped I would be able to put up a resistance to the toxins of the water body. I clothed my mouth and nose to reduce the intake of those poisons that might be stopped by a simple cloth. It was possible. If cloth could block the fatally potent rays of the sun, it might be able to obstruct some airborne toxins.

We boarded the ship and set sail with the blessing of a slight wind blowing in from the east. I stayed on deck, straining to watch for the first glimpse of my homeland mountains as we slowly rocked forward. I thought about my journey and the knowledge that was bestowed upon me.

I had witnessed many adaptations I wished to pursue as a result of my venture. Shelter and cultivation in the caves of my home were high on the list. Could Alexandra have survived longer in the caves? I wondered. The thought was painful, but painful with a purpose.

What of the seed inside me? Would it take hold? How long should I hold secret to this event if, indeed, I was with child?

The majestic mountains were now in view with the clouds dividing their base from their peaks. Who would be there waiting? Would children be hiding on the ridge among the wind deformed trees? Would nausea soon set in? Amidst my questions was calmness. A calm reinforced by the cradling motion brought on by the rippling waves of the sea. I was not afraid nor worried because, soon, I would be home.

Edwards Brothers Malloy
Thorofare, NJ USA
October 30, 2013